Someone else is in the house . . .

I turned to leave the house, deciding my brief career as a detective was over, when I caught a glimpse of flashing light in the room just beyond the kitchen. My curiosity pulled me forward instead of out the door—which my common sense told me I should be exiting through right now. Oh well. I was a redhead. Blame it on poor impulse control. I slowly walked toward the place where I had seen the flashing light, when I was suddenly blinded by a powerful beam.

In that one brilliant moment, it was all horribly—and dangerously—clear.

Someone was inside this house with a flashlight. Someone, who, like me, had no business being in this house.

Someone who was most likely a killer.

I turned to run but was stopped by a sudden sharp pain in my head.

I awoke to a light that hurt my eyes, and some sort of metal pointed directly at my head. When I could get my eyes to focus, I saw that the metal was attached to the hand of an extremely attractive, very tall, very angry man wearing a nicely tailored dark blue suit. The metal was also a gun.

I allowed myself a brief moment of panic and sheer terror, and then forced myself back to reality. *Come on, criminals were not this good looking . . .*

TUTU
DEADLY

NATALIE M. ROBERTS

BERKLEY PRIME CRIME, NEW YORK

THE BERKLEY PUBLISHING GROUP
Published by the Penguin Group
Penguin Group (USA) Inc.
375 Hudson Street, New York, New York 10014, USA
Penguin Group (Canada), 90 Eglinton Avenue East, Suite 700, Toronto, Ontario M4P 2Y3, Canada
(a division of Pearson Penguin Canada Inc.)
Penguin Books Ltd., 80 Strand, London WC2R 0RL, England
Penguin Group Ireland, 25 St. Stephen's Green, Dublin 2, Ireland (a division of Penguin Books Ltd.)
Penguin Group (Australia), 250 Camberwell Road, Camberwell, Victoria 3124, Australia
(a division of Pearson Australia Group Pty. Ltd.)
Penguin Books India Pvt. Ltd., 11 Community Centre, Panchsheel Park, New Delhi—110 017, India
Penguin Group (NZ), 67 Apollo Drive, Mairangi Bay, Auckland 1311, New Zealand
(a division of Pearson New Zealand Ltd.)
Penguin Books (South Africa) (Pty.) Ltd., 24 Sturdee Avenue, Rosebank, Johannesburg 2196,
South Africa

Penguin Books Ltd., Registered Offices: 80 Strand, London WC2R 0RL, England

This is a work of fiction. Names, characters, places, and incidents either are the product of the author's imagination or are used fictitiously, and any resemblance to actual persons, living or dead, business establishments, events, or locales is entirely coincidental. The publisher does not have any control over and does not assume any responsibility for author or third-party websites or their content.

TUTU DEADLY

A Berkley Prime Crime Book / published by arrangement with the author

PRINTING HISTORY
Berkley Prime Crime mass-market edition / April 2007

Copyright © 2007 by Natalie M. Roberts.
Cover art by Mary Lynn Blasutta.
Cover design by Rita Frangie.
Logo design by axb group.
Interior text design by Kristin del Rosario.

ISBN: 978-0-425-21486-2

BERKLEY® PRIME CRIME
Berkley Prime Crime Books are published by The Berkley Publishing Group,
a division of Penguin Group (USA) Inc.,
375 Hudson Street, New York, New York 10014.
The name BERKLEY PRIME CRIME and the BERKLEY PRIME CRIME design are trademarks
belonging to Penguin Group (USA) Inc.

PRINTED IN THE UNITED STATES OF AMERICA

10 9 8 7 6 5 4 3 2 1

To Misty Robbins, dance teacher extraordinaire, who can choreograph her way out of a hostage situation. When the stress is high, the deadlines near, the performance on the edge—then you see that she is pure and unadulterated magic. What more can you ask?

ACKNOWLEDGMENTS ·

To all the dance moms who inspired this book (you know who you are!) along with the dancers at EDF, and, of course, my own little Dancing Daughter, Cambre. Without the craziness of the world of competitive dance, I could never have created a wonderful, flighty, and ditzy character like Jenny T. Partridge. And of course, to my fabulous agent, Karen Solem, and my editor at Berkley, Sandra Harding, it's been a joy to work with both of you. I hope Jenny is around for a long, long time so we can continue this collaboration. As always, I must thank the ladies at murdershewrites.com, Jennifer Apodaca, Deborah LeBlanc, Allison Brennan, and Karin Tabke; especially Karen and Jennifer, who took the time to read and critique Jenny's exploits.

ONE

DESPITE what my mother would probably tell you, my greatest fear in life was not dying alone with only four hundred cats for company. My greatest fear in life was staring me right in the face—and she was colossal. She was the mother of all dance moms, and she was steaming mad. Any minute now, she was going to do one of those sumo-wrestler moves and land on top of me, and then it would all be over. I'd slowly suffocate, my dance studio would go bankrupt, and my mom would be left mourning over my grave with nothing to remember me by except a few dead plants, dust bunnies under my bed, and some stuffed animals. *This* was my worst nightmare. I really needed to get a life.

Every dance teacher knew that the worst part of trying to instruct children was not the kids themselves, but their parents. Sure, an occasional kid threw up on you, or peed in the middle of class, but that was nothing compared to dealing with an irate mother who didn't think her little darling was getting enough attention or the starring role she deserved.

I didn't particularly like chubby little Ella Anderson, who was just six years old, and I cared even less for her mother, Emma, whose picture was probably in the dictionary under "stage mother." I just hadn't looked yet.

Emma Anderson believed that her daughter was the next big thing in the world of dance, and was determined to convince me of the same. I was afraid if I didn't kowtow to her demands to keep Ella on the front-row fifty—the prime spot for dancers to be placed, right in the center of the front row—Momma Anderson was going to end my life. I'm sure plenty of people have been killed for lesser things. For a dance mom, there was nothing more primo than seeing her daughter in the front-row fifty. And of course once a dancer earned that coveted spot, her mom would do just about anything to keep her there. It was scary. Kind of like Emma Anderson.

Today's argument—we had one nearly every week—was over whether Ella deserved the part of the Sugar Plum Fairy in the Jenny T. Partridge Dance Academy's annual production of *The Nutcracker*.

I'm Jenny T. Partridge—no jokes please—and no, I do not have a pear tree. Christmastime, which was just around the corner, usually brought out the worst in the name punsters—mostly male—who took great joy in asking to see my plumage. I rarely replied to that. Guys didn't listen to what you said, anyway. They were too busy staring at your chest, or moving around their equipment in front of God and the whole country. At least that's what my last boyfriend did. I broke up with him when I realized he couldn't pick my face out of a crowd, but could describe my chest in great detail.

At any rate, my production of *The Nutcracker* was not your typical classic. We did a jazzy version with loud music—you know, that thrashy pop and hip-hop mix—and elegant, flashy costumes that was well-known for hundreds of miles around Ogden, Utah, which is where my studio is located. It was the one thing I did that allowed me to scrimp by the rest of the year. Entire families made attending our production an annual event.

But back to Ella, who at six had no talent, and even less desire to learn to dance. She spent most of the class burying her finger up her nose, and the rest of it whining and crying; there was very little dancing going on in her neck of the forest—probably a good thing, actually, considering she had two right feet.

"See, Mrs. Anderson, the Sugar Plum Fairy is a hard role, and it usually goes to one of the older girls, those who have danced for years. Those who can stand on relevé, and dance en pointe."

"But fairies are little," the woman protested, as she pushed in closer to me, giving me a whiff of her odiferous perfume. She had absolutely no sense of personal space. I got claustrophobic just hearing her name. I was right, I thought. My nightmares were coming true. She was going to pin me to the wall until I gave her daughter the role. Emma was very tall—at least six feet—and broad shouldered, and she towered over me. "Ella is just right for the fairy. She *is* the fairy. She can relevé. Show her your relevé, Ella."

She pointed her left arm back at her daughter without turning away from me. Mrs. Anderson's little sugar plum fairy was about twenty pounds heavier than she should have been at her age, and "little" was a relative term. She might be little to her Amazonian momma, but she was two to three sizes larger than my other Minis. I knew one day she would grow into that weight, but right now . . . She stared blankly at her mother's face for a moment then brightened. "You mean ice cream?" she asked, obviously relating the term "relevé" to Chocolate Peanut Butter Revel. I understood. That was good ice cream.

James Marriott, who taught my Seniors and Petites, and who was the world's biggest yellow-bellied coward, had taken off with a crazed look in his eye the minute Mrs. Anderson stepped foot in the door, so I was on my own. That was his usual reaction. I could hear the loud music from the other room, which meant that James was pretending to be busy, choreographing a routine or designing a new move. Since the Seniors weren't due at the studio for at least another hour, I was on to his pretense. He'd get his later.

Marlys Fulton, whose daughter, Carly, danced in my Petites, and whose other daughter Maribel danced in my Tots, and who worked in exchange for her daughters' dance lessons, had just left to make some copies of the dance calendar. She usually ran interference for me with the pushy dance moms, but she couldn't be with me 24-7.

"Look," I said, moving backward away from Mrs. Anderson, who only pressed in closer, "my Minis usually play the role of the buffoons, and that's just how I've always done it." I found I was stuck—I'd hit the barre, which was attached to the mirror on the wall. There was no escape.

"A buffoon? You want my daughter to be a buffoon?" Her voice nearly cracked with strain and outrage, and I groaned as she moved even closer. She waved her arms and got so close I could see the pores on her face. "Listen, here, Jenny T. Partridge, I know talent when I see talent and Ella has talent. I wouldn't even bother to come in here if I didn't know she was right for the part. You *have* to put her in that role."

At that point I got a little light-headed. There was a very big unstated "and if you don't I'll make your pay" in her proclamation. It was going to make the newspapers, I just knew it.

LOCAL DANCE TEACHER
SUFFOCATED BY STAGE MOTHER

Ogden, Utah—Local dance teacher Jenny Partridge was flattened today by the mother of one of her students, after an altercation over a sugar plum fairy. Police said they had to peel Partridge off the mirror of her dance studio after she was cornered by Mrs. Emma Anderson, mother of fairy-wannabe Ella

Anderson. "She called my daughter a buffoon!" said an indignant Mrs. Anderson. "Nobody calls my daughter a buffoon!"

Luckily for me, Ella picked that very moment to pee her pants, staring down as her pink leotard and tights darkened, a pool of urine puddling under her feet. She seemed fascinated by her bodily functions. This amazed me, as I figured by the time you were six you pretty much had that stuff figured out. Despite the fact I didn't like Ella a whole lot, I was very grateful for her interruption.

"Oh, Ella! You made a naughty on the floor! Oh no!"

Mrs. Anderson ran over and hustled her daughter out of the room, her face flushing, while the other mothers watched, giggled, and whispered behind their hands. She turned in my direction before she exited and said, "I'm warning you, Jenny. You don't want to mess with me, or you'll be sorry."

Yeah, I was already sorry. Sorry I didn't study tennis or piano when I was younger. The other moms were still whispering and laughing. Mrs. Anderson was *not* particularly well liked by the other dance moms. The little girls also giggled and moved away from the puddle that was beginning to spread and seep toward them. My studio was old, and there was a certain slant in the floor that was usually unnoticeable—unless something liquid was placed on it. As the puddle picked up speed, they began to scatter and run and squeal, most of them heading to their mothers—who sat in chairs and on the floor on the other side of the room. I understood. Someone else's urine usually made me want to run and squeal, too. Unfortunately, Mrs. Anderson had left the building, and I was left with the mess—the story of my professional life. All the moms sitting there watching me without offering to help knew they weren't supposed to be inside the studio, where the girls were dancing. The sign on my door clearly said "No parents allowed." Yeah, right. Over the eight years I had been in business I had gotten a little lax. I had grown tired of fighting. I just let one in, then another, until they just kind of took over. How was I supposed to enforce this rule now? I was nothing but a dance teacher. I'd need a bodyguard to keep these women out.

"What's up?" my assistant dance teacher Amber Francis asked, as she sauntered into the room—ten minutes late, as usual. Amber's long blond hair was casually tied back in a ponytail and she wore no makeup. She didn't need it. She had large blue eyes, dark eyelashes that never had to endure the horror of an eyelash curler, and plump full lips. She also had a strong, lithe body with a large chest and a tiny waist. Those breasts had been the only thing keeping her from a real career as a ballerina, and she wasn't willing to give them up for the craft, so she concentrated on jazz dance, which is what she taught for me. "What's the puddle?"

I looked down at my own short legs, thick waist, and slightly bulging middle—I needed to lay off the ice cream and Cheetos—and sighed. It's a good thing I still danced, or I'd probably weigh four hundred pounds. "Ewwww," I said aloud, and Amber gave me the same look she always did when my mental processes got ahead of my mouth.

"Ella peed her pants. Mrs. Anderson thinks Ella should be the Sugar Plum Fairy, and she's appalled I'd call her daughter a buffoon. And she almost suffocated me again," I explained.

Amber peered at my face. "You've got bags under your eyes. You dreaming about her squishing you again?"

"Hey, it could happen."

"Man, Jenny, you seriously need a life. Or a boyfriend, or something."

With that pronouncement on my pathetic existence—all of which I was perfectly aware of without her pointing it out—she clapped her hands and called the girls to attention. No one listened, as they were fixated on the puddle.

I got a rag and cleaned up Ella's urine, because it was hard to teach little girls to dance when they were all huddled on one side of the small studio trying to avoid the river of pee headed swiftly in their direction.

That was where I was—on the floor, sopping up little girl pee—when I saw the shoes advance on me. Black, polished dress shoes—man shoes. "No street shoes in here!" I shouted. "Out! Get out!"

The shoes didn't move. I followed them up to see a nice pair of dress pants, well pressed and very well fitted, a dress shirt and jacket, broad, athletic shoulders, and on top of the entire package, an impossibly handsome face, saved from pretty-boy status only by a one-inch scar over the left eye. Dark hair. Cobalt blue eyes. I almost melted on the spot, except then I would have been puddled next to Ella's pee, and that was something I did *not* want to experience.

After exchanging with me what I wanted to believe were looks of instant and mutual attraction, Blue Eyes took himself over to the door where he slipped off his shoes and then padded back over to me. "Jenny Partridge?" Even his socks were elegant—no holes. I thought of the pair I was wearing under my dance shoes. They were mostly one big hole. There wasn't much sock left.

"That's me." I finished cleaning up the pee, and stood. "I'd offer my hand, but I don't think that would be a good idea." He wrinkled his nose as the smell of urine from the rag drifted over to him, and he waved a hand.

"Not necessary. I'm Detective Tate Wilson. I'm here about Sandra Epstein."

I groaned aloud. Sandra Epstein, the worst stage mother of them all. Worse than four Emma Andersons. I'd taught her daughter Taylee dance for three years now, and the girl was incredibly talented, but her mother was going to be the death of any career she might have.

Epstein was mentally unstable at best, downright loony tunes at worst, and last week we'd had our final blowup. After Taylee had shown up for class a half hour late, with only one shoe and a pair of tights that were missing an entire leg, I'd kicked her out and told her to come back when she was ready to be serious. Of course, I was really mad at her mother, because Taylee was just a kid. I think she clued into that, because she just stared at me with those big, mournful eyes, and I immediately felt like a total creep.

"Do you need me to get you some new tights and shoes,

Tay?" I'd asked her gently, dropping the harsh tone. I could hardly afford to buy anything—including food—on my income, but something about the little girl just spoke to me.

"No. Mom can do it," she'd answered quietly.

Her mother had stormed in shortly after that, calling me an imbecilic moron and a joke of a dance teacher, and I said a few things I'd rather not repeat. Hey, I'm a redhead. Everyone knew how fiery we were. I also mixed up a few clichés, something I always did, too, but it resulted in me telling her that I was going to stick her head where the moon doesn't shine and . . . well, it's best not to go there. I was very ashamed of my behavior.

"What is she saying now? She filed charges against me? I didn't touch her. She's whacko. She grabbed *me* and wouldn't let go. Look, I still have a bruise." I thrust out my arm toward him.

"I did mention I'm with homicide, didn't I?" Detective Wilson asked.

"Homicide?" Horror slowly dawned over me. Someone had killed Sandra Epstein, or worse, her daughter? And they were questioning me? "I'm sorry, but who was killed?"

"Sandra Epstein," he explained patiently, talking slowly as though I were an imbecile. Right now, I felt like one.

"Was it an accident?" I asked, feeling faint, the blood rushing from my head.

"No," he patiently explained again. "I'm with *homicide*. Mrs. Epstein was poisoned. In the course of our investigation, we discovered that the two of you had a recent altercation, and so I need to talk to you if you don't mind. It would be best if we went to the station."

"To the station?" I repeated, like a parrot. "Poisoned? But, but . . ."

Next thing I knew I was on the floor, and Amber was kneeling over me, fanning my face with her hands. James knelt next to her, his big blue eyes trained on Detective Wilson, who stood above all three of us, staring down at me. I tried to scramble to my feet. Big mistake.

"Oh, man, the room is spinning. Did I land in the pee?"

"No, you cleaned it up, remember? Take it slow. Should I call the paramedics?" Amber asked, helping me to my feet.

"No, no! No paramedics, I'll be fine." Dance teachers don't have insurance, at least not those of us barely scraping by, and I knew I had fainted only from shock. And probably lack of food. Tuition wasn't due for another five days, and all I had in my fridge was some old bologna I was saving for a dire emergency—such as the immediate threat of starvation—and two light beers.

I knew why Detective Wilson was here. I knew someone had told him what I'd yelled at Sandra Epstein right after she grabbed my arm and gave me an Indian burn, and just before she stomped out of my studio dragging Taylee behind her like a small, forlorn rag doll.

"You better watch out or someone is going to give you what you deserve!" I'd yelled.

And someone had, although I wasn't entirely sure she deserved to die. What I *was* entirely sure of was that someone hadn't been me. But the police weren't, and now I was probably their main suspect.

Detective Wilson might be passionate about me, all right. Passionate about seeing me in jail! This was not good. Jail clothes were orange, and everyone knew that orange was not a good color for a redhead. Especially a redhead who needed Mary Kay concealer to cover her freckles. I doubted there would be a Mary Kay distributor in jail, anyway—they mostly hung out in upper-class neighborhoods wearing pink clothes and driving pink cars. Another color that wasn't good for me. Pink.

Good Lord. This was bad.

Two

I left Amber in charge of the Mini class, and sent James off into exile to wait for the Seniors and Petites. I swear he said, "Yum, spicy hot," as I left with the homicide detective who, it was entirely possible, wanted to put me behind bars.

James Marriott was one of my best friends. He felt the same way about me, although he constantly bemoaned my lack of fashion sense. He was also a very talented dancer, a great teacher, a patient angel with young children, and a flaming queen. Despite the fact that his every mannerism screamed "gay," his mother remained blind to the fact that her only child, a son—a late-in-life baby—liked men as much as I did. Because of his Mormon heritage, and the fact that he loved his mother dearly, James pretended to be something he was not. I had no idea how Sister Marriott (she insisted on being addressed this way—James said it was best not to argue) could possibly not know her pride and joy was playing for the other team.

James and I had danced together with the Camelot

Dance Troupe in Salt Lake City, and our professional careers had ended around the same time. Mine because I suffered a knee injury that took months to recover from, and James's because he stole the director's boyfriend.

Somehow I became his cover. Whenever James required a date of the female persuasion, I got dragged along. This meant I had been to *way* too many Mormon weddings and get-togethers, where they did not serve alcoholic beverages, thereby preventing me from numbing my pain, but where the food was usually pretty good and always plentiful.

That's how I became addicted to potato salad, but that's another story. Thinking of potato salad, I heard my empty stomach rumble, and I quickly coughed to try and hide the noise. Since I was riding with Detective Wilson down to the police station in his blue Ford Taurus, and since I was trying to impress him, even as I feared he'd be throwing me into jail, I did not want my bodily noises to drive him off. I'd thrown a jacket over my leotard, tights, and dance shorts, but I was still woefully underdressed for the cold late-November wind that was blowing, and I shivered uncontrollably until the officer took pity on me and turned on the heat full blast.

"Look, Detective, I didn't kill anybody, okay? I mean, the woman was a wretch, but you see a lot of that in this business."

"Let's save it for your statement, okay?"

"I have to make a statement?" I felt faint. "But, isn't that what you have suspects do? Which means you seriously think I might have done this . . . Oh good Lord." I felt the blood drain from my face again and Detective Wilson kept giving me short, nervous glances while trying to keep his attention on the road. It was starting to snow—big wet "hey-it's-winter-in-Utah-flakes," and they were sticking to the windshield.

"Lady, you seriously need to relax. This is routine. I'm not arresting you, nor am I accusing you of anything. I just need you to answer some questions. If you aren't guilty, then you'll be fine. You must watch too much TV."

"Don't call me 'lady,'" I muttered under my breath.

"What?"

"Nothing." My cell phone rang in my pocket and I pulled it out and looked at the caller ID. A dance mom. I didn't answer it, nor did I speak again—a world record for me, by the way; I almost always had something to say— until we were sitting at a table in a small conference room at the Ogden City Police Department. Detective Wilson and another detective he introduced only as Benson were sipping coffee from foam cups. I had not been offered any. Could this be considered police brutality? Judging from the grimaces each cop made as he took a sip, I decided it was probably a favor, although some hot cocoa would go a long way toward making me feel better—and warmer. I glared at Detective Wilson. Where were his manners? My mother would be appalled. I bet *his* mother would be appalled.

My cell phone rang again, and I looked at the ID. Another dance mom.

"I just have to read you your rights, okay? It's standard procedure, so don't freak out on me."

"My rights?" The words squeaked out of me, barely audible, as my day went from totally rotten to almost as bad as it gets, in just a pulse of my rapidly beating heart. Somewhere in my twisted psyche I heard his words and registered that he now knew enough about me to understand that being read my rights was going to cause me to freak out. My heart did a weird little flutter at that thought. I was seriously twisted.

"Now, we're going to record this, just to make sure we get it all right, okay?" Wilson said, pointing to the video camera that had *not* escaped my notice. I nodded nervously, willing my heart to slow down, and he flipped it on, and then sighted it in on me. I felt like a deer in the spotlight— or maybe a deer in the scope of a rifle.

"Now, Mrs. Partridge . . ."

"Ms. Partridge, please."

"Okay, Ms. Partridge, now for the record, where were you yesterday evening . . ."

My cell phone rang for the third time, and Detective Wilson got an extremely pained look on his face, while Benson's eyes hardened in suspicion. I turned it off. My phone never stopped ringing. Dance moms were neurotic.

"Where were you around seven o' clock yesterday evening?"

I wasn't about to own up to the carton of Häagen Dazs I had been devouring in front of the television while I watched *The Bachelor*. Some guilty pleasures were not to be shared. It had taken all the spare change I could find under my couch cushions and on my car floor to buy that Häagen Dazs, but it had been worth it. Pralines and cream. Yum.

"Ms. Partridge?"

"I was home watching television."

The two detectives looked at each other, and I almost groaned. Isn't that what all the guilty people said? At least on television . . . *Ack!* I needed a life. If I didn't get sent to prison for a murder I didn't commit, I was going to do something . . . save the starving children, or maybe build houses for Habitat for Humanity.

"And can anyone vouch for your whereabouts?"

"No, I live alone." So far, I hadn't done a lot to disprove my guilt. Bring on that hammer: I was ready to construct.

"So no one saw you and you didn't talk to anyone?"

"Well, I did buy some ice cream at the 7-Eleven. The one on 40th? The clerk might remember me." The time had come to be honest about my ice cream addiction. Embarrassment about my junk-food habit in front of the hunky cop and his partner was better than prison. Again, my only experience with women's prison had been television, but it had to be close to the truth, didn't it? I didn't particularly want to be a woman named Bertha's bitch.

"And what time was this?"

"Seven, seven thirty?"

"And what did you do after that."

"I went home."

"And?"

"And I watched television." I was *still* hoping *The Bachelor* could stay my little secret, but the way things were going, I knew the chances of that were slim.

"And no one saw you after that? Did you talk to anyone on the phone?"

"No, I pretty much just watched TV and then went to bed. My phone rang a lot, but I didn't answer it."

"Hmmph," Benson snorted. He didn't sound like he believed me. Who would have known that my pathetic life would get me sent to prison?

"So you are saying that around 8:30 p.m. last night you did not deliver two cartons of cookie dough to Mrs. Epstein's doorstep?"

Cookie dough? Good Lord, our cookie-dough fundraiser! I'd been out all day delivering the dough that had been ordered, and had just finished when I stopped at 7-Eleven for ice cream. "I . . . I . . . well, I delivered cookie dough, but not to Sandra. See, she and I had sort of a small disagreement, and I asked one of the other dance moms to take her order to her. I didn't want to see her."

"And does this woman have a name?"

"Well, yes. Her name is Emma Anderson. She's Sandra Epstein's neighbor. This all happened before Emma got mad at me over the Sugar Plum Fairy incident today. But that's nothing new. She's always mad at me."

"The Sugar Plum Fairy incident?" Benson asked, his eyes narrowing, confusion tingeing his voice.

"Yeah, right before Ella peed on the floor."

"Who is Ella?"

"She's Emma's daughter, and she's a little bit short and chubby to be the Sugar Plum Fairy. Plus she can't dance and when she—"

Wilson rolled his eyes and I shut up immediately. When cops roll their eyes, it means trouble. Everybody knew this—at least everybody who watched television.

"Well, see, here we have a problem," Wilson said, his eyes back in a normal position. I bit my lip to keep from telling him if he kept doing that his eyes were going to stay that way. "We talked to Mrs. Anderson this morning, and she says you didn't give her the cookie dough for Mrs. Epstein. In fact, she says you told her that you were going to personally deliver it even though she offered. And deliver it you did, right? Left it on her front porch, but added a little something extra to make it special?"

"Whoa, hold on there, cowboy. I told you, I didn't deliver the cookie dough to Sandra. I delivered it to Emma. She said I didn't? She's lying!" Oh no! It was the big "if you don't" warning. *This* was what she meant. She was going to get me back for not making Ella the Sugar Plum Fairy. But was it really necessary to frame me for murder? This was worse than I thought. Much worse.

"Cowboy?" Wilson said, interrupting my frantic rambling thoughts. He had one eyebrow raised higher than the other, and he wore a smirk on his lips.

"It's just something I say. I'm eccentric, okay?" Everyone knew that artists were expected to be a little bit off, after all. And I was an artist of a sort—a starving one, even. My art was dance and choreography. My biggest fault was I couldn't shut up. "Just what is it you think I added to the cookie dough?"

"Arsenic." Benson spoke dully, with little expression on his face. Nevertheless, the pronouncement gave me a major case of racing heart and high blood pressure.

"Arsenic? Are you kidding me? I don't even know where you would get arsenic!" I felt like I'd fallen asleep and woken up in a B movie. I shook my head and closed my eyes tightly then opened them again, praying I'd be looking at a group of little girls in a ragtag line, hopping around on one leg as they tried desperately to hold up their heel extensions. No luck. Still impossibly gorgeous Detective Wilson and his morose, crew-cut partner Benson.

"So, you're saying you have no knowledge of who might have delivered the fatal cookie dough to Mrs. Epstein?" Death by cookie dough. This was surreal.

"Hell no, I mean, no! I promise you, I gave that dough to Mrs. Anderson. I don't know why she's lying except she wants her daughter to be the Sugar Plum Fairy in our production of *The Nutcracker*, and I won't give in to her manipulations. Maybe she thinks if she holds out on telling the truth I'll cave and give Ella the role, to keep myself from going to prison."

The two detectives glanced at each other and fought to keep from laughing. Even morose Benson had a twitch at the corner of his mouth where his lip was trying to smile, something I just knew was against his nature.

Could this be any more over the top?

"So, you have no alibi, you have motive, you had access to the murder, uh, weapon, and the one person who can absolve you says you didn't give her the dough. You did have the cookie dough in your possession before you allegedly gave it to Mrs. Anderson, correct?"

I could see the court case now. I could see the news media. I'd be tagged the Cookie Killer for the rest of my life. Other criminals at least had cool or frightening crimes. Not that I was guilty, but if I was going to go to prison, I'd prefer it would be for something other than killing someone with a fundraiser. I doubted that would hold a lot of weight with the prison crowd. I felt tears threatening to spill over and fear took hold, causing me to breathe in deep, ragged pants. "I'm telling you right now I didn't kill her. I didn't kill anyone. I don't know how to find arsenic, and even if I did, I wouldn't do it. I can't even kill spiders or bugs. I'm just a dance teacher, okay? That's all I do is teach dance."

To my embarrassment, the tears couldn't be held back and I began to sob helplessly. Detective Wilson watched me closely, occasionally handing me a tissue, and Detective Benson looked away as though uncomfortable with the emotions of a killer. Except I wasn't a killer. I was a dumb dance teacher who was just trying to make a living doing the thing I loved most.

When the tears subsided Detective Wilson handed me the last tissue and threw the box in the garbage. I was pretty sure it had been full when I started crying.

"I normally don't cry this much. I think it's because I'm hungry. Tuition isn't due for five days."

Wilson gave me an odd look before saying, "All right, Ms. Partridge, that's all for now. I'll take you home, but I have to warn you not to leave town." They said that on television all the time, too.

He didn't talk much on the way to my small apartment, and I was surprised when he pulled over into a Burger King drive-through that was a few blocks from my home and turned to ask me what I wanted. My mouth stayed open but no words came out, so he just turned and ordered a Whopper combo meal and then drove forward and paid for it. After the teenager at the pickup window handed him the food, he passed it to me and without another word reentered Harrison Boulevard headed in the direction of my apartment, located on the corner of Monroe and 26th Street.

The food smelled so good I couldn't help but inhale, and I closed my eyes as the aroma of French fries and hamburger grease wafted up around me. My stomach rumbled in response, and I opened my eyes to see we had stopped in front of my little apartment building. Detective Wilson stared at me with a huge grin on his face, and my face went hot. I knew from experience it matched the color of my hair.

"Thanks for the, uh, dinner," I said hastily, embarrassed that every time I turned around this man was seeing my worst side. Little girls who pee on the floor, clothes with holes in them, neurotic dance moms, a tearful crying jag, and a junk-food addiction were everyday occurrences for me. Although I'd never been a suspect in a murder before. In the space of three hours, I'd managed to cram a lot of eccentricity into the detective's knowledge of me. I could kiss that passionate future with him good-bye.

He turned off the car and escorted me to the door. I was even a little surprised he knew where I lived, although I shouldn't have been. He was a detective, and I was somewhat of a suspect.

My little place was on the bottom floor of a very old building. It had a lot of charm and style, as well as noisy pipes, and was always impossibly cold. The strong points included a wood-burning fireplace, high ceilings, and hardwood floors that were a dancer's dream. I spent a lot of nights dancing with an imaginary partner on those floors. I doubted they had hardwood floors in prison. I sure didn't want to find out.

"Look, Detective," I said, turning awkwardly toward him after I had put the key into my door, pushed it open, and dropped the food bag on the small table located in the entryway. "I didn't kill anyone. I've never killed anyone in my life." .

"Your fingerprints were on the cookie-dough container."

I didn't ask why they had my fingerprints on record. I already knew. During a short stint of my life, when I was trying to hold down nine-to-five jobs like everyone else, I had worked for the Weber County Sheriff's Office as a dispatcher. Fingerprinting was required of all employees who worked with the Bureau of Criminal Identification database. I'd only lasted four months among the fighting, bitchy, backstabbing women who made up the dispatch department before I quit and returned to teaching dance—probably the only thing I had ever truly been good at.

I didn't play well with other grown-ups.

"Of course they were. I divided the containers out when they arrived. They come in big boxes, and I had to separate them so that we could deliver each order to the moms. It's a fundraiser, Detective, for my dance team. And I'm the dance teacher."

He didn't look convinced, but he wasn't really looking at me like I was a coldhearted killer, either. Instead, his blue eyes were burning into me, probing me, and I felt a warmth and a flush I hadn't felt for a while.

Great. Attracted to the man who wants to put me away for life. Maybe he'll come visit me in prison and we can have conjugal . . .

"Go inside," he said. "Lock your door. If you didn't do

this, then whoever did is still out there, and if they figure out you haven't been charged, you could be next. If you didn't do it, someone wants us to think you did."

He waited until I shut the door and turned the dead bolt, and then I could hear him walk away. I peeked out my four-paned side window and watched as he got into his car. He spoke into his car radio and just sat there for a minute, making notes on a pad and occasionally turning to look at my apartment. Each time I would ease back, hoping he couldn't see my bright eyes at the window. Hoping he didn't know the effect his incredible physique and handsome face had on me. The man most likely wanted me in prison and I wanted to jump his bones.

Ain't life grand? This situation called for French fries. After all, they were from the potato family, and were as close to potato salad as I was going to get tonight.

THREE

$\mathcal{A}$ lot of people had preconceived notions about what it was like to live in Utah. Most of that had to do with the image people had of Mormons, and how they thought everyone who lived here was Mormon. While to a certain extent this was true—everyone who lived in Utah probably had a relative who belonged at one time or another to the church—Utah was not quite as hostile to non-Mormons as everyone thought.

I was born to a Catholic mother and a Mormon father. Neither one was religious, although my paternal grandmother, Nana Marian, took me to Mormon Sunday school when I was a kid. I liked it, but that's just because I got to wear fancy dresses that my grandmother bought me just for that reason, color, and eat cookies after the Sunday school lesson. I didn't do much listening, so it was best not to ask me about their theology. My entire extent of Mormon knowledge could be described this way: Jesus wants me for a sunbeam.

That said, I'd lived here in Ogden all my life. I knew a

lot of Mormons who knew a whole lot more about their church than I did. I also knew a lot of ex-Mormons, non-Mormons, and even quite a few Catholics. I didn't know much about that religion, either, but as a kid, I didn't like it as much because my maternal grandmother only took me to Sunday Mass once and didn't buy me any new clothing, and they only served food—wafers and wine—to the real members. Plus Grandma Gilly always crossed herself and squinted at me with despair and anger, after I'd broken yet another one of her precious saint figurines, or ran the water over in the tub so it flooded her bathroom. It gave me an aversion to the sign of the cross that was totally unrelated to Jesus.

In more recent years, my other grandma, Nana Marian, had begun regularly bringing me copies of the Book of Mormon. I thought she was getting Alzheimer's, although my father denied it, because I had a whole closet full of those books stashed away. We met for lunch once a month in Salt Lake City at the top of the Joseph Smith Memorial Building. Once there, my white-haired grandmother, who stood only about four feet, eight inches tall, would hand me a Book of Mormon and a ten-dollar bill. We'd order lunch—her a light salad, me something substantial and greasy; who knew when I'd eat again—and then we'd dine while we discussed the weather and my mother's Catholic-bred eccentricities. When lunch was done, Nana would pat my hand with her leathery, cold one and urge me to "read it, dear. It's true, you know. I want to see you when I die! I want you there with me."

I'd agree to read it, she'd pay the bill, and we'd part ways until the next month, when we'd go through the same routine. I got twelve copies of the Book of Mormon a year. Luckily, for Christmas and birthdays Nana Marian gave me clothes. During the summer months, my apartment building would have a large "garage sale," despite the fact none of us had a garage, and I'd put out a table laden with all my copies of the Book of Mormon, selling them for a buck apiece. I'd get a lot of strange looks and enough money to buy an inexpensive dinner at the Chinese place down the street. Some of the older residents of the building probably thought I knocked over the Mormon-owned Deseret Bookstore once a year or so. I also think they bought the books because they were afraid that if they didn't their sacred book would end up in the wrong hands. At least that's the way they looked when they were forking over the dollars, but I wasn't going to question their motivation too deeply.

Now I admit I never actually cracked open those books, but that had more to do with the fact that I was essentially very lazy—it was much easier to watch television than to concentrate on a book—than with my rejection of Mormon theology. I was an equal-opportunity rejecter of all things religious. I didn't care for Mass, got the heebie-jeebies when the Jehovah's Witness missionaries knocked on my door, and made it a habit to pray only when I really, really needed something—like blueberry ripple ice cream. Now that was worth praying for.

Every once in a while I would get visits from the Mormon missionaries, looking to increase their membership numbers, and I was usually nice to them, although my niceness didn't extend itself to agreeing to baptism ten minutes after we'd met. I felt sorry for them. Can you imagine waiting your whole life to serve a mission for God, and being told that you were being sent to the only state populated almost entirely by Mormons? Since I'd never been baptized in any religion, it was no wonder they kept showing up at my door. I was fresh meat.

So it shouldn't have surprised me when my doorbell rang at 8 a.m. Saturday. I was startled out of a restless sleep, and I almost screamed. I remembered being chased by Emma Anderson and Sandra Epstein, who were both screaming "Buffoons? Buffoons?" Behind them followed Detective Wilson, holding a pair of handcuffs in one hand and an orange jumpsuit in the other. That's enough to make anyone scream, and not with pleasure, although just before the dance moms crashed my dream I remembered a wave of pleasure running through my body . . .

The doorbell rang again and I threw aside the covers and padded to my front door, shivering from the cold. Four days until tuition was due. I was out of fire logs.

I looked out the peephole and saw the same two missionaries who had visited me three times before. I was starting to regret being nice to them.

I opened the door slightly and said, "Hullo?"

"Hi, Jenny!" said Elder Martin, who hailed from Tennessee and had the twang to prove it. "Hope you don't mind we're back. Can we come in?"

Sometimes, you just gotta be tough on these missionaries, or they can't see the river for the trees. Obviously, I had been too nice before. Time to pull out the big logs. "I'm sorry, but I haven't cleaned the place up yet from last night's animal sacrifice."

The smile on Elder Martin's face faded, and Elder Tuatuola, his companion, who came here from Samoa, stepped back from the door.

"Gosh, Jenny, did we do something to make you mad?" Elder Martin asked.

"Sorry, guys, I'm just really busy right now." I shut the door then leaned back against it, guilt consuming me. I quickly opened it again. They were just walking away, shoulders slumped, backs rounded in defeat, when I re-opened it. Elder Martin's face perked up when he turned around and saw me standing there. I'm not sure why, as I'm sure I had bed hair from hell. I was also wearing my rattiest pajama pants and a big T-shirt, and was at least five—okay *maybe* seven—years older than either one of them. Okay, fine, probably ten years. But hey, Mormon missionaries didn't get a whole lot of female interaction. The rules against that kind of thing were pretty strict. On the first visit, Elder Martin even confided to me that the only time he was allowed to be separated from Elder Tuatuola was to go to the bathroom.

I told James about this, and for about a month he talked about going on the mission he had opted out of years before. For a Church so adamantly against homosexuality, the missionary pairing seemed like a breeding ground for switch-hitters, at least to me. From the way the two elders at my door were staring at me, I didn't think that was a problem for either one of them.

"Uh, Jenny? Can we come in?"

Could they come in? Was I in the mood to deal with Mormon missionaries and their theology I had no interest in? Elder Tuatuola stood behind Elder Martin, nodding and smiling. After all the time they spent together, they appeared desperate for some different company—female company. Unlike James, they clearly were not so enamored of being around other men all the time. Of course, James was never really serious about Mormon missionary work. The other rules for missionaries—combing the streets daily for possible converts, always wearing a suit fresh off the rack from Mr. Mac, begging meals from strangers, incessant church meetings, and of course, the old "abstaining" rule, which was basically no sex, no alcohol, no fun—just weren't so appealing to a man who liked designer clothes, expensive food, Broadway shows, and $350 bottles of wine.

I stared at Elder Martin's cheerful face, and sighed. I supposed after a few months on the beaded path I might look pretty good to them, even though they were both just at the end of their teens. My thirtieth birthday had come and gone, which in Utah made me old-maid material. Some of the dance moms tried to set me up with friends and relatives from time to time, usually with little success. Did I mention I was a little eccentric?

"Look guys, I'm sorry. I had a really rough night, and right now all I want to do is go back to bed and get some sleep." Again the crestfallen look on Elder Martin's face. This poor kid really needed a girlfriend, which of course he would not be able to even think about until his service for the Lord was over.

"All right, all right, come in." They bounded together through the door—evidently, as long as missionaries are together, it is not taboo to enter a female's apartment—and headed for my kitchen. Once there, they sat in my chairs and looked up at me expectantly, like children waiting for dinner. They didn't know me very well.

"Look guys, I really don't have any food, okay? I'm sorry. You can look around, but don't be too hopeful. Unless you can perform one of those Bible miracles with loaves of bread and prime rib, you're out of luck. I'm going to go brush my hair and teeth. I'll be right back."

"It was fish, Jenny," Elder Martin said as I left the room.

Yeah, whatever. Like I said, religion wasn't my strong suit.

I figured they couldn't get into too much trouble in my nearly empty kitchen. In the bathroom, I washed my face and brushed my teeth and tongue, and cringed when I looked in the mirror. My straight, long red hair looked fuzzy from a night spent restlessly rubbing the pillowcase as I tossed and turned. I looked like a pom-pom!

I wetted a comb and ran it over my mane, taming it as best I could. I left the bathroom and went into my bedroom to throw on sweats. I heard the clanging of a pan from the kitchen, and wondered what in the world they could have found to eat in there—maybe the Mormons really did have the true gospel, and those two were in there making the bologna multiply into huge mounds of filet mignon—or something like that. Like my morning hair, my Bible knowledge was fuzzy.

I had to spend extra time finding socks that didn't have holes in them bigger than my feet. Four more days until tuition payments were due, and I could buy some groceries, and some new socks, and possibly a new car that started on the first try. Yeah, right. Maybe Top Ramen and cheap socks.

When I reentered the kitchen I could smell the vanilla-buttery flavor of baking cookies, and Elders Martin and Tuatuola were sitting on my counter, eating raw cookie dough from a container, both of them dipping into the unbaked dough with spoons and savoring the sweetness. I was impressed. Rarely did men appreciate the qualities of unbaked cookie dough. Perhaps there was depth to these two that I had not yet recognized.

"This good," Elder Tuatuola said in his broken English.

"Of course. Unbaked cookie dough is one of the true pleasures of life," I answered them. "Smells like you baked some, too, though. But I didn't have any cookie dough. Where did you find the . . ."

Uh-oh. Warning bells went off in my head. Cookie dough. Dead Sandra Epstein.

"Stop! Stop eating!" I screamed as I frantically grabbed the carton and pulled it from them, both of them staring at me wide-eyed as they held their spoons full of raw cookie dough just inches from their mouths.

"Quick, where did you find this?"

"In your freezer," Elder Martin answered, a little breathlessly. I suspected after this slightly psychotic behavior from me that he wouldn't be so eager to visit again, despite his desire to baptize me. Especially if what I suspected was true.

I ran to the phone and dialed 911, my hands shaking.

"You've got to send somebody quick. I think the missionaries have been poisoned."

FOUR

ELDERS Martin and Tuatuola were carted off to the hospital despite their protests that they felt fine. I watched with despair as the ambulance departed, lights flashing, sirens wailing, wondering just how I was going to explain this one.

An old guy in a suit had shown up, called by the police, I guess, as he was in charge of the missionaries. After conversing with Detective Wilson—who had shown up shortly after the paramedics, shaking his head, a grim set to his mouth—the Church man gave me a very nasty look before he got into his blue sedan and took off behind the ambulance. I suspected I was in deep shit with the Mormon Church, something I could hardly afford in my line of work. Since the majority of Utah residents were Mormon, and I taught dance to young Utah residents, it stood to reason that lots of my students were Mormon. I imagined my name going onto some list somewhere—a "stay away from this heathen" kind of list—and my stomach churned with fear and angst.

"Oh, God. Oh, oh God." I knew I was muttering out loud, but the events of the morning were not exactly calming. Surely one could not be blamed for being slightly hysterical?

As he walked toward me, Detective Tate Wilson gave me a funny look. Not a good funny look, either, but a "what have you done now?" kind of look, like Grandma Gilly used to give me when I broke something in her house.

"Tell me again what happened," he said, his lips tight, his words terse. I'd already informed him that there had been no cookie dough in my freezer just yesterday, and that I knew someone had put the dough there to frame me—boy, did that sound like an old movie line. "Start with last night after I dropped you off. I know you didn't leave." He'd been watching me. A warm rivet of pure adrenaline ran through my body, although I wasn't quite sure why. Of course he was watching me. I was a suspect, and these newest events just cemented it. Still, he was watching me . . . Watching *me*.

"Jenny?" he prodded. I ran down the events of my evening after he dropped me off. Nothing, nothing, and more nothing. Then bed. He gave me another look. Truthfully, the look Tate Wilson was giving me was not the kind of look you wanted to get from a man you had erotic dreams about, and truthfully, the night before, in my dreams, just before he tried to hand me the orange jumpsuit, I had been seduced and was naked on a bearskin rug in front of my fireplace. Of course, in the dream my body was perfectly smooth and thin, with nothing bulging out in an unsightly way. In my dream, tuition had been paid and I had fire logs. Dreams were great. Then reality barged in, and I had a sudden, sharp vision of myself in the orange jumpsuit, behind bars, looking like a creamsicle. A tasty treat for Big Bertha . . .

"Oh God. Oh, oh God," I repeated. Detective Wilson rolled his eyes. I ignored him.

"Tell me again what happened last night," he said slowly, as though trying to be patient, and not really succeeding.

"You dropped me off, I watched a little television, and then I went to sleep."

I needed a life.

"And you locked the door, right?"

I nodded.

"So, you didn't hear anyone come into your apartment? There is no sign of forced entry. Have things been moved? The chain lock isn't cut or altered, so I think that . . . Uh-oh. I know that look. You didn't lock it, did you?"

"I always forget. I locked the dead bolt. No one can get through that, right?" He didn't nod in agreement, which meant I had been totally wrong for years. What was new? "Nothing bad has ever happened to me here. I live with old people. I have nothing to steal. And even the stuff that is not worth stealing is not gone. The only thing different is I just have cookie dough in my freezer where there was none before."

"Your own life should be enough to make you lock that chain, Jenny. You should use every defense you have against the bad guys." He shook his head. "You're sure nothing else is missing or gone? And you are also sure you didn't have any cookie dough in your freezer?"

"Hell, yes! You think I wouldn't know if I had something edible in my freezer? I'd have eaten it last night! Four days until tuition is due! Stale bologna! No sane person would say no to cookie dough." I was pretty sure I had waved my arms in the air when I said that, but that's got to be understandable.

He grinned, and I felt butterflies in my stomach as he showed off his white, even teeth and perfect dimples. My knees felt a little weak. Must have been all the excitement. Or the fact that if I had eaten the dough, and if it had been poisoned, I could now be just as dead as Sandra Epstein. Did someone want me dead—beside a slew of dance moms?

"Well, the suspect dough is now at the crime lab, and it'll be tested to see whether there is anything in it, and if so, whether it matches the poison we found in the dough Sandra Epstein was eating."

"Suspect dough? Heh. That sounds funny."

"You're kind of weird."

He had no idea.

After the police cars and the ambulance and the detective left, my apartment felt pretty big again. The neighbors were all out gawking, so I stayed inside. I didn't want to have to explain why the missionaries were getting their stomachs pumped. They might have thought I was some radical anti-Mormon, and they were already suspicious because of my annual Book of Mormon sale. This whole mess was not conducive to receiving Christmas cookies and homemade candy.

Inside, my phone was ringing, and, thrown off my usual check-the-caller-ID-stride—and being very worried about the missionaries—I answered, only to hear the one voice I was not prepared to deal with this morning. "Hello, Jennifer, dear, it's Auntie Vi. I hear you tried to kill the missionaries."

Auntie Vi was my father's sister, and she never had children of her own. This was somewhat of a cardinal sin in Utah, so to compensate she had schnauzer dogs she dressed in clothing, took shopping, and fed from the table, perhaps thinking that no one would notice her children had pointy ears, long snouts, and very wet black noses. My father called her eccentric. My mother called her a nutbag. Her poor dogs looked incredibly stupid in sweaters—especially the fat one named Sweetie—but no one dared to tell her that.

My aptly named Uncle Mort owned a local mortuary—get it? Mort? Mortuary?—and thus made a good living burying the big families Utahns were prone to have. This allowed Auntie Vi to live a life of leisure, since dogs were not known to require as much maintenance as human children.

With all this spare time on her hands, she had become the biggest gossip in Ogden, and had sources planted all over the city. "I didn't try to kill the missionaries, Auntie Vi. Someone put some cookie dough in my freezer that might have been poisoned, and they found it, that's all."

"And why would someone want to poison you, dear? I mean you're just a dance teacher. Perhaps if you had kept your important job with the sheriff's office, then I could understand it, but . . ."

It always happened. After a moment of listening to Auntie Vi, all I heard was blah, blah, blah, blah, blah, sort of like the adults sounded in the Charlie Brown cartoons I watched as a kid.

She blathered on, and I finally cut her off. "Gotta run, Auntie, I'm going to be late for class." This was a bald-faced lie because I didn't teach on Saturdays or Sundays. Good thing I wasn't religious, or I might be worried I was going to hell for lying.

The phone rang again before I could get two steps away from it. This time I looked at the caller ID, and sighed. There was no running from this one. "Jennifer? What in tarnation is going on?" It was my father, using his "you are in deep shit young lady" voice. Somehow, the fact I was now thirty years old—well past the legal age for parental scolding—had no effect on him.

Auntie Vi, the rat, had informed on me. Called them before she even called me.

"Look, Dad, someone killed one of my dance moms two nights ago. They poisoned her with cookie dough that we were selling for a fundraiser. The police have questioned me because I didn't exactly get along with her, but I'm not in any trouble."

"What's this I hear about you trying to kill the missionaries?" I was going to get Auntie Vi—and maybe her little dog, too—if it was the last thing I did.

I sighed heavily. "I didn't try to kill the missionaries. They found some cookie dough in my freezer that I didn't put there, and they ate it, so the paramedics took them to the hospital as a precaution."

"You know, Jenny, you can just tell them no. You don't have to kill them to keep them from coming to your door . . ."

"Dad!" I yelled into the phone. I didn't like yelling at

my dad, but I couldn't help myself. Things had been a bit stressful lately. "I did *not* try to kill the missionaries."

There was a pause, and then my father pulled the trump card. "Your mother isn't going to like this."

"Yeah, well her daughter isn't too crazy about it, either. Good-bye, Dad."

"Jenny?"

"Yes?"

"Are you in some kind of trouble?"

"Yes, Dad, I am in trouble, because I don't know who is doing this, or why. But I'm sure the police will get to the bottom of it. Love you. Kiss Mom for me."

I hung up the phone and grabbed my purse and keys. Mrs. Emma Anderson had some explaining to do.

FIVE

EMMA and Ella Anderson lived on Polk Street, just far enough east of Harrison to be safe from the decay that had beset the downtown area. All the downtown Ogden streets were named for United States presidents, but I couldn't tell you much more than that. I know about Washington, and even Madison (there was a musical based on that president's wife! I know my musicals), but I'd always thought Harrison was an actor. You know, Harrison Ford? Anyway, the Andersons had a nicely maintained older brick home, set in a nicely maintained neighborhood, directly across the street from the not-so-nicely maintained abode of Sandra Epstein. A pack rat and garage-sale junkie, Sandra collected other people's trash for a living. I knew about her collecting habits because I often took Taylee home after dance when Sandra failed to show to pick up her daughter from class. Even before her home was draped with yellow crime-scene tape, it had been rather unsightly, with bicycles, lawn gnomes, wheelbarrows, and oddly unrelated decorations strewn about the entire area. A fresh coating of snow made all the junk in Epstein's yard look eerily threatening, like monsters or gremlins holding perfectly still until you got close, and then they'd come to life and jump out and get you and . . .

Breathe, Jenny, breathe. I'd always had an overactive imagination, and today it was working in double time. I had to keep it under control. I turned away from the Epstein's and turned to look at the home on my left.

The Anderson residence was exactly the opposite of Epstein's home. The yard was immaculate, even in the bitter cold of winter, and Christmas decorations were placed all around the snow-covered lawn. Here in Utah, Christmas season officially begins on Thanksgiving Day, so it was no surprise that Emma Anderson's yard was decorated. White wire reindeer, intricately wrapped with Christmas lights, pranced through the yard. Christmas bulbs draped perfectly along the eaves, and on the porch, two elves stood with outstretched hands, beckoning visitors to come forward and stay a while. It was very inviting, even during the daytime, and I cringed a little as I thought about what I knew. Mrs. Anderson was a single mom whose husband had left her for another woman. The dance-mom rumor mill—famous for getting things horribly distorted, like the old game of telephone I used to play when I was a kid—said that after she was unable to produce more children, she became desperate to make Ella the perfect child, and began spending all her time and energy—and husband's money—on creating FrankenElla. Mr. Anderson got tired of being ignored, and took up with his secretary. From that point forward, Mrs. Anderson began to strive to be the perfect mother and wife, as well as to have the perfect daughter. She spent hours fixing up her house. Hours fixing up her yard. Hours trying to fix up her daughter, who had absolutely no interest in being fixed.

As I stared at the yard now, it all came to me, and a deep sorrow flooded my veins. Maybe Emma Anderson wasn't a psycho dance mom for the same reasons other women became psycho dance moms. Maybe she was trying to create the perfect scenario—wonderful home, fabulous meals, talented beautiful daughter—that would bring her husband back home. It would explain a lot.

I turned and caught sight of the untidy Epstein house with the snow-coated demons in the front yard. I didn't know her story, even though, after a few years of teaching dance, I knew everyone had a story. Sandra Epstein had come to the studio with a daughter whom she believed to be the next Leslie Caron. No one knew much about her. No one ever really bonded with her, even though most dance moms can find someone else who is like them, or gets along with them. All we knew was that her daughter was very talented. Sandra Epstein was a study of all or nothing. Either she came to every practice, and stayed the entire time, or she didn't show at all. Sometimes, for weeks at a time, Taylee took the bus to class and I often gave her a ride home, because it bothered me to see her sitting on the bus bench all alone, so small and defenseless.

She opened up a little to me during those times, and we would talk about her dreams and aspirations. And I could keep her talking, as long as I didn't question her too closely about her dance background or personal issues like who or where her father was.

When Sandra did come to class, she sat there sullen and icy, and didn't speak to the other moms, which immediately made her an outcast and object of suspicion, particularly among those trying to curry favor with me. Epstein became my mortal enemy shortly after Taylee joined Jenny T. Partridge Dance because she believed that Taylee should be the focus of every routine. I had seventy-two other girls to worry about, with seventy-two other moms, so I tried to be at least a little bit fair. This was hard to explain to strident stage moms.

"Taylee is the best dancer you have," she would say in her high-pitched, rapid-fire voice, tinged with a sharp, nasal, "back East" accent. And in a way, she was right. Taylee was good. She was fluid and strong, and had excellent ballet training and flawless technique from some prior studio that Sandra Epstein would not reveal. I had a hard time not placing her in front-row fifty in every routine, just because she could carry the dance. Your eyes found her and that was it. The entire team looked good because of her. Taylee would be my Sugar Plum Fairy—or at least that had been what I had planned. Now that her mother was dead, who knew what would happen?

But I couldn't stand the grief from the other moms if I didn't give their daughters equal dance time. And I really didn't care much for Sandra and her situation, whatever it was. I found the whole thing rather odd, just like the woman herself, with her dark brown unkempt hair, circles under her eyes, and large baggy clothing.

I wondered where Taylee was now? As far as I knew, Epstein didn't have any relatives in the area, and my heart pinged a little bit at the thought of the quiet, forlorn little girl in the care of strangers.

Maybe I could take her home with me. *Yeah, right.* I couldn't even keep plants alive. I sincerely doubted I was mother material. And right now, I was kinda the prime suspect in her *real* mother's demise. But as I stared at her house, the memories of Taylee sitting on the floor before last year's *Nutcracker* performance, carefully applying her own makeup while her mother watched, made me feel even worse. She had been only eleven then, but seemed so self-sufficient. Her mother's strident rages and incredible pushiness didn't translate into caring for Taylee—only into pushing the people surrounding her daughter into giving in to her demands. The more she yelled, the quieter Taylee became.

I remembered the stormy and cold night she couldn't get her mother on the telephone, and so I took her to my house after dance, because when we drove by her house it was dark. I made popcorn and we watched the movie *Honey*—the one where Jessica Alba is a really hot dancer—and we laughed and chatted, and when the movie was over, Taylee turned to me and said, "How come you don't have kids? You'd be a great mom."

Of course, I knew she was wrong. I would not be a great mom. I couldn't even take care of myself.

"Where do you think your mom is, Taylee?" I'd asked.

"Home," she said quietly. "She's probably asleep and didn't hear the phone. She does that a lot." She hesitated, then spoke again. "Don't be mad at me, but I have a key. I could have just gone in. But I didn't want to be alone tonight."

Right about then I started to believe that Epstein might have a tiny drug or alcohol problem, although I couldn't really remember smelling booze on her. I'd wanted Taylee to stay over that night, but she'd refused, and I'd dropped her off around 11 p.m. There was a light on in the kitchen, so I figured Sandra had roused herself.

Now I stared at the abandoned Epstein house as I thought of Taylee. Old beyond her years, she was one of my best students—quiet, reserved, respectful, always following directions. She truly was a natural dancer who lost herself while performing. What would happen to her now? Furthermore, where *was* she now? In all the rush and concern for myself, I hadn't asked anyone where Taylee was. What kind of person was I?

I sighed deeply and pushed the breath in and out of my lungs, watching it billow in white clouds after it left my pursed lips, as I contemplated my character—or lack thereof.

I would have to ask Detective Wilson. Or Emma Anderson. Or probably Auntie Vi, who knew everyone in and everything about Ogden.

I stared more determinedly at the Epstein house. I should go over there and look around. They did it on television all the time. The spunky heroine always solved the crime. Maybe I could figure out what had happened to Sandra Epstein, rescue Taylee, and get my own ass off the hook for the murder. I was spunky . . . wasn't I?

I could do this. If only someone was with me . . . Because my true nature was that of a big, fat scaredy-cat, I had called Amber to meet me here. She didn't answer her cell phone. James was otherwise engaged, getting an "absolutely vital pedi and mani," and my other friend, Alissa Miller, the only connection I still had with the Weber County Sheriff's Department, had to work. Marlys had four kids so her Saturdays were jam-packed with indoor soccer and swimming and other mysterious mom duties that I could not comprehend. I was on my own, so it was best to start at the house where a woman had *not* died. I walked up the stairs to the Anderson's front door and knocked. Everything looked like it was locked up tight, and I rang the bell several times but didn't get an answer. I walked around the side of the house to the back porch, my feet crunching loudly in the snow, making me wince, and tried to peer in the back window but could see nothing. At only five-two, I mostly had a bird's-eye view of the nicely painted white windowsill.

I surveyed the backyard for a moment, lips pursed as I thought, and then crossed over to the detached garage, also tightly locked up. I peered through the garage window, and saw nothing but a neatly maintained space, empty of any vehicle.

Walking back to my car, I looked across at the Epstein house and got a glimpse of something shiny reflecting out one of the front windows. The house faced west, and was not currently in the favored path of the miserly winter sun, positioned mid-sky but mostly hidden by thick clouds, so the reflecting flashes struck me as odd. Curious, I crossed the street and wandered as close to the crime-scene tape as I dared. I squinted my eyes to see if I could see the flashes again, but there was nothing. My mother always squinted when she was trying to see something, too vain to admit she needed glasses. My own vision was twenty-twenty.

"Squinting is stupid," I said. Time for a more proactive stance. Glancing carefully from side to side, but seeing nobody watching, I purposefully pulled up a small amount of the crime-scene tape and sashayed under it. I'm pretty limber and have sashaying down to an art, so I moved fairly quickly up the driveway and to a side window where I would not be seen by the neighbors, passing cars, and possibly a certain policeman who seemed to have a burning desire to see me behind bars.

Staring through, I caught another glimpse of reflecting light, although the house was totally dark. One flash, then another, and my curiosity welled up, uncontainable as it had been when I was a kid. It was my curiosity that had made me overflow Grandma Gilly's tub. I'd wanted to see if her falsies would make me float. To do that, I had to have a lot of water, and it was an old, deep tub. Sure enough, strapped around my skinny chest, the falsies did indeed float, and I was so intrigued I didn't notice the water flowing onto the floor and out under the crack of the door.

That same curiosity led me to ignore a big catch of fear in my throat—and the sense of the forbidden—and I walked farther back to the side door of the golden-color brick house. I passed by pink flamingos stuck haphazardly into dirt, identifiable up close from the patches of pink showing through where the snow had melted, and little lawn decorations made up to look like people with their big butts sticking out as they tended to the yard. The door, to my surprise, was slightly ajar, and I looked around guiltily before sliding inside, my heart pounding so loud I couldn't hear anything but a steady thump-thump-thump. In the dark, I couldn't see too much, and I stood there waiting for the pounding in my head to go away and my eyes to adjust to the dark. I stood in what appeared to be a kitchen, messy and unkempt, the smell of rotting food causing my stomach to churn and my eyes to water.

I turned to leave, deciding my brief career as a detective was over, when I caught another glimpse of flashing light in the room just beyond the kitchen.

My curiosity pulled me forward instead of out the door—which my common sense told me I should be exiting through right now. Oh well. I was a redhead. Blame it on poor impulse control. I slowly walked toward the place where I had seen the flashing light, when I was suddenly blinded by a powerful beam.

In that one brilliant moment, it was all horribly—and dangerously—clear.

Someone was inside this house with a flashlight. Someone who, like me, had no business being in this house.

Someone who was most likely a killer.

I turned to run but was stopped cold by a sudden sharp pain in my head.

SIX

I awoke to a light that hurt my eyes, and some sort of metal pointed directly at my head. When I could get my eyes to focus, I saw that the metal was attached to the hand of an extremely attractive, very tall, very angry man wearing a nicely tailored dark blue suit. The metal was also a gun.

I allowed myself a brief moment of panic and sheer terror, and then forced myself back to reality. *Come on, criminals were not this good looking.* Only in movies. In real life, criminals were ugly, stupid, and usually, kind of stinky. Often they were drunk, and sometimes they had even forgotten their collective mothers had potty-trained them years before. Crime does not pay. Rather, it sucks the little intelligence you might have out of your brain. One of the big reasons I taught dance instead of robbing banks for a living. That and the fact I looked awful in the brighter shades on the color wheel.

This guy was not your average criminal. In fact, he looked a lot like a cop, although not one I'd ever met. His dark green eyes shot daggers at me and I could see the hint of a dimple on each cheek, above his square, strong jaw.

"What have you done with her?" he asked in a commanding, but surprisingly silky voice.

"Done with who? And why the hell did you hit me?"

I was starting to get cranky. Lack of a good meal and jonesing for potato salad will do that to you, even when a gun was pointed at your head—a head that throbbed with every pulse of blood flowing through my veins. For a second, a brief flash of joy ran through my veins—joy that I wasn't twelve feet under. I could be dead, but the pain reminded me I was not. I was, however, in a bit of a pickle.

"I didn't hit you. Why are you trespassing on a crime scene?" he asked, changing tacks, the gun still aimed at me.

Crime scene. Yeah, he was a cop. Probably. Until I knew for sure, I was proceeding with caution. At least as much caution as I was capable of. "Who are you? Why are *you* here? I'm Sandra's friend, and Taylee's dance teacher. I was trying to find out why Taylee didn't come to dance." That was a big fat lie, and just another mark against me in God's black book.

"Taylee's dance teacher? As in the *prime suspect* in her mother's murder?"

Ooops. Guess I should have thought that one through. It was that poor impulse control again.

"I did not kill anybody. But someone is doing an awfully good job of trying to convince the police I did."

"And you came here to prove your innocence? Or perhaps to hide some evidence?"

Man, this was just like television, and everyone knew that when your criminal case was proceeding like it did on television, you were in deep doo-doo. I decided to be honest. Lying had never gotten me anywhere. But before I proceeded, I wanted to know exactly who this man was.

"Who are you?" I asked him again. If he said something like, "I am your worst nightmare," I was going to pee my pants. It would not be pretty.

He finally dropped the gun to his side, but did not holster it.

"You're Jenny Partridge, aren't you?" He was still avoiding answering my question. "Why did you come here? Tell me the truth." The look he gave me made me want to confess every sin I'd ever committed, in mind-numbing detail. Except I still wasn't exactly sure what I was dealing with, even though I was fairly certain he was a cop. I just couldn't put a finger on his connection with the case. So I fudged a little. Just a little.

"I actually came to find Emma Anderson. She lives across the street. I gave her the cookie dough to deliver to Sandra, and she told the police I didn't. I came to find out why she lied. But she's gone. Her house is locked up tight. And then I looked over here and saw something flashing, so I came in to investigate. But why did you have to hit me?"

"I didn't hit you," Mystery Man said, finally holstering the gun. Further proof he was a cop. Criminals tucked their guns in the waistbands of their dirty jeans. "Do you need medical attention?"

"No, I'm fine," I said weakly, reaching up to touch the back of my head and growing dizzy when I pulled my fingers back and could see they were covered with blood. "Or maybe I'm not."

The world started spinning then, and he eased me back down onto Sandra's dirty floor, while images of germ spores crawling into my wound danced through my head—no sugarplums to be found in this disaster of a kitchen. "This floor is not clean. This cannot be sanitary," I muttered as I tried to get my vision to clear and the world to stop rotating.

He moved out of my vision for a moment and came back with a semiclean couch pillow, in a horrid shade of puce. He lifted my head up gently, then put the pillow beneath it and lowered me back down onto the pillow, and talked in his cell phone all at the same time.

He was multitalented, as well as being incredibly handsome.

"Who are you?" I asked Mystery Man again.

He didn't get a chance to answer before the troops arrived.

"OUCH," I complained to the paramedic who dabbed at the back of my head with some sort of antiseptic cloth.

Mystery Man was chatting with a local uniformed police officer over on the other side of the messy kitchen. They'd been the first to arrive on the scene, apparently called before I woke up on the floor of Sandra's trashed house. I saw no sign of Detective Wilson, but I imagined he'd show up any time now. After all, this was his case. But if that was true, who was tall, dark, and handsome?

"Well, you should be okay, and don't need stitches, but I really think you should get an MRI or something, Jenny," the paramedic told me. His name was Bones. Really. Well, that was his nickname. It occurred to me that I had no idea what his real name was. I also did not know why that was occurring to me right now, when it had no relevance whatsoever to my situation.

I'd been on ride-alongs with him before I bailed on my dispatch job, so I knew him fairly well. The other cops and medics called him Bones for two reasons. One, from time to time he was called to pick up the "bag of bones" that used to be a person. And two, because he was so skinny there wasn't any meat at all on him. I could loan him some of mine. There was another possible reason they called him Bones, but I was *not* going there. Cops were great for giving nicknames. Everybody who worked at the Weber County Sheriff's Department ended up with one. For example, the sluttiest dispatcher was called "McDonald's" because of all the officers she had "served."

I was lucky I'd quit the job when I did, before I could end up with a nickname like "Cheetos," both because I liked to eat junk food and because I had red hair.

I assured Bones I would be fine, and he helped me sit up slowly. Every light in the Epstein house was now blazing, where before it had been dark.

It was also filled with people, along with a ton of junk. Man, Sandra Epstein had been a serious pack rat. Mystery Man was done talking to the uniform, and he headed toward me purposefully, his stride long and strong, and I found myself drawn to him, with his square, strong shoulders, full head of dark hair, and long legs.

When the side door opened and Detective Tate Wilson walked in, I stopped my perusal of Mystery Man. Now I was in deep shit. He was either here to arrest me or to beat me to death because I was checking out another cop. Hmm, that bonk on the head must have done more damage than I realized . . .

He reached me about the same time the hunky stranger did. "Lucy, you got some 'splainin' to do," Wilson said to me as he waggled a finger at me.

I burst out laughing at his comment. Wilson was familiar with *I Love Lucy*, which had been popular long before both of us had been any sort of twinkle in our parents' eyes. Be still my immature heart.

One side of his mouth quirked up in that half grin I found so irresistible and I remembered that was exactly the look on his face when I'd been naked before him on the bearskin rug—in my dream. Well, not completely naked. I think I probably had a diamond anklet on, too. But nothing else. I could live in my dreams.

"United States Marshal Andrew Fallon," Wilson drawled, pointing to me, "meet dance teacher Jenny Partridge." *Marshal? Get the heck outta Dodge!*

"Jenny, are you okay?" I looked up to see that Alissa had arrived, still in her uniform from work. She was everything I was not—tall, willowy, brunette, and long legged like a runway model. I should hate her. She even made the ugly dispatch uniform look good. I didn't miss the looks Marshal Fallon and Detective Wilson gave her. I was used to it.

She ignored them. "I got the call and the supervisor let me come and make sure you were okay," she said. Alissa was the one tie I had left with the sheriff's department, other than my passing acquaintance with all sorts of law enforcement personnel. We had bonded over lattes and man trouble, and had become fast friends, even though I was jealous of her personal assets. Alissa was the rare person who truly was just as beautiful inside as she was on the outside. *Ugh.* I sounded like a Hallmark card.

"I'm okay. Sore. But okay."

"I'm taking you home," she said, pulling me to my feet unceremoniously, while the paramedics and the police officers all watched her with their mouths open. Disgusting. Why didn't I have that kind of power with men?

"Wait just a minute," Wilson said, finally closing his mouth to quit drooling and then opening it to speak. I fought off the twinge of jealousy. I'd met this man only by the unfortunate circumstances that were my life. It's not like I owned him. I barely knew him. So he got kind of slack jawed and Neanderthal-like at the sight of Alissa. Men always did. I should be used to it. "We need to talk to Jenny."

My cell phone, which I had stuck into my pocket just before I got out of my car, chose that opportune moment to ring. Saved by the bell!

"Hello?"

"Jenny, it's Amber. We've got a major problem here. Monica's had a meltdown. She showed up here at the studio about ten minutes ago raving about the ostrich feathers on the Sugar Plum Fairy costume. Now she's locked herself in the bathroom and won't come out until you agree to let her use fake feathers."

Monica Finch was my costume designer, sometime friend—when she wasn't going off the deep end—and a creative genius when it came to sewing. Unfortunately, a little too much genius also led her to be very flighty and more than a little unbalanced. It goes without saying that I understood her, but that doesn't mean she didn't irritate the living hell out of me.

"Oh my hell. Doesn't she understand that the fake feathers *look* fake? Only ostrich flows the right way, and when the dancers are doing their jetés . . ."

"Ostrich feathers?" Marshal Fallon asked, an eyebrow raised.

Detective Wilson rolled his eyes and said, "You don't want to know. It's always something."

"Hey," I interjected, "don't make fun. This is serious business. I have a reputation to uphold."

"I'm not making fun, Jenn, but did you remember this afternoon is the Golden Age Center's aerobics class?" Amber asked, not realizing I was talking to someone else.

Crikey, I *had* forgotten. Since I didn't teach dance on Saturdays and Sundays, I allowed Amber to teach aerobics in exchange for a slight rental fee. The Golden Agers, most of whom were in their late seventies, spent more than half their time in the bathroom, as they had reached an age when continence was somewhat unreliable.

"Good Lord. This is bad. Really bad. There'll be rivers of pee."

"Yup," Amber answered. I looked up to see about six pairs of eyes watching me. It was going to be hard to explain that "rivers of pee" comment. I probably wouldn't try.

"Um, Amber, try and talk her out, okay. I'll be there in a minute." I clicked disconnect on my cell phone, and faced my audience. "Gotta go guys. Sorry, it's an emergency."

"You can't go. We need to talk to you," Wilson said, a scowl marring his handsome face, taking some of the twinkle out of those dark blue eyes.

"Is she under arrest?" Alissa asked Wilson.

"She could be," he answered unhelpfully.

"Trespassing, maybe?" That helpful suggestion came from Marshal Fallon. Great. Now I had *two* men who wanted to see me incarcerated. My life was *really* looking up.

"Oh, please," Alissa said, rolling her eyes, and glaring at Detective Wilson. "You know as well as I do that everything she told you is exactly what happened. You are so annoying, Tate."

Tate? Did my best friend just call the man who wanted to see me dressed in prison garb—and the one I kinda wanted to see in absolutely nothing—by his *first* name? Figures. Lovely Alissa, with all her assets, would appeal to a man like Detective Tate Wilson. Why, she even looked good in orange.

"There're lives at stake here," Fallon said, and I turned my attention to his dark green eyes.

"There's an already warped wood dance floor at stake here, and my life's business down the not-so-proverbial toilet, such as it is. I have to *go*. Er, I mean I have to get to the studio *now*!"

"We'll go with you," Wilson announced cheerily.

"We will?" Fallon answered, a quizzical look crossing his face.

"Yeah, you'll enjoy it. Nothing is ever dull around Jenny."

"Okay, cool," Fallon said, and they both crossed their arms and watched as Alissa shepherded me out of Sandra Epstein's pigsty. I turned, and sure enough they were following, talking about something that sounded like sports scores. My head was still pounding, and seeing them all buddy-buddy was not helping.

Weren't federal agents and local police personnel supposed to hate each other? And furthermore, when did I become the local entertainment? The situation did not look good for me. A chill shot through me, and Alissa asked if I was okay, just as Detective Wilson sped up his pace and pulled me in the direction of his car, holding firmly on to my elbow.

"I'll drop you back to get your car later," he said, his voice a deep timbre with a hint of what I could swear was amusement. He was enjoying this. Was it possible he didn't really suspect me, and was hanging around for another reason?

"*You* aren't taking her anywhere," Alissa said, her voice full of commanding order.

"You don't run the show here, *chickie*," Wilson said, a

comment that immediately dropped him down in my esteem. *Chickie?* How could Alissa stand for that? She was fire and brimstone, and do-it-my-way-or-the-highway. *Chickie?*

"You, Wilson, are an annoying little peasant with no social skills and even less education. I could mop the floor with you, you are so low and so very, very pedantic. Please."

With that, she turned and walked away. What the hell did "pedantic" mean? And, given the derisive manner in which she had delivered her tirade, what did that say for my taste, since I thought Tate Wilson was pretty damn hot?

My boring life had gotten a lot more interesting in the last few days. Not that I was courting this kind of interesting. This was the kind of stuff that made a girl run for cover.

"Nice, Alissa, really nice," Wilson said, anger and something else crossing his handsome features. "But I'm not playing your game. I won't be the jerk you want me to be. Sorry. And Jenny is riding with me."

Apparently, whatever it was they had going was still going, or something. And I was riding with Wilson, so I rushed up to meet Alissa's long stride and asked her, "What does 'pedantic' mean? Just so I don't look dumb. And what the hell is up with you two, anyway?"

" 'Pedantic' means he is caught up in all the rules and is boring the hell out of me, and you should stay away from him." Her long strides soon saw us beside her car. "Outside of this whole mess you are caught up in, anyway. And I'll meet you at the studio. I'm not throwing you to these particular two wolves. See you there."

With that, she opened her car door, got inside, and fired up the engine.

These two wolves? Did she know Marshal Fallon, too? Where the hell was I when all these hot girl genes were being handed out? Life was not fair.

Wilson stepped up quickly behind me and grabbed my elbow, guiding me into the front seat of his Ford Taurus, as Fallon headed to another sedate blue sedan parked behind Wilson's police car.

I sighed heavily as the door slammed shut, and Wilson walked around to the driver's side of the vehicle.

My future? Not looking good.

SEVEN

My studio was located on Ogden's historic 25th Street, in the top half of a building originally built in the early 1900s. It should have been way out of my price range, as far as paying rent went, since 25th Street was the happening place to be in Ogden. But since it was located above a store that was closed more than it was open, due to the impressive vacationing schedule of the owners, I got a great deal. It was easy for me to keep an eye on things since I almost always had students going in and out of the building, and that was part of the bargain. Of course, what I would do if I was ever faced with an intruder remained to be seen. Even though our street had a lot of homeless people, and some criminal element, due to its proximity to the Union Railroad Station, it also had a pretty impressive police presence.

I loved the atmosphere of my building, and the entire street. Of course, I didn't share the history of the old structure with most of my dance moms. In the early days of Ogden, it had been a bordello, and there were still tunnels under the buildings—although most had been closed off in order to meet earthquake codes—where all manner of illegal activity used to take place. I found it ironic that such a history-filled building now saw most of its excitement from crazy costume designers, geriatric bladders, and little dance feet.

As we walked in the front door of the studio, Amber stared wide-eyed as I came in trailed closely by Wilson, then Fallon, and finally Alissa, glaring at both policemen through lowered—and sexy—lids.

"Yo, Lissa," Amber said to our glowering friend, then turned to me and raised her eyebrows, but made no comment. She'd been with me a long time. Weird things usually happened around me, although I don't remember ever being a murder suspect, or even showing up at the studio with two incredibly hunky lawmen.

Amber was surrounded by three elderly women, who were already doing the geriatric version of the pee-pee dance, easy to identify since I worked with little girls every day. With the older set, there was a little less hopping, and their movements were a little more jerky, but these women needed to *go*. Since the class was scheduled for 2 p.m., and it was 1:55 p.m., I believed their bladders had been spurred on by the very thought that they might *not* be able to get into the bathroom if nature called. I prayed for them to be wearing Depends and went to the bathroom door.

"No luck getting her out, huh?" I asked Amber.

"Nope, but she's been quiet for a while. No raving or blubbering. Just tell her whatever the hell she wants to hear and get her out of there. I have a date after this class." Everybody had something going on, in the romance department, except me.

One of the elderly women, a blue-hair dressed up in tight-fitting aerobics gear, wildly patterned in migraine-inducing pink and green colors, sidled up to Detective Wilson, and drawled, "How you doing, honey? Watcha doing here? Come to join our class? I could show you some moves."

Detective Wilson got a panicked look on his face and opened and closed his mouth a few times. I guessed he wasn't used to being hit on by septuagenarians—especially septuagenarians wearing tight-fitting, not entirely flattering leggings and a tank.

I turned away to face the bathroom door, ignoring his plight. About time he got himself into something he couldn't get out of. Maybe then he'd have more sympathy for my necessity-driven fundraiser that had caused all this trouble.

"Monica," I called, rapping on the door gently. "Monica, you need to come out. People need to use the restroom."

There was no answer.

"Monica," I said, knocking harder. "Monica!" Still nothing.

"Monica!" I yelled, my voice several octaves higher.

James chose that moment to saunter in the door. He was dressed immaculately, and his nails were perfectly manicured. I wasn't exactly sure why he was there, but was glad for the reinforcements. Someone who was on *my* side, instead of hoping I'd soon be locked up in county jail. Hearing me yelling Monica's name, he asked, "What's the nutbag done now?" His eyes scanned the crowd, and stopped on Detective Wilson, and then moved to Marshal Fallon. "Oh my," he murmured softly but quite audibly. "It's a smorgasbord!" Both officers moved back a bit, and I grinned, for the first time in days. About time someone else felt the heat of the furnace. This inspired me a bit. Maybe things were turning my way.

"Monica!" I yelled at the top of my lungs. "If you do not answer me, in my next performance, I will use pleather and bootie shorts in awful shades of puce and chartreuse on the Seniors, some of whom you know well should not be wearing pleather and absolutely *not* bootie shorts, and I will tell everyone in the local community that you did the designs, and you are open to more business of that nature." Like me, Monica had a reputation to uphold. Although I didn't turn students away, I did attempt to not dress them up in vulgar ways, and truthfully, bootie shorts were only cute on little girls. With little booties. And vulgar didn't hold a lot of weight in our Mormon community.

"This is like taking a left on Harrison Boulevard and landing in Oz," Marshal Fallon commented.

"It'll get better," Detective Wilson assured him.

I ignored them both. There was a brief silence, and then we heard, "I am not coming out until you promise I can use the faux feathers." Her voice was high and tinny, a mixture of Mickey Mouse and helium. I used to think she was faking it, using that voice, but soon came to realize that no, this was Monica, creative design genius with the Betty Boop voice. When she got excited, dogs everywhere dove for cover.

"Come out and we'll talk," I promised, my voice within normal range now.

"No, no, I can't. I can't do this anymore, Jenny. You put too many demands on me, and I just can't handle it."

Demands? Good God, I paid the woman more money than I made, and I was making demands? I needed a new life. A new career. Disgust filled me and I turned away from the door, only to spy both Detective Wilson and Marshal Fallon watching me intently, unfathomable looks on their faces. There were also four elderly ladies standing there watching me, their eyes starting to look slightly yellow, and I knew time was running out. I gazed back at the two cops, and their intent looks, and I knew they were probably wondering what strange or kooky thing would happen to me next.

I turned back to the bathroom door.

"Dangit, Monica, get the heck out of there, or I am going to freaking kick your ass!"

"Did she just say 'dangit,' 'heck,' and 'freaking'?" Marshal Fallon asked.

"She works with kids. And Mormon kids, to boot. You have to understand," Alissa said gently, giving me a knowing glance. I didn't like it when she got gentle. It meant she was explaining away my eccentricities, like she used to do when I worked—briefly—for the sheriff's office. I might be weird, but I was capable! My blood began to boil. I could swear with the best of them, except I didn't choose to. Another reason I didn't fit in at the sheriff's office. Even the most Mormon of the law enforcement agents put sailors to shame. And I'd never really picked up the cursing habit.

"She did say 'ass,'" James piped up helpfully.

"Monica, you are seriously pissing me off," I screamed at the door. Even though she was part of the problem, she didn't deserve my intense anger. But my life had gone to hell in a go-cart in the past few days, so she was getting it.

"I will *not* make your wedding dress if you don't stop yelling at me, and if you don't agree to use the faux feathers," was her reply. It was as loud as she got, and I knew she meant it. "I have spent *days* trying to find the real ones, at a reasonable cost, and it's a nightmare you cannot . . ."

"Wedding dress?" Wilson said, interrupting the helium voice from the other side of the door. "You're getting married?"

Things went from bad to worse in the blink of an eye.

EIGHT

"Ooopsies, forgot about an appointment I have," James said rapidly, backing toward the door, staring at his left wrist where there was no watch, since he couldn't afford a Rolex just yet and he wasn't about to settle for anything less.

"Do. *Not*. Take. Another. Step," I said to James, putting my hands on my hips in my best dance-teacher authoritative stance. Amazingly, he stopped. I'd had enough happen in the past few days that he must have realized I was about to go dancing off the edge.

"Monica, get your damned ass out here, now!" Compelled by my tone, and of course the profanity that I rarely used—because I was afraid that once I started I wouldn't be able to stop—Monica unlocked the door and stepped out. Tiny, with short blond hair, she was almost elfin, and she looked more like a kindergarten teacher than a costume designer for dance teams. But she had a gift. I could tell her what I wanted, and she could produce it, sometimes inside of an hour. Of course, it didn't take much to push *her* off the edge.

"Move aside, I gotta go," boomed the most aggressive

of the elderly women in aerobics gear, as she pushed Monica out of the way and zoomed into the bathroom, slamming the door behind her. The other ladies continued their pee-pee dance, lining up in front of the door.

"I asked for ostrich feathers, because that is what I wanted. The others don't flow right. You, Monica, can do anything. I've seen you create miracles with a bolt of fabric and some sequins. You can find the right feathers. Now go do it."

Chagrined, Monica lowered her head and aimed her body for the door, where James was standing, probably looking for a good opportunity to skedaddle before I got hold of him.

"Wait, Monica," I called. "Why did you think I needed a wedding dress?"

I pretty much already knew what had happened, or at least some semblance of what had happened, but I wanted as much information as I could get before I tried to fix this latest mess. Ogden was not a big enough town for this type of information to stay undercover. I was going to have to do damage control.

She looked at me for a moment, a wary look on her face, her eyes darting frantically back and forth, as if she were trying to discover whether this was going to get her into more trouble with me. Monica was in deep need of some psychological counseling, but I was afraid if they ever got hold of her, they would lock her up and throw away the key, so I'd never suggested she seek help. I needed her warped genius. I needed costumes.

"Sister Marriott called and said you'd finally come to your senses. She said probably to figure on June for the wedding dress."

"She did, did she?" I started to steam. I didn't mind helping James out with his impossible mother—who, by the way, seemed to like me, but never let an opportunity to convert me to Mormonism pass her by—but planning a faux wedding? My mother was going to have kittens. "And tell me what else she said."

I knew Sister Marriott wouldn't have left it at that. She didn't approve of me as a partner for her baby boy, but I was the only female she'd seen in James's company in the past five years. She probably figured she was stuck with me. She had no idea. I liked to imagine she wouldn't find me nearly so abhorrent if she compared me to the artsy males James preferred.

"Well, she mentioned maybe you could start going to church a little bit," Monica said, using her prevaricating skills, finely honed from years of telling me costumes would be ready weeks before they actually were. Did I mention her design genius, which is why I still dealt with her? Oh, and I kind of liked her, too, in a strange way.

"Monica . . ."

"Oh, hell, Jenny, she's in denial. She has no idea James is a flaming queer, and if you don't know that by now, you are never going to!"

James gasped, putting his right hand to his chest. "I beg your pardon. How could you . . ."

"Oh shut up, James," I said crossly. "Nobody here is fooled. We all know you're gay and we're all wondering when the hell you are going to find the balls to tell your mother. You do still have those, right?"

There was another indignant gasp from James, and then he turned and stalked off into a corner, very dramatically. I knew he'd be mad for about ten minutes. He knew he was gay, too. Although the balls comment might stick in his throat a little.

I turned to Monica. "You thought I didn't know?"

"Um, well there was that whole wedding thing from his mom, and the dates and stuff, and well . . ."

"You know, I have been dealing with all of you nuts for quite a while now. And I've never said anything. But I really need some help now, Monica. Right now, my whole life is riding on this performance. Hell, it is *always* riding on this performance. I run my whole studio for the year based on what I earn from *The Nutcracker*. And so I need your help. Please help me. Just get the costumes done.

Please." I knew desperation tinged my voice, but I was unable to control it. I glanced at the two cops watching the whole scene, and saw a funny expression cross Detective Wilson's face. God, please tell me it wasn't pity. I didn't want his pity. What I *did* want from him was more complicated.

Monica paused for a moment, and then spoke. "I'm not a nut, Jenny, but I do understand. I'll find the ostrich feathers somehow."

She turned and scurried out of the studio.

During the entire event, old women had been entering and exiting the bathroom, giving the two cops a once-over and me strange looks.

I could hear the sounds of KC and the Sunshine Band pounding out from the main studio, where Amber was teaching aerobics to the geriatrics.

"Well, that was fun," Wilson said, amusement in his voice. "I've got to hand it to you, Jenny. Things are never boring around you. This is the most fun I've had investigating a homicide in . . . well, ever."

Homicide investigations were supposed to be fun?

"Look, it's been a long afternoon. Ask me any questions you have, and then can I please just go home and die?" I winced as I said the words. "I mean relax."

James was trying to inch his way toward the door. "Stop!" I ordered him. He froze.

"Sure, Jenny. We'll pick the questioning up tomorrow. I'm sure you've told us all you know," Detective Wilson said, surprising both me and Alissa. She raised her eyebrows and stared at him. Fallon's face remained blank.

"Okay, but tomorrow is Sunday. Surely you won't be working tomorrow?" I needed a day off. I would stay in my bed and not move. I wouldn't answer the phone, I wouldn't answer the door. Unless I could find a place that delivered potato salad. I'd answer the door for them, but they'd want money. I considered inviting myself to my parents' house for dinner, but that would require answering questions. I'd already said I was not answering *anything*. Maybe I could make my own potato salad. No, that would require money to purchase ingredients. Although today had seemed eternal, it was *still* four days until tuition was due. Also, cooking anything would require an ability to do more than boil water. Maybe I could afford some Top Ramen.

"Earth to Jenny," Alissa said. "Are you okay, girlfriend?"

"I'm fine, just beat. It's been a trying couple of days."

"When I'm on a case, I work it until it's solved," Wilson said. "But we'll let it go tonight."

"Okay, I'm out of here," Marshal Fallon said, but not before casting a lingering look over both me and Alissa, and a look of sheer terror at James, who was gazing at him longingly from his self-exiled corner, apparently having forgotten he was in deep doo-doo with me.

Fallon quickly exited the building, holding the door open for someone entering. Rushing through, along with the cold air, was a voluptuous, overly made-up woman with big hair. And she was making a bee path right for me.

Not now, I moaned to myself. *Please not now*. I closed my eyes tightly, then opened them, hoping she would be gone, but she wasn't.

Krystal Glass was larger than life, even though she was extremely petite, and when she moved into a room, it became suddenly smaller. She knew all eyes were on her, and that's the way she liked it. I personally felt like she had been reading too many magazines like *People* and *US Weekly*, because she seemed to be channeling Paris Hilton, albeit not the bazillionaire version. As it was, I think Krystal had plenty of money; I wasn't sure what her husband did, but I knew that now he was semiretired and worked with her in her shop. And whatever he had done before was still providing at least enough to keep her little Krystal Klear Designs alive. I wasn't thinking her shop and business alone were enough to survive on, but I could be wrong. She might make more money than I did. Everyone made more money than I did.

Krystal had a New York hairstyle and clothes, a year-round California tan (courtesy of a fake bake, of course), and the aspirations of a social climber. Unfortunately, there wasn't much "social" to climb in Ogden, so she'd kinda already reached the top of the pile. After that, she had to turn her attention to her washed-out, overweight, bland daughter Marilyn. And that's where I came in. Marilyn despised dance, and the woman who taught it—me. Still, Marilyn's mother was extremely forceful, so week after week the brutish teen glared at me and reluctantly clomped across my dance floor.

The fact I didn't give Monster Marilyn—a moniker assigned to her by Amber, who claimed she was about as graceful as Frankenstein—the role of the Sugar Plum Fairy really pissed off Krystal. Even worse, when I'd chosen the cookie-dough fundraiser over her more expensive, and lower profit margin, crystal mobile fundraiser, she was livid.

Given the way my day was going, I knew she was there for one reason alone. To make me regret I'd ever agreed to the cookie-dough fundraiser.

She didn't even have to try. I never wanted to see another tub of raw cookie dough as long as I lived.

"This isn't really a good time," I told Krystal, before she could even say a word. She stared at Detective Wilson, Alissa, James, and the never-ending line of old ladies entering and exiting the bathroom, and smiled smugly at me. Her long blond hair was teased high, and her makeup was intense, with a dark red line around her lips, emphasizing their fullness. Black eyeliner ringed her eyes expertly, and her lashes were long and lush. She wore tight, frayed jeans—the style that was in now, which she probably paid $130 for and which she could have found in my closet for free—and a long camisole top with a lacy bottom, covered by a short jacket, which couldn't possibly keep someone warm in this weather. But Krystal was all about the fashion.

"Jenny, I just came by to see how you were," she cooed

at me. "I heard about Sandra. It's just terrible. And cookie dough! Who would have thought it? But don't worry. I called up everyone, and let them know that there was a problem with the dough. So no one else will die."

Alarm bells went off in my head. Good God. Poisoned cookie dough meant that every tub of dough we'd sold, and delivered, and even those already consumed, were suspect. And that also meant that I would not be getting any money for the dough, and that it was entirely possible I was going to end up in the hole, and since I was already always in the hole, this could be the end of me. The end of Jenny T. Partridge Dance Academy.

"Gee, thanks, Krystal. How good of you to help me out," I muttered, trying to keep myself from reaching out and strangling her.

"No problem. I told them all to bring the dough back here to the studio Monday morning. I'll be here to help you round it up. After all, you can't exactly expect people to eat the dough, knowing that it might be poisoned. I told them to expect their refunds when they bring the dough back."

"Krystal, I had to write a check to pay for that dough. I could only write that check because they all paid for it up front. I don't have the money to give all those people refunds."

"Well, perhaps the cookie-dough company will reimburse you." She put an immaculately manicured finger up to her cheek. "I should probably give them a call, too. Would you like me to do that for you, Jenny? I'm willing to do whatever is necessary to help out."

Alissa saw the look on my face and put a hand on Krystal's arm, leading her to the door. "Thanks for your help. Jenny's had a long day. I'm going to take her home now."

"Okay, well, bye. I'll be here bright and early Monday morning to help with the cookie-dough return," Krystal said, her voice low and breathy. She turned before she left. "Oh, just one more thing. Since Taylee is missing, you'll need a Sugar Plum Fairy. Marilyn is the obvious choice. I'm sure you realize that. Just thought I'd mention that."

She sashayed out the door, aware that all eyes were on her. Wilson was eyeing her with something akin to confusion on his face. I wasn't sure if he was interested in her, found her alluring, or just thought she was weird. She was that kind of woman. James was just disgusted; he couldn't stand Krystal.

"Well, thank God she's gone. I better get, too. Lots to do, you know. Busy, busy," James said, trying to head toward the door again.

"Busy my ass. You are not going anywhere. Office. Now. *We* are going to talk."

NINE

I left Alissa and Detective Wilson in the entryway to the studio, and shepherded James into the office, shutting the door.

"You had better spill and spill now, or I will never, ever, ever escort you to another event. Ever! You can find another hapless moron to go with you."

"Hapless moron? Jennifer, I have never treated you that way. I am deeply offended."

"Good try. Not buying it. Spill."

He sighed, a big, dramatic, exaggerated sigh, and then finally spoke. "It's getting serious now, Jenny. I don't know what to do. My mother has decided she must have grandchildren before she dies. And since I am her only child, it is up to me to give her those grandchildren."

"Well, don't look at me."

"I wasn't. Jenny, as much as I love you, you're hardly my type."

"Yeah? Well, your type is not capable of producing offspring, or did you miss that somewhere along the line?"

Another big sigh from James. "Jenny, my mom is sick. She's got fluid around her heart, and the doctors aren't sure why, and so she's getting frantic to see me do some of the things I've been promising her I would do for years."

"Wouldn't it be easier to just tell her the truth?"

If eyes could shoot daggers, I'd be dead. His handsome face contorted with emotion a few times, and then softened, despair settling in on him. That damn pity gene kicked in and I felt myself begin to soften. *No, no stay strong. Resist.* After another long silence, he spoke. "I can't tell her. She has to have some idea, Jenny, because I am a walking cliché of gayness, but she lives in denial of everything I am. Sometimes I think I go overboard just so she will figure it out, but she never does. It's like the more outlandish I get—the more stereotypical—the blinder she gets. Or she knows, and just thinks that if you don't accept it, or talk about it, or think about it, it will go away. And I know this one's not going away. I've tried every way I can think of, without coming right out and saying, 'Hey, Mom, guess what, I'm queer.' I've hinted. I've introduced her to friends. She remains blissfully clueless, probably because she chooses to be. And if I told her the truth, she would probably die right there on the spot." Tears filled his beautiful blue eyes, and I caved. How could I hold up under that? James was my friend. I was a huge sucker.

"Okay, so it's not easy. But I'm not sure how you think this is going to turn out. My answer would be *not well*. Obviously, you and I are not ever going to be together, and there will be no wedding or grandchildren. Only bad things can come of this, James."

"Please, just play along. Just until I figure something else out, and until we find out if Mom's heart is going to hold out."

"James . . ."

"Jenny, I'm begging you."

"But she is trying to order me a wedding dress! She's probably shopping for invitations! Booking the ward house for a wedding under the basketball standard." I couldn't help but shudder. That was not my idea of a wedding. I was more a "wedding-on-the-beach-under-the-stars" kinda girl, although the only beach we had close was the briny, salty, bug-infested shores of the stinky Great Salt Lake. *Focus!* "And, what if *my* mom hears about this?"

"Just tell her we are talking about it, but we have not decided yet."

I didn't have the heart to tell James that my mother had long ago guessed that his sexual proclivities did not lend himself to the members of my gender. I can just imagine the lecture that would arise out of *that* discussion. I did not want to go there.

"What about me? What's going to happen when I get married and have my own kids? Well, I mean, if I decide to have kids. What then?"

"Uh, Jenn? They aren't exactly knocking down your door, are they? When's the last time you even had a date?"

I didn't know why, but James's comment stung and I felt the tears fill my eyes. I blinked rapidly, trying to hold them back, but of course he saw.

"Oh, Jenny, I'm so sorry. That wasn't very nice. I'm thinking of me, and not you, and you've had a rough time the past few days. Of course it works out great for me if you never get married or even have a boyfriend."

The tears started to flow after that comment. Never. Never was a long time, although it didn't make a lot of difference if my "boyfriend" was named Big Bertha.

"Don't cry. I said I'm sorry. I wish that we weren't such good friends and hadn't been together so much, so then I could convince my mom that someone else was my intended."

"You wish we weren't such good friends?" Even more tears. I must be premenstrual. This was nuts. I was hungry. That was it. I needed substantial food and that wouldn't happen until tuition was due, four days from now.

"Something tells me that it doesn't matter what I say, you're going to cry. So come here."

He opened up his arms and I fell against him and he

held me while I sobbed a little. So much for being stern and in command while I told him he could not use me anymore.

When I finally stopped crying, I sniffled and rubbed at my eyes, and then pulled away from him.

"Hey, look at the bright side," James said, rubbing at a mascara stain I'd left on his shirt, but kindly not commenting on it. "Those two law enforcement officials are pretty hot. Perhaps something will come of that."

"Yeah, sure it will. Prison orange will come of that. Not good. Not good at all."

"Oh, you are so right. Orange is just not a good color for you."

So much for being comforted.

"You have two weeks to figure this out, James. I have enough on my plate without dealing with your mother's delusions. Either come clean—and come out—or find another mustache."

"Another mustache?"

"You know, when the girl covers for the gay guy, so people won't know he's gay, they call her the mustache."

James cracked up. "Jennifer, you are a totally delightful human being. It's not a mustache, it's a beard, but I think I like your terminology better."

There was a rap on the door, and then Detective Wilson's voice sounded through the door. "Uh, Jenny? Is everything okay in there?"

Oh yeah, everything was just great.

TEN

ALISSA refused to leave until I assured her I'd be fine in Detective Wilson's care. She gave me a warning look before exiting out the door. Of course, I had no idea what she was trying to convey with her glare. Perhaps, "Don't sleep with him, he has a small Johnson," or "This one uses them and loses them." She gave me too much credit. I sucked at reading nuances. James left with a wink, following closely behind Alissa. Amber was still teaching dance to the geriatrics, who continued to file in and out of the bathroom every few minutes.

"Well, since this is my day off, I think I'll go home. Things haven't gone too well for me today."

"I noticed," Detective Wilson said, with a sardonic drawl coloring his voice. "Is your life always like this?"

"Pretty much. Minus dead bodies and bonks on the head, of course."

"Let's go get something to eat."

My stomach rumbled at the mere suggestion. But did I really want to be in this man's company any longer? It was exhausting, trying to decide whether he wanted to trip me up and get me to confess to a murder I had not committed, or wanted to strip my clothes off and make passionate love to me.

I was slightly terrified that the "love" part of it was totally in my head, and very one-sided, so it was easier not to think about it.

"Come on, my treat." That decided it. I didn't get that opportunity very often. And there was nothing to eat in my apartment.

We ended up at Rooster's Brew Pub, a hop, skip, and fairly substantial leap from my small studio on 25th Street. They made a killer French onion soup that was to die for. *Erk.* I really needed to watch those clichés.

After the hostess seated us on the main floor, handing us two large menus, I looked at the handsome man sitting across from me and reality settled in. "Look Detective Wilson . . ."

"Tate," he said interrupting me.

"Okay, look Tate," I said, starting again, "I'm not sure if you invited me here thinking you could soften me up and then I'd spill all the sordid details of my plot to murder Sandra Epstein, but I just have to tell you there is no plot, and I did not kill anyone."

"Yeah?"

"Yeah. I'm not a criminal mastermind. And Sandra always paid her tuition on time. She was a huge pain in my ass, but she paid! Not everyone does that, and I can't even begin to tell you how many people write me checks that bounce."

"Really? They realize that is illegal, right?"

I stared at him closely for a moment. "I guess not everyone has your legal sensibilities, Det . . . er, Tate. And I also guess I understand it. I live day to hour every single month. But it doesn't make it easier for me when people's checks bounce. Sandra paid six months at a time, and always in cash. That's kind of weird, huh, considering she had no job. At least that I know of."

"Kinda weird," he agreed. Was he agreeing? Or just trying to lead me astray? His face was emotionless, and he stared around the restaurant, his glance serious, careful, controlled.

"Hi, my name's Cullin, and I'll be your . . . Oh no." The waiter who had just walked up to our table took one look at me and turned a pasty white, his mouth falling open on the "o" and kinda staying that way for what seemed like five minutes.

"Uh, hi, Cullin. You should probably shut your mouth. Not attractive."

In compliance, Cullin shut his mouth, and then opened and shut it a few more times, like he was trying to regain control of muscles that had gone slack at the sight of me. Finally, he clamped it shut and it stayed that way. In both hands he'd been balancing glasses of ice water, and he slammed both on the table in front of us, with a resounding thwack, water sloshing over the sides and onto the table.

Tate's eyebrows lowered and his eyes tightened, and he gave Cullin a hard stare. "Is there a problem here, Cullin?"

"You have no idea what you are getting into," Cullin muttered, and then took off for the back without taking our drink order or even asking us if we wanted an appetizer. I really wanted that artichoke dip, so Cullin was going to pay.

"What now, Jenny? Old boyfriend?"

"Heck no," I said, appalled he couldn't see what to me was terribly obvious. Of course, I'd been around Cullin before. "Old boyfriend of James's. He was always jealous of our friendship. Decided he hated me, and the horse I rode in on. Did everything he could to get James to quit teaching dance for me and stop hanging out with me. In the end, I, uh, sorta helped James see the light."

"You got him to switch teams?" There was a gleam of humor in Tate's eye as he fought back a grin.

"Uh, I think it's pretty obvious that isn't ever going to happen. No, no, see I spotted Cullin with someone else, and so I did a little reconnaissance work, and got some pictures of him in a compromising position."

"So, you blackmailed him?" Man, this guy really wanted me to be a criminal bad.

"Blackmail is a harsh word. I just showed Cullin the pictures and threatened to out him."

"Out him to James? But isn't he . . . Okay, now I'm really confused."

Another man approached our table, slightly wary, but determined. Who knows what manner of lies Cullin had told. "Hi, my name is Jake, and I'll be your waiter."

"Where's our old waiter Cullin?" Tate asked, his eyes taking on that "what-the-hell-is-going-on-here" look I'd seen more than a few times in the short time I'd known him.

"Suddenly got sick. Had to go home. Can I get you an appetizer?"

"Artichoke dip," I said, speaking up quickly before Waiter Jake could discover some connection to me— *please God, don't let him be a relative of the woman I'm accused of murdering*—and bolt, too.

"Right. I'll get that coming."

"I'll take a honey wheat draft," Tate interjected.

"Oooh, can I get one of those piña coladas? With the little umbrella?"

"It'll be right out."

"A piña colada? A foo-foo girlie drink."

"I'm a girl. I've had my foo-foo moments, too."

"Yes, I am aware you are a girl. All girl. I guess you're entitled to your foo-foo drink."

Be still my beating heart. He thought I was all girl. Whoa. Hey, wait a minute. Did that mean he thought I was immature, because technically I was a woman. *Argh.* I had to stop overthinking things.

"Back to Cullin and his story. I'm kind of curious what happened."

"Well, Cullin plays on both teams. He's married with two kids. Something he didn't bother to tell James. Marlys drives a school bus, and she picks up Cullin's oldest. Of course, she didn't know the child belonged to him until the day she saw Cullin standing there, waiting for the bus, holding his daughter's hand."

"Who is Marlys, and how does she know James?"

"Marlys's daughters Carly and Maribel dance with me. And since Marlys has four kids, and they are all in one sport or another, and her husband is a teacher, she works for me in trade for her tuition. She does books, answers the phone, and mollifies the psycho moms before they go postal."

"And she drives a bus."

"Yes, she works for the Weber School District."

"So, Marlys saw Cullin. How did she know it was him?"

"Because James was parading him around like arm candy at one of our competitions last year."

"Competitions? I thought you did a *Nutcracker* performance."

"You don't know much about dance, do you?"

"Only child."

"And of course you don't have any kids, so you wouldn't have a daughter who . . ." I stopped as the realization that he could certainly have some children running around hit me. I was assuming he was feetloose and fancy-free, but he could very well have luggage—perhaps even luggage of the small human kind.

"I don't have any kids, Jenny, and I've never been married, and I don't have a fiancée or anything else lurking in my closet."

"Why haven't you ever been married?"

"Why haven't you?"

"Me? Isn't it obvious? I'm weird, I'm unstable, I live from foot to mouth week by week, and I spend all my time around raving lunatic dance moms and little kids with hygiene problems."

"Hand to mouth."

"Huh?"

"You live hand to . . . Never mind." He leaned back in his chair and shrugged off his suit coat, turning to drape it over the back of his chair, his strong arms rippling through the light fabric of his dress shirt as he completed the motion.

"So back to this competition thing. How does that work?"

"Well, I have teams that compete in local and national competitions. Usually just local, because I'm so poor I can't afford to take them anywhere but places that I can drive to. There are hundreds of dance teams up and down the Wasatch Front, so there's plenty of competitions to attend."

"And do you earn money when they win? Assuming they win."

Pride filled my heart, and the invisible voices of Nana Marian and alternately Grandma Gilly played in my head. "Pride goeth before a fall, Jennifer," said Nana. "You're going to hell in a handbasket," was Grandma Gilly's contribution. You'd think the two old women were dead and speaking to me from the otherworld, instead of both alive and kicking and, at least in Grandma Gilly's case, playing Bingo every Friday night at St. Joseph's. I shook them off.

"I win. My teams are good and they win almost every time. Usually they win overall awards. Best of show awards. But no, I don't get money. We get trophies. I have a lot of them."

"But no money?"

I sighed. "No, that's not the point. What I do earn is a reputation, and that attracts kids to my studio. I started out with fifteen dancers. Now I have more than seventy. There are a lot of bigger studios around that make a ton of money, but they have become businesses, and are no longer about the dance, in its pure form. I can't stand to have someone with my team name out there dancing and doing a crappy job. Dance is not a business. It's an art."

"Maybe you can sell the trophies and earn a little money."

I snorted. I wanted to be irritated at his comment, but the quirk of his lips highlighted a strong dimple in his right cheek, and I found myself fanning the flames of attraction instead. Damn, why did I snort? That was not attractive.

"Artichoke dip," singsonged our waiter, setting down a tray carrying the dip and our drinks. He put the dip before us, and then placed Tate's beer in front of him and my foo-foo drink in front of me. "Gave you two umbrellas," he whispered loudly, and I blushed. Then he pulled out his notepad and said, "Have you made a decision about your entrées?"

I already knew what I wanted. I'd had it a few months before, when James treated me to a birthday celebration. The Pacific Coast bisque was to die for. *Ack!* Needed to watch those clichés. But it was seriously good food. It even had a creamy mound of mashed potatoes in the middle. I'd been craving it since about three hours after I stuffed myself the first time. Potatoes were my crack. Was there a twelve-step program for a complex-carb addiction? Thinking of potatoes only reminded me how hungry I was.

"I'm ready," I said loudly, so my stomach rumble would not be audible. I ordered the bisque, snapping shut my own menu to drown out the second stomach rumble. I had voices in my head, and now my stomach was talking. What was next? I was not going to go there. I figured I'd better start stuffing that artichoke dip into my mouth before my stomach rumbling disturbed everyone in the restaurant.

"What do you recommend?" Tate asked the waiter.

"Well, do you like steak? My favorite is the center-cut tenderloin."

"I'll take it." Tate slapped shut his menu and handed it to the waiter, who then asked us for our side and soup or salad choices, and then left us alone again.

The dip was warm and flavorful, and I hoped I wasn't drooling. I forced myself to eat slowly and act like this was not my last supper—even though it might be. You never knew in my world. After I swallowed my dip and bread, I said, "This is nice. So peaceful and quiet. No ringing phones, no dead bodies . . . No . . . hey, where is my phone?" I pulled my purse off the seat next to me, where it had been resting, and dug through it, looking for my phone. Nothing but a bunch of junk. I really needed to clean this purse out.

"No phone?"

"Nope, must be at the studio. I hope."

"You don't seem too worried."

I sighed, wondering whether to tell the truth or just make something up. Considering he was a cop, I decided on the truth. Grandma Gilly would be so proud. "I lose it about every other day. It usually turns up. Once or twice it hasn't and I've had to get a new one. Good thing it's tax deductible with my business. Although the IRS might start to wonder if I lose it one more time before the end of the year."

"How many times have you lost it this year? A few more than one or two?"

"Um, I think six. Maybe seven."

He shook his head and an amused grin lit up his sometimes stern countenance. "Maybe if you didn't have to buy so many new phones, your finances wouldn't be so tight."

"Maybe," I agreed, trying to interpret what he thought of me, and coming up short. It was probably not good, so I figured I shouldn't think about it too hard. "Um, I'll try harder?"

He laughed again, and then my stomach rumbled and I put a hand to it to try and disguise the noise. Didn't work.

"You are really hungry. Do you know your stomach rumbles a lot?"

My faced turned a bright red, aware that my attempt at camouflaging my gastric noises had not worked.

"I do without a lot. But it's okay. I love what I'm doing." I didn't want to talk about my stomach anymore, so I changed the subject. And it was one that had been weighing on my mind for quite a while. "I'm really worried about Taylee. I'm such an awful person, I haven't even asked where she is. Does anyone have any idea?"

"No, not really," he said.

"Um, are you even looking for her?"

Detective Wilson—Tate—was looking around the

restaurant, classic evasive tactics. This I had not learned from cop shows on television but from watching my costume designer Monica avoid answering my questions about costumes that were supposed to be ready months before they actually were. If he knew, he wasn't going to tell me. Or he was going to wait for me to own up to the fact that I had stolen her.

"This is getting really annoying," I said, reaching over and pulling my piña colada toward me and taking a big slurp. It was only a few seconds before the brain freeze hit. Why the hell did I order a frozen drink in the middle of winter, anyway? Furthermore, why did I order an alcoholic drink? I was already seriously worried about my common-sense skills. I suspected I did not need to tamper with them further by drinking. I slapped my hand to my forehead, unable to control my actions, and through the fog of pain located in the front of my head, heard Tate chuckle.

When the pain dissipated, I pushed the foo-foo drink away and tried to focus on him again. "I'm serious about this. Where is Taylee, and why are you being vague? And do you and Marshal Fallon seriously believe that I could have taken her or"—I shuddered—"hurt her?"

"Well, I don't think that."

Hmm. More vague answers. He wasn't including Fallon in that declaration.

I sighed heavily, just as the waiter came back with our main dishes. I decided I was getting nowhere with Tate, at least as far as finding out Taylee's location, so I might as well just shut up and eat. I was starving.

I closed my eyes as the first bite of the warm, flavorful bisque dripped down my throat. "Mmmm."

"Looks good."

I opened my eyes to see Detective Tate Wilson watching me closely, ignoring the steamy, fragrant steak sitting in front of him. Instead, he was looking at me like I might be his dinner. Or at the least, a midnight snack.

Ulp! I swallowed hard.

He watched me for a moment, a bemused and sensual

look on his face, and then he picked up his fork and knife and started carving his steak.

Three days before, my life had been crazy boring, frantic, stressful, and lonely. Now it was just plain terrifying.

Eleven

DESPITE the looks Tate had been giving me during the meal, he only walked me back to the studio, watched as I scoured the place for my phone—which I finally located on the desk of my office under a mountain of invoices for the cookie-dough fundraiser—and then helped me lock up before driving me to my car, which was still parked on Emma Anderson and Sandra Epstein's street.

He watched silently as I unlocked the door, and then commented, "Pink. Should have guessed."

I'd had the Volkswagen Bug painted last year, at one of those cheap ninety-nine-dollar paint places, and in a fit of whimsy, had decided on pink. I couldn't wear the color, but no fashion dictates said I couldn't drive it. Of course, as so much in my life had been, it was a huge mistake. My car looked like a misshapen large Pepto-Bismol tablet. Even worse, I was identifiable from a hundred yards out . . . two hundred on a clear day. Everyone knew when I was coming. Good thing my business didn't rely on stealth as a key factor to success.

"Does it work when you have indigestion?" he asked.

Lovely. Everything about me was a joke. I turned on the engine and let it warm up, knowing if I tried to take off before the engine was comfortable with itself I'd look like a sixteen-year-old taking her driver's test, lurching and peeling out. Why I was worried about impressing him, I didn't know. Since giving me that bemused and, I thought, sensual look over dinner, he had done nothing more to indicate he saw me as anything other than a suspect, and a pretty strange one at that—although he did pay for my dinner.

It was hardly a date. And I was hardly dating material. A murderer was on the loose, and he probably still wasn't sure it wasn't me. Was I the only one who knew I didn't do it?

After a few moments, I knew the Bug would cooperate and so I drove off, sneaking glances at Detective Tate Wilson, standing on the street, arms crossed, watching me leave.

When I reached my street, I coasted into an open spot in front of my apartment building, shut off the car engine, and sat there for a moment. Where was Taylee? Honestly, even if I did go to jail, that was more important. Was she hurt? Kidnapped? Terrified? Crying for a mother who would never answer?

"God, please let her be okay," I muttered. I never ever learned my lesson. No good ever came of praying, at least for me. Was it because I had not chosen a religion to stick with? "I'm sorry, God. Just let Taylee be okay."

I opened up my door and grabbed my purse off the front passenger seat, then scooted out and snapped down the lock before shutting the door. I headed toward my apartment and was almost there when I was suddenly aware of slight—very slight—but very definite noises behind me. Being a dancer, even an older one, I was still pretty agile, so I spun around and stared at the empty sidewalk in front of me—no sign of anyone around. But the hair rose on my arms and I felt all my muscles tighten. I had my keys in my hand, and I carefully slid each separate key into my fingers as I had seen people do on television. One day, all this TV watching was going to pay off. I hoped today was that day. I still saw no one, so I slowly backed toward my door, my left hand behind me feeling for it, my brain quickly plotting out how I would turn, jam the key into the lock, and rush inside, locking the villains of the world outside.

I glanced around. Still no one. But I couldn't relax. Every nerve was screaming danger at me. I figured I better listen. "Is someone there?" I called, trying to sound tough and confident. No sooner did those words leave my mouth than I heard a rustle in the bushes and a large, dark-clothed figure jumped out at me, grabbed me, and twisted my arm behind my back, while a hand covered my mouth.

My scream was muffled by the gloved hand, but I had not survived for thirty years, barely eking out a living teaching other people's children to dance, just to see myself die tonight. It was not going to happen. I rammed my elbow into my assailant's stomach and heard a muffled "ooomph," and the grip on my arm loosened. I wrenched myself away and turned to face the masked man, using the maneuver I'd been waiting all my life to try. I had taken assault classes. I had learned how to incapacitate a man. My knee connected solidly with groin, and there was a high-pitched squeal, and then the assailant ran off. I jammed my key into the lock, having to push it in three different times, my shaking hands making it hard to get the metal into the small keyhole. When I finally got inside my apartment, I slammed the door shut, locked the dead bolt and then the chain, and leaned against the door, sobbing.

A rap-rap-rap on my door made me jump and scream again, and I turned and peered frantically out the peephole, just as a somewhat familiar voice said, "Jenny, open up. It's me, Andrew Fallon." My eye finally focused on his face, worry dotting his features, and I could hear the wail of sirens in the background. In the back of my mind, questions raged. Why was he here? How had he arrived so quickly? More sirens wailed, and I knew that it was safe.

I undid the locks and opened the door to see Marshal

Fallon followed by four or five uniformed police officers and another man in a suit.

"Are you okay?" he asked gently.

I was not okay. Tears started to run down my face and I felt his strong hands support me and guide me to my couch, which was so old it had the tendency to swallow people whole. I sat and sank, nonetheless. I wasn't able to stand right now. I shivered there, my arms held tightly around my body. Why was this happening to me?

I looked up at the concerned face of Marshal Fallon and I wondered about him again. "Why were you here so fast?"

A grimace crossed his face, and he turned away.

"You were watching me, weren't you? You were outside my place and saw the whole thing happen."

"It went down really quickly," offered the man I had not seen before tonight, obviously another marshal, judging by his suit and the bulge under his jacket. "You move really quick for someone your age."

Someone my age? My *age*? Okay, he was only about twenty-five, but I had maybe five years on him. Someone my *age*? I did not like him, nosiree. "I'm a dancer," I told him by way of explanation, aware that my tone was not friendly. Maybe he'd just write that off to the fact that I'd just been assaulted. I turned to Fallon. "But why are you watching me? Never mind, stupid question. You are watching me because you think I killed Sandra Epstein and I have Taylee somewhere, or maybe even that I killed her, too." I was filled with a mixture of emotions I could only vaguely identify as anger, disgust, despair, and a deep, deep exhaustion.

"You're not the prime suspect," Marshal Fallon said from between clenched teeth, his compassionate persona from a moment ago gone. "However, we do not have a clear suspect or motive, and so we have to follow what we have. Because it all revolves around you; *you* are all we have. It only makes sense we would be watching you."

And it only made sense that is why Tate had taken me to dinner, and was acting interested in me, if that in itself wasn't a figment of my lonely imagination. He was watching me, too.

Sadness took over all the other emotions and I wanted to climb into my bed and never get out again. "Can I just go to bed, please?"

"We need a statement," said one of the officers.

"Well, do it quickly, and then we'll leave Jenny alone," Marshal Fallon said. Alone. Did I dare be alone? Not really.

"I'll give you my statement in a minute. First I need to call someone."

I picked up my phone and dialed Alissa's number. "Can you come over? Somebody just tried to attack me, and I don't want to be alone."

After making sure I had called the police, that I was following proper procedure, and that I would allow an officer to stay there until she showed up, Alissa said she would arrive in twenty minutes.

I gave my statement to the police and then waited for their questions. There wasn't a lot to tell.

"Can you remember anything about your attacker, anything more, such as his face? You said his build was short and stocky, but did you see any part of his body, any identifying marks?"

"No, no identifying marks," I said, "but you have the sex wrong. That was no man. I've never kneed anyone in the nuts before, but I can guarantee you that this person *had* no nuts. I was attacked by a woman."

TWELVE

AFTER Alissa arrived and the officers left, she showed me her friend, Mr. Smith and Wesson, which she kept in her purse, and which, I suppose, she thought would make me feel safer. It just terrified me more.

I was experiencing a strange sense of loss and hurt, and I knew part of it was because Tate Wilson had not shown up at my house, when he had to have known I was attacked. It emphasized even more what I already knew. He was only interested in me to solve this crime. Still, I felt like crying, and I had the feeling ice cream or funeral potatoes weren't going to make this one better. Thinking of the hot, gooey, cheesy potatoes commonly served at Mormon funerals made images of Sandra Epstein dance through my head, like troglodyte sugar plum fairies. *Ugh.* Not good thoughts. But who was going to bury her? Especially with Taylee missing. And was anyone even concerned about it? Should it concern me that I was concerned about it?

"What do you think will happen to Sandra's . . . uh, remains?" I asked Alissa.

"Whoa, where did that come from?"

You'd think she would have been used to me by now.

"Well, I was just thinking about funeral potatoes, and that made me think of funerals and from there . . ."

Alissa laughed and shook her head, something she did a lot when she was around me. "Well, normally, after an autopsy, the body would be released to the family so they could give it a proper burial. And without family hanging out anxiously waiting for the body, I guess she'll be cremated."

The only one who cared about Sandra Epstein here in Utah was her daughter, and nobody knew where she was. And now Sandra was going to be turned into ashes and dust.

I felt like crying again.

"Let's talk about something else," Alissa said. "Like the fact you are obviously in some danger here, and we didn't realize it. Or at least *more* danger than we realized."

"At least I won't look as much like a suspect as I did before. I think."

"Do you have any idea at all who might have attacked you? I'm guessing you didn't get a look at his face."

"It wasn't a he. I finally got a chance to use all that self-defense we were taught for years, and I kneed him, only to discover there was nothing there to knee. I'm sure it still hurt. But that was no guy."

Alissa was silent as she digested the information that a woman had attacked me. "Well, I suppose it makes sense, in a crazy, warped, Jenny T. Partridge kinda way. You spend all your time around psycho dance moms. Remember that time one of them tried to run you off the road, and said it was just because she needed to discuss her daughter's performance spot?"

"Yep, people have nearly died for front-row fifty. Up until now, though, I just never thought someone would want to kill me. I mean, usually, don't they go after the rivals of their darling daughters, like that crazy cheerleader mom in Texas? Killing the dance teacher seems to defeat the purpose. You'd just have to find another dance teacher to harass."

"I'm guessing that, despite the fact a woman attacked you, this isn't about the front-row fifty," Alissa answered. I knew she was right. I just wished I knew what it *was* about.

"This is so frustrating."

"I know. Just remember that somehow it does tie in with your studio and your students' crazy parents. To Sandra. I mean, she didn't know anyone else here in Ogden, as far as we can tell. So let's go over the facts."

"You sound just like a cop."

Alissa blushed a little, and I tilted my head at her, studying her face. "Okay, spill it girlfriend. What's going on?"

"Well, why should I be content to send the guys out to solve the crime when I'm just as capable as they are? I just turned in my paperwork to Weber to attend the police academy."

"Wow." I was stunned, but I shouldn't have been. Mr. Smith and Wesson was the first clue that Alissa had gone beyond dispatcher. "Look out, Ogden. It's all good, I guess. Stupid criminals are even easier to catch when their tongues are hanging out and their eyes all googly."

"Jenny, this is not about how I look and you know it."

"You're right. I do know it, but you look hot, and you know that, too."

"Well, in this case, how I look is probably going to work against me."

I had a hard time comprehending that. In fact, it seemed patently unfair that she would even say that, given the fact that how I looked was never that good, and she always looked like a goddess. If you wanted to talk about things working against you . . .

"Anyway, let's look at the facts here. You were attacked by a woman, trying to pretend to be a man. Or at least that is what it sounds like to me. Right?" I nodded. "Who else in Ogden, Utah, would have wanted Sandra Epstein dead, except for another dance mom? Unless she was involved in some sort of intrigue or espionage or dirty dealings. At least that is how it looks on the surface, and perhaps it's even what the killer wants us to think. But maybe there's more. There is obviously a lot more that we don't know about her, and somehow, we have to figure it out. Maybe she stole some money from someone, or witnessed a crime."

I didn't know about that. But I didn't know much else, either. In fact, I knew next to nothing about Sandra, and so any of the things Alissa mentioned were entirely possible. But I was fixated on the one connection I had with her; she was a nasty psycho dance mom who regularly gave me grief but paid her tuition bill on time.

Thank goodness Alissa was a broader thinker than I was. She made me boot up the computer my parents had bought me on my last birthday, and pulled chairs over for both of us. I couldn't type, and didn't really understand how this Internet thing could possibly work, so there was quite a layer of dust on the computer, but Alissa dusted it off with a rag and then sat down.

She selected the triangle AOL login that was on the desktop, and clicked the connect button. My parents were paying good money for my monthly AOL hookup, "so we can stay connected," as my father said, but I rarely looked at it or even turned the computer on. It gave me a headache, and I had enough of those in my life.

"You've got mail," the deep male voice intoned. The little mailbox said I had 127 messages.

"Do you ever read this?"

"Um, once in a while?"

"Jenny."

"Okay, once. There was an e-mail from my cousin Kim inviting me to her singles ward dance, and fifteen e-mails from people who think I have an erectile dysfunction and need medication for it. I figured that was a bad sign, so I didn't come back."

Alissa sighed heavily. My refusal to move technologically into the twenty-first century drove her nuts. It was also another reason I was not a fit at the sheriff's office.

She quickly scanned through the e-mails, deleting those

that were clearly spam, and when she was done, there were just five. Two were from my mother—how was it she was more computer literate than I?—another from my cousin Kim that I told Alissa to delete quickly before it infected my computer with some sort of religious virus, and the other two from an e-mail address I could not identify.

"Who is this?" Alissa asked.

The address was "dancedancedance14@hotmail.com."

"I guess one of my students," I said, giving her a "duh" look. I didn't get to do that very often, so I was taking advantage of it when I could.

She clicked to open it, and inside we saw just three words: "SHE DID IT."

There was no signature, and no identifying name on the e-mail.

"Well. Who did you give your e-mail out to?"

"Um, just about everybody, at first. Because I was a little excited about a new way to reach me. Then of course I realized that these people never leave me alone as it is. Like they need one more way to contact me." As if to emphasize my point, my cell phone rang in my purse at the same time as my house phone rang. I ignored both, and let them go to voice mail. "Marlys sent out a flier with the e-mail on it, and then I got a few and then I sort of forgot I had e-mail, and so I never checked it again."

"Hmm," Alissa said, clicking open the second e-mail. It also had three words, all uppercase. Again, there were no identifying names or signatures in the header or the body copy, and no way to tell who had written it. This time, the words read, "SHE'S A KILLER."

"Great, cryptic messages from a medium I do not understand, sent by someone anonymous, about someone named She."

"Jenny, you need some sleep. Or sex. One or the other."

Maybe both, but I wasn't owning up to it.

Alissa messed around with the messages some more, then printed them out and clicked on the Save to Hard Drive function.

"Looks like they were both sent yesterday, one at 5 p.m. and the next one at 7 p.m. I'll give these to Tate tomorrow, along with the headers, to see if they can trace them, or at least track down the ISP location. In the meantime, I have an idea."

"Ice cream?" I asked hopefully. In my world, that was a *damn* good idea. Even though I was still mostly full from my dinner, I could make room for ice cream.

"No, not ice cream." Alissa laughed. "Here's the thing. I've been perplexed as to why the U.S. Marshals Office is involved in this investigation. If it were about Taylee and her being a missing minor, if they brought someone else in, it would be the FBI. And I keep running into shut doors at work, which is unusual, and which means whatever is happening is being highly guarded. And so, it occurred to me. Maybe Sandra Epstein was in the Witness Protection Program, because that is handled by the Marshals Office. And they don't let out any information at all about the people in it. None."

"Witness protection? Alissa, this is not television. And you are always getting mad at me for having an overactive imagination."

"Jenny, I'm serious. I mean, think about it. Why the secrets? Why the very attractive Marshal Fallon standing guard over her house? And watching you so closely? It makes sense. You have to admit it."

I supposed it did in my world, but usually, things like that did not click in Alissa's world. That meant either she was right, or she'd been hanging around me too much.

"I thought I'd do some searches, although where it will get us I don't know, because obviously, she would have changed her name to Sandra Epstein before she came here."

Just to check, Alissa typed in "www.google.com," then typed "Sandra Epstein" into a box, and hit Enter. A bunch of information about horse shows and a couple of sites that were in a foreign language came up, but there was nothing that linked to the woman I knew as Sandra Epstein.

"What about Taylee? Would they change her name, too?"

"Yes, they would have to. It's standard op. They have to leave everything behind. The only way to protect them is to hide them from the people who want them dead."

"Well, if Sandra Epstein was in witness protection, she did not turn over a new leaf in this new life, because obviously people wanted her dead here, too!"

"Was she Jewish?"

"Uh, how would I know that?"

"Epstein is a Jewish name. Did they go to a synagogue, or anything like that?"

"Not as far as I knew."

Alissa sighed. "Okay, did you ever hear them talk about anything of religious significance, or see anything that might have indicated . . ."

Something clicked in my memory, an event that happened the year before just as we were ready to go on to perform at a team competition in Bountiful.

Taylee stood before the mirror in the dressing room, her face tight and solemn, her eyes dark and cloudy, and watched as I tugged at the wrinkled costume she had pulled out of her bag.

"Tay, you have got to take better care of this stuff. It looks awful," I lectured. "You're the strongest dancer I have and now you are going to go out there in a wrinkled costume and all eyes will be on you, front-row fifty, and all they are going to see is this costume that looks like road-kill." I continued to fuss at the costume, pulling it this way and that, and Taylee held perfectly still, head straight ahead, watching the entire thing in the mirror with no comment and without moving. Until I caught a glimpse of a small gold chain around her neck.

I reached for it and pulled, but her hand snapped up and held mine, firmly, stronger than I ever could have imagined for a child her age. Our combined movements brought out a small gold cross that she had tucked into her costume, sure I wouldn't see it.

"No jewelry, Tay."

"I'm not taking it off. I never take it off."

"Taylee, you know the team rule is no jewelry . . ."

"I don't take it off." Her voice was even quieter than it had been a moment before. And I could tell she wasn't messing around. I saw something in her eyes I couldn't define, and decided to let it go. Besides, no one would notice the cross with the state her costume was in . . .

"She wore a cross," I said to Alissa, who had been watching me closely, as though aware a memory had been triggered. "I only saw it once, but it obviously meant a lot to her, and she was not about to take it off."

"I wonder why you only saw it once."

"She kept it pretty well hidden, under high-necked shirts and shrugs at dance, and . . . well, I really never saw her anywhere else but dance, and sometimes here after dance, but she was still in dance clothes."

"Hidden. This just adds to the pile of clues we are coming up with. We should go talk to her teachers. We should . . ."

"Alissa, we are not detectives. You are a bit closer than I am, but we need to leave this to the police."

"The same police who are camping on your doorstep waiting for you to slip up and make a mistake so they can send you to prison?" Yikes. This really was serious. Alissa was kind of in the know, and so maybe they really did suspect me and only me of Sandra Epstein's murder. Either that or she was bored—and she *was* between boyfriends—and was looking for a little excitement to spice up her life, and was going to drag me along with her.

"They really do think it's me, don't they?" My voice trembled a little.

"Jenn, they don't know anything. That's the problem. They have a tub of cookie dough that killed a woman, and it had your fingerprints on it, and a witness who says that you were the last person to touch the dough before it was delivered to Epstein. Do I think they really suspect you?

Not unless they are total idiots. But people have been tripped up by lesser things."

"There's that other tub of dough, too, the one that almost killed the missionaries."

"Actually, that one came back clean of any poison. The Church was not thrilled they had to pay the medical bills of two missionaries, who both had to drink charcoal and have their stomachs pumped, and all that good stuff . . ."

"Great. I don't know how to feel. Relieved they weren't poisoned, or stupid because they weren't poisoned and I caused such a ruckus."

"You did the right thing. Someone put the cookie dough in your freezer, and you don't know how it got there. Or how they got in. How did they get in? Who has a key?"

I thought hard. "My mom and dad. Marlys, of course, because I keep locking myself out, and she is always there to let me in. And I think that's it."

"You think?"

"Well, I can't remember for sure."

"Jenny, someone came in here, through a locked door, and put cookie dough in your fridge. I would think you would try to remember."

"I am remembering!" I thought harder, even though my head was already pounding. "No, no one else has a key. I've never had a roommate. Certainly never had a husband or a live-in boyfriend. Oh, no, *that's* never happened. I've certainly not ever handed out a key to anyone like *that*." My voice had taken on a desperate edge I wasn't really thrilled to hear.

Alissa sighed. "Let's get some ice cream." I guess Alissa heard that desperate edge, too.

ALISSA and I fell asleep in front of the television—she in the beanbag chair, and me on the couch—watching old moves like *Pretty in Pink* and *Mystic Pizza*, me dreaming of life as a glamorous redhead like Molly Ringwald or Julia

Roberts, instead of the pom-pom head I actually was. The next morning she treated me to breakfast at Village Inn—still three more days until tuition was due—and then asked me where I was going to stay that afternoon, as she had to work swing shift at the sheriff's office.

"I'll be fine at my apartment," I assured her. She wasn't listening. Lucky for me—was it luck?—when we pulled up in front of my apartment building, Detective Tate Wilson was waiting there, arms crossed in front of him, leaning back against his car. He was casual today—Doc Martens, worn Levi's, leather jacket. Half a sexy smile on his face, causing anticipation to rise up in my stomach. Being a murder suspect would do that to you. Really. I couldn't possibly be this easily turned on by a man who wanted to see me in handcuffs. Could I?

"Well, I guess he wasn't kidding about working this case every day," I said to a glowering Alissa.

"That's not all he's working," Alissa said.

I wasn't in the mood for a lecture, so I hopped out of the car and waved good-bye to her. She drove off with a scowl on her face, obviously displeased by my unwillingness to take her advice and steer clear of Tate Wilson, although how the heck I was supposed to do that when he was the detective investigating a murder of which I was somewhat of a suspect, I don't know.

As I walked toward Tate, I remembered his absence the night before, and my stomach began to churn. I didn't know what to think about this whole thing anymore. I was terribly attracted to this man—there, I admitted it!—but very insecure about him and his interest in me.

When I reached his car, he stood up and grabbed my shoulders, pulling me toward him until we were about one inch apart, and I was forced to tilt my head to look up at him. Electric shocks coursed through my body as the smile disappeared from his face. I wanted to be aloof and distant, to keep myself protected from the feelings he stirred in me.

"Are you okay?" he asked, and I melted like room-temperature ice cream.

"No," I said, hearing the catch in my voice, and wanting to choke down the tears, but unable to do so. "No, I'm not."

The tears coursed down my face, and he just held me, tight up against him, while I prayed that his leather jacket was waterproof and that I wasn't ruining it. I could hardly afford to buy him a new one.

Finally, the tears stopped coming. I pulled away from him and he smiled that half smile again. "We're giving the neighbors a show. Maybe we should go inside."

"Danger, danger, Jenny T. Partridge!" screamed my internal alert system. Good thing I had no common sense and never listened.

He followed me to my front door and I pulled my key out of my purse, preparing to insert it into the lock when the gentle pressure on the door made it swing open wide.

Tate immediately went into cop mode, pulling his gun from the holster located under his jacket and aiming it into the room.

"Jenny," screamed a familiar voice, and then I heard a thunk as Auntie Vi fainted dead away on the floor.

"Jennifer Tamara Partridge," came my father's scolding voice. "Just what in the dickens have you gotten yourself into now?"

T HIRTEEN

APPARENTLY, word had leaked back to Auntie Vi, via her many sources, about my assault the night before. So, of course, she shared with my parents and convinced them they needed to stage some sort of intervention before I ended up dead. I always thought interventions were for drug addicts or alcoholics, not potato addicts, but I guess one never knew.

I could see by the look on my father's face that he was genuinely worried about me. I could see by Auntie Vi's face that she was genuinely pissed off that she had fainted and missed even an ounce of the action, although having a gun pointed at her gave her a great story to tell to all her cronies. Ogden would be abuzz the moment she left my house. Maybe before.

At any rate, both Auntie Vi and my father were now urging me to stay with my parents until the murderer was found. A rapid knock on my door meant reinforcements. Unfortunately, it was for their side, not mine. My cousins

Kim and Terri had arrived. The only one missing was my mother, who was undoubtedly home in bed, with a migraine, wondering what horrible thing she had done in her life to be cursed with such a daughter.

"Gotta run," mouthed Detective Wilson, tapping at his watch, as soon as Terri and Kim turned to him, a gleam lighting up their very-single eyes. He scooted out the door before I could protest. Or ask him where he had been the night I had been attacked.

"Who's that?' Kim asked.

"The policeman who is investigating Jennifer's murder case," announced Auntie Vi, even as she fanned at her face from the kitchen chair my father had pulled over for her. Obviously, a beanbag chair was not a suitable place for a sixty-five-year-old queen-bee gossip maven, and the living room couch was too far from the action for her liking—plus it was old and soft and ate people for a living.

"Is he single?" Terri asked.

"Is he Mormon?" Kim asked.

"Is he a returned missionary?" they asked in unison. God, give me strength *Ack. No praying!* Both Kim and Terri were well past marrying age, with good reason. Terri resembled a horse, or maybe a small donkey, and Uncle Jim had spent thousands of dollars on braces trying to fix the problem. It hadn't worked. She still looked like a donkey with a very good orthodontic and dental insurance plan. Kim was a little round—okay, a lot round, and she tended to speak really, really fast in a high, breathy voice. She was one of those women about whom comments like "She has such a pretty face" were always made. Like me, Kim had a serious carb addiction. Unlike me, she did not dance off all those extra calories.

"Seriously, Jenn, is he a single returned missionary?" Kim asked again.

"I have no idea," I answered. "Dad, please . . ."

He took the hint, thank God, and I almost forgave him

for bringing them here in the first place. I was pretty sure my mother had sent him to make sure I was okay, and Auntie Vi and the cousins had just managed to tag along somehow. My mother had a low tolerance for my father's family. They must have been visiting, so she had seen an excuse to get rid of them all in one swoop. Great. Lucky for Mom, not so lucky for me. My mother thought Auntie Vi's obsession with everybody else's business was crude and vulgar. She thought my father's brother Jim, who worked as an accountant and served in the bishopric of his ward, was pedestrian and chauvinistic. It was probably best not to ponder what she thought of her daughter the dance teacher. Uncle Jim's two daughters were just like Auntie Vi. The three used to have sleepovers, where they would play dress up and "Who will be my eternal mate?" while crying over Mormon-themed romances that Auntie Vi would read aloud to them. I only got invited once. After I picked David Lee Roth as my eternal mate, and laughed out loud at the sappy parts of the romances, I was not invited back.

"Girls, everything is fine here. Let's leave Jenny be."

"Larry, everything is not fine here. Look at your daughter. Just look. She's past thirty, no sign of a mate or any children, and now she's gotten herself tangled up in this horrible murder case. Why, I would think you would want to do something about the way her life is going into the toilet, and . . ."

"Vivian, Jenny says she is fine. You are fine, right, Jenn?" I saw the concern in his eyes, and felt tears pricking at the back of my own. But I was tough, and I was not going to have a meltdown in front of Auntie Vi and my cousins.

"I'm fine, Dad."

"Okay. You sure you won't come stay? Your mother is worried sick."

It sounded inviting for all of ten seconds, until I remembered my mother's meaningful sighs and baited questions.

Plus I needed to figure out what was going on, and I couldn't do that if I had to answer questions about every step I made.

"I'll be fine." I wished I could convince myself of that.

The next morning, I said a little prayer as I pulled my Bug into the tight parking spot on the side of my studio building. "Please God, let today be normal. Please. No dead bodies. No psycho dance moms. No unflattering jail wear." That was a prayer that, at least partially, would not be answered, for lovely Krystal Glass had scheduled my cookie-dough refund for this morning. God did not like me. I could hear Auntie Vi's voice in my head: "Sorry, Jenny dear, but God only answers prayers from the worthy." In her book, that didn't include me, since I hadn't embraced Mormonism as God's true religion. "Hell is a very real place, Jennifer," intoned Grandma Gilly's nasal, tight voice. Great. The voices were back. Granted, they were voices I'd been hearing over and over again all my life, saying the same thing over and over again, but still. Voices. Did they have a dress code in mental institutions? I quickly got out of my car and slammed the door shut, hoping the voices would stay behind. I wrapped my scarf tightly around my neck as the bitter cold wind whipped around the corner of the building next to mine and hit me full force.

The back lot of my building—which had lots of atmosphere and almost no insulation—was closer to the stairway entrance to my upper-floor studio. But I had to leave the back lot for the dance moms, because if they had a hard time finding parking, they would badger me until I pulled all my hair out. Not a good look for a fair-skinned, freckle-faced redhead. That left only a small space on the side of the building, but luckily, my old Bug was small. There'd been a few close calls with cars whipping through the alley, but so far the Bug had survived intact. In a way, I almost wished someone would sideswipe the car so I could get it repainted on their dime, but of course, it didn't happen. I was stuck with Pepto-Bismol pink.

I shivered as I climbed the stairway to my studio, and struggled with the lock, cussing as the wind whipped through my thin jacket. The lock finally clicked in and I pushed through the door and then shut it behind me, leaning on it and breathing a sigh of relief, waiting for a modest amount of warmth to flood over me. Nothing. I let out a breath and alarm filled me as I saw a white cloud in front of me.

"No, no, no, not again. I know I paid that bill." It was still two days until tuition was due, but I knew I had already sent the gas bill. I hurried into the small office and checked the thermostat setting, which was in the same place I had left it—sixty-three degrees. The thermometer, however, said the inside temperature was a nippy thirty-eight. This was not good. Children did not dance well in freezing temperatures. Hell, some of my students did not *ever* dance well, but it was certainly made worse by the cold. I pushed the thermostat knob up slightly to sixty-eight, waiting to hear the hiss of the old furnace. Nothing. I pushed it up a little more to seventy-two, waiting to hear something click, or the noisy pipes bang a bit, as they always did when the furnace was firing up, but still nothing.

Damn. This was bad. See what I got for praying? No wonder I never went to church—any church. I walked to the desk in my office and picked up the cordless phone, hitting the speed dial for the store located directly below me. "Hello, you've reached Priceless Pearls. This is Marco. Jack and I are out of the office until December 26, and the store will be closed until that time. If you would like to leave a message . . ."

"Damn," I swore as I hung up the phone. Marco and Jack were probably in Mexico again, on one of their countless fishing trips. They went at least four times a year. Maybe I needed to open a pawn-slash-antique shop, and name it using a thinly disguised play on the title of one of the important religious books—*The Pearl of Great Price*—of the predominant Utah religion.

If the furnace was out in our building, life would not be good. I couldn't call the landlord, because Marco *was* the landlord. He was a great guy, but he usually forgot to tell me when he was going out of town, and I had no emergency contact. Things were dire. I couldn't call in a furnace repairman, because it was still two days until tuition was due, and I was about to have a ton of cookie dough returned to me that I could not afford to refund the money for.

I was going to have to call in reinforcements, and I didn't know anyone who had better fix-it abilities than my dad.

Of course, calling Dad meant listening to long-suffering sighs and inquiries into when I was going to get my life on track and inferences that I was a huge disappointment to my mother, who had expected several grandchildren by now. During his time teaching school, Dad had followed the "love and logic" method of teaching. Basically, he always asked his students what they thought would be the consequences for their actions, instead of telling them what he was going to do. He liked this method so much, he transferred it into his parental skills. I grew up hearing the words, "And how do you think that's going to work out for you, Jenny?" The answer, almost always, was "not good." Almost anytime my dad was around, I could expect to hear a form of this question. Just once I wanted him to say, "You really screwed up this time, Jennifer, and you are grounded for the rest of your life," instead of making me own up to my behavior in my own words. But he never did say that. He just let me wallow in my own acknowledgment that feeding the neighbor's four cats from my mother's finest china—it was a tea party!—would not have good consequences.

James sashayed through the door of the studio with what looked like a rodent tucked under his arm. He stopped and looked around, a perplexed expression on his perfectly waxed eyebrows. "It is colder than Paris Hilton's heart in here. I know money is tight, Jenn, but I have to be warm to teach . . ."

"*What* is that?" I said, interrupting his self-absorbed patter.

"Oh this," he said, practically cooing. "This is Winkie. Isn't he cute?"

"Winkie? You have a rat named Winkie, and you think he's cute?"

"A rat? Jenny T. Partridge, have you no class and breeding?" James's voice let me know he was appalled. "Winkie is a miniature Chihuahua. He has papers and everything. A rat! How could you?"

"He looks like Madison Pratt." Madison was one of my more unfortunate-featured Tots. It wasn't her fault she looked like a rodent. She was the spitting image of her father. If her mother had passed down her genes, the child would have resembled a bulldog. These were thoughts I needed to keep to myself. "You brought a dog to my studio, to teach dance? And even more appalling, you brought a dog named *Winkie* to my studio?" I couldn't decide which was worse. The rodent under James's arm, the fact the rodent was considered a dog, the fact the rodent's name was Winkie, the fact I had no heat and moms with cookie dough would be arriving in fifteen short minutes—moms expecting cookie-dough refunds I did not have the cash to cover—or the fact that James was now glowering at me in a way that meant a temper tantrum was sure to follow. Take your pick. I'd say things couldn't get much worse, but in my estimation, they always did.

"Never mind," I said. I picked up the cordless phone and called my dad. I needed heat in here, and I needed it quick, or things were going to be ugly. I'd have to cancel dance, and then the psycho dance moms would be calling me 24-7, on both my cell phone and my home phone, wanting to know when I was going to make up the lesson that their precious daughter had missed, because God knew one lesson missed was going to guarantee that New York Broadway career went down the tubes.

"Jenny, are you okay?" James looked genuinely concerned. "You are mumbling under your breath."

I ignored him.

"Dad, I need your help. The furnace isn't working in the studio, Marco and Jack are fishing, James has a rodent under his arm, and I have dance moms due in fifteen minutes."

"I'll be right there." I heard some muffled whispering and then my dad uttered the words that chilled my blood another fifteen degrees, putting me dangerously close to hypothermia. "Mom's coming with me."

My father was a miracle worker, despite the fact he had no real religious inclinations. He went with Nana Marian to church on occasion, mostly to appease her, and had even attended Mass with my mother once or twice, enduring Grandma Gilly's glares through the entire service. But as a whole, Sunday football and NASCAR was his religion. He'd worked for forty years for the Davis County School District as a junior high school science and math teacher, and was now retired. He didn't much like kids anymore, especially after years of seeing them at their teenage worst, but he did have mechanical inclinations that had been tightly honed by years of surviving as a homeowner on a tight budget.

My father could fix anything. Give him a roll of duct tape and he could fix decapitated Barbies, leaking hoses, and probably even perform major surgery. Within ten minutes— minutes through which I'd endured my mother alternately cooing over Winkie the Rat and giving me heartfelt, angst-filled glances—I heard the familiar hiss and clang and warm air started to fill the studio. Just in time for the moms carrying tubs of cookie dough who began to surge through the door. My heart sank. How the heck was I going to get out of this?

Krystal Glass pushed through, today wearing a light denim jacket with a turquoise cami top underneath it, and another pair of frayed jeans. On her feet she wore stylish black boots. In her arms she carried a ledger book. Behind her trailed Marlys, the look on her round expressive face telling me she would be more than happy to hit Krystal from behind and once she had her on the floor, slap her until Krystal screamed uncle.

Marlys had less tolerance for psycho moms than even I did. Behind Marlys was Camari Stone, a dance mom with a younger dancer, and apparently today's flunkie of choice. Krystal usually picked moms she could easily manipulate. Since Camari was a hamburger short of a French fry, she was easy pickings.

"Well, let's get this going," announced Krystal, in a bright, too-happy voice.

"Jenny and I can handle this," Marlys said, her voice a low growl. Standing next to Krystal, she looked almost the complete opposite. Her face was bare of makeup, her hair was pulled up into a ponytail, and she wore a sweatshirt over old jeans that had probably come from Wal-Mart. Even so, she was much more beautiful than Krystal, in an understated, earthy way. She was confident, even in her natural state. She just didn't need the bells and whistles that comprised Krystal Glass.

"Oh, I'm happy to help," Krystal replied, giving Marlys a nasty look that usually worked to shut people down and made small children everywhere run in fear. But Marlys had been dealing with pushy psycho dance moms for quite a while now. She knew every trick in the book, and then some.

The only way Krystal was going to push herself into this situation was over Marlys's dead body. *Urk.* I had to stop thinking in clichés.

"Jenny, can we help?" my mother asked kindly, eyeing the two women warily. I could tell by the look on my father's face that he was done, and needed to get out of here quick before too many female hormones rubbed off on him and made him cry at Jell-O commercials.

"No, but thanks, Mom and Dad, thanks so much. I really appreciate you fixing the furnace."

"Glad to help," my father said.

"Jenny, can you come over to lunch next Sunday?" My

mother's voice was a higher pitch than normal, which meant she was up to something—again. She'd been trying to set me up with nice Catholic boys for the past two months. I think it was because Auntie Vi kept hinting that if I didn't meet someone and marry soon my ovaries were going to shrivel up and die, and my mother would never get any grandchildren. The problem was, nice Catholic boys who weren't total dog meat were hard to find in Utah. Here, the majority of people were some form of Mormon—active, jack, or former. Nice Catholic boys grew up and went to Notre Dame and didn't come back to Utah. The ones who did stick around were nancy momma's boys. Not my kind of guy.

"Uh, I'll have to let you know, Mom."

"Please do, dear. I'm making funeral potatoes and prime rib." Oh, that was a low, low blow on my mother's part.

"I'll let you know, Mom."

My parents bid their good-byes, and I turned back to the mess at hand.

Marlys and Krystal still glared at each other, even as the studio entryway began to fill up with moms carrying tubs of cookie dough. Tubs that I was going to be expected to return money for. Money, that, of course, I did not have. Camari stood expectantly behind Krystal and watched for my reaction.

I think I'd rather be in a pigpen during slop time than in the middle of a room filled with psycho dance moms who are about to be told they would have to wait to get their money back until I got the money back from the owner of the cookie-dough company. Since I'd already called and spoken with someone in his office that morning, and she had pretty much told me that it would be a cold day in hell before I saw any money from him, I knew that would not be soon. At any rate, I was in possession of some knowledge which I did not intend to share with the psycho dance moms. At least for now.

"Look," Krystal finally said, through gritted teeth, "I am here to help. Let's get this done and over with." Marlys stood matching her stare, hands on her hips, legs apart.

"Fine," Marlys said, through teeth gritted equally tight.

She turned and clapped her hands, and called the dance moms to attention. "All right, listen up everyone. First of all, you need to form lines one to the left, and one to the right. Mrs. Glass will handle the ones on the right, and I'll handle the ones on the left."

A murmur started in the crowd, and then grew up to a loud roar as they all began asking questions at once.

"Please, everyone, please, just calm down . . ." I yelled, trying to be heard above the roar.

"My friend's daughter ate some dough last night, so they rushed her to the hospital, just in case. Are you going to pay her medical bills?"

"Are you going to get more cookie dough so that we can raise money to pay for our costumes? I really can't afford to pay for costumes without a fundraiser to help."

"Does poisoning cause a rash, because this really ugly one formed on my . . ."

A sharp whistle pierced the room, and everyone turned to stare at Amber, who watched the melee from the hallway. She stood for a moment and shook her head disapprovingly, and all the moms kind of bowed their heads as though they were very respectful and sorry that they had not been quieter. How did she do it?

Alissa got the hot-girl genes, Marlys got the organized genes, Amber got the "I can get your attention and respect the moment I walk into a room" genes, and I got pom-pom hair and carb-addiction genes.

"I think you all need to listen. Line up. Be prepared to tell us how many cartons you are returning. You should know that you will not be getting refunds until we settle this with the cookie manufacturer, and since there is also an ongoing police investigation, we are unsure how long this might take . . ."

That did it. The mention of no refunds and long time in her statement set the psychos off and even Amber couldn't bring them back into control.

But Detective Tate Wilson could. He strolled through

the door, taking his jacket off as he walked, his gun, tucked neatly into a shoulder holster, displayed for all to see. The room grew quiet. I wasn't sure if it was the gun or the package toting the gun that had these moms silent, but I was thankful for whatever it was.

"Change of plans, ladies," Detective Wilson said. "Jenny will be writing each of you a check for the amount of the dough you purchased, and settling with the manufacturer later." I gasped. Had he lost his mind? I had no money. I had checks, but everybody knew where writing checks when you had no money in the bank got you—jail, that's where. Jail! *Ack!* He really did just want to see me behind bars.

"But, but, but . . ." I tried to stop him. It was too late. Perhaps worried if they didn't act now, they would never get their money, the women divided off nicely into two lines and handed over their cartoons of cookie dough to Amber and James, who began stacking them against the wall.

"What have you done?" I asked him, tears filling my eyes. "I don't have this kind of money. In fact, I have no money. Did you miss that somewhere? Oh God, I'm going to have to borrow from my parents, or maybe Nana Marian, and they will all know what a failure I am and . . . Oh, how could you do this? Do you really want to see me in jail this bad?"

He gave me a puzzled look and then pulled me toward my office. "We'll be right back," he told Marlys, who nodded and continued to add up containers of frozen cookie dough.

After he shut the door, I turned to him and just shook my head, unable to find words to express what I was feeling. "I . . ."

"Before you speak, or call me names, or any of that, let me explain. I grew up in Brigham City, which is where Ponds Cookie Dough is made. In fact, my mother taught all of the Ponds children in school, and they still invite her to every family occasion. I simply reminded Mr. Ponds that refusing to refund money in light of a possible disaster, where people could be hurt, was not good business. Especially since the person who sold the cookie dough was a small business owner—a dance teacher—just trying to make a living. And since he was a multi million-dollar conglomerate, it wouldn't look good to have him refuse refunds to that teacher, and to have that teacher go under, due to his sheer greediness. He agreed. After I threatened to go to the press."

Stunned, I could not find words. Finally, I spoke. "He gave you the money?"

"Not exactly. But he will be giving you the money. It takes time to get things rolling in the corporate world."

"But the vultures out there want their money now."

"And they shall get their money."

He pulled out his wallet and took out a folded check, and handed it to me. I could see it was from his personal account, signed by him, but the amount was blank. It was made out to me.

"You're going to pay for the dough?"

"It's a temporary loan. As soon as Ponds pays up, you will pay me back."

"You have that kind of money? Do you know how much it is? We sold four thousand dollars worth."

"I'm single, I own a small condo, a modest car, and I don't have kids or pets. It's easy to save when you live that way."

A glimmer of hope was replaced by complete darkness. "I can't do this. What if Ponds doesn't pay up? It would take me years to repay you. Literally. I barely scrape by, Tate. I make just enough each month to pay my rent here, my rent at home, put gas in my car, and buy a week's worth of groceries. I scramble the rest of the month."

"We'll work it out some other way then," he said, a strange glimmer lighting his eye.

"I am not that kind of girl," I said, putting all the disgust and anger I could find in my voice, all the while thinking how much fun it would be to work off all that money. I *was* bad.

"You aren't?" he said teasingly, and I knew he didn't really mean it as a proposition. He really wanted to help me.

"Thank you," I said quietly, leaning into him and standing on my tiptoes to kiss his cheek. "I don't know how I'll repay you—and that's probably literal—but somehow I will."

Tate pulled me into him and I gasped as electric shocks coursed up and down my body, my breasts pressed against his firm, sturdy chest, my legs pressed up against his, and me, on tiptoe, wondering if my body was going to spontaneously combust.

He leaned his head down and kissed me on the lips, not too gently, and I swear I heard sparks fly somewhere around us. Then he let me go.

"Go out there and pay those crazy women back. Then I want to buy you some food—so your stomach won't complain—and then take you home and get to know you a little better." There was promise in his voice, and my eyes opened wide as I considered it. Perhaps I had not been imagining, all along, that he found me attractive.

"I can't," I said, a mixture of disappointment and relief tingeing my voice. "I have classes until 9 p.m."

"Damn," he said, a sexy smile turning his handsome face into an irresistible lure.

"But maybe if you came by after lessons . . ." What was wrong with me? This man was dangerous. Eh, who was I kidding? This man was hot. Dangerous or not, I wanted him.

"Maybe," he agreed. "Maybe."

Then he leaned over and gave me another soft kiss, one that hardened and turned passionate and which resulted in me throwing my arms around his neck and wishing we weren't in my little office so I could rip off his clothes and find out . . .

"Later, Jenny. Psycho moms? Outside the door?"

"Psycho moms," I parroted, not really comprehending. "Oh, psycho moms!" Yikes.

I straightened my hair and dance clothes, and he watched me, his arms crossed and muscles rippling, leaning back against my desk, as I opened the door and went out into the fray, emboldened and strengthened by the fact I was not going to go to jail today, or anytime in the next, oh, week. At least.

Each mother gave the total amount of containers they had returned to either Krystal or Marlys, and I sat down on a chair and wrote out check, after check, after check. I'd never written so many checks in my life. But finally, the moms started to file out, just in time for afternoon classes to begin. The Tots came early, since they did not have school, and would be arriving in less than thirty minutes.

And of course, some of them came with their mothers to return the dough, so they were already here, milling around, and in some cases, looking for something to destroy.

I grudgingly thanked Krystal for her help, and tried to get away before she could corner me about making Marilyn the Sugar Plum Fairy again. It didn't work. "Now, Jenny, you are going to need a new fundraiser. Perhaps the full Krystal mobiles were too much. How about I make a mini version, and you can sell them for ten dollars, and I'll give you three dollars of that?"

While it was a much more reasonable deal than the one she had pitched to me before, I knew it was still too costly for a fundraiser, and besides, if I never did another fundraiser again, it would be too soon."

"Can we talk about it later, Krystal?"

"Of course. Now, about Marilyn and the Sugar Plum Fairy . . ."

I sighed, and everything that had built up over the past few days came rushing back. I just couldn't take any more. "Krystal, Marilyn will never be the Sugar Plum Fairy. In case you haven't noticed—and apparently you haven't— Marilyn does not like to dance. In fact, she hates it. She despises it. She tells me every week she despises it, and the only time she actually dances is when you are here, glaring at her. The rest of the time, she does nothing. She is not gifted in dance. I'm sure she has other gifts, but dance is not one of them."

Krystal gasped. "How can you say something like that? She has my genes! Of course she can dance. I was Marvelous Miss Dance and Drill Utah for all three years of high school. I was the drill mistress of our drill team. I danced in college. She can dance. Oh yes, she *can* dance, because she is *my* daughter, by God, and she can and will dance. And you better put her in *that* role and give her a chance to show you that she can dance, or I'll make you regret the day you were born."

With that, she turned and stomped out of the studio.

Some of the other mothers tittered at the display, and then turned to each other and started gossiping, and I sighed heavily. Marlys came over to me and put her arm around me.

"That woman is a whack job," she said.

"Unfortunately, she's one of many. This is a pretty frustrating business."

"I'd say," Amber added from behind us. James was showing Winkie off to the Tots and their moms, who apparently had more appreciation for rat dogs than I did.

"Jenny, I don't mean to pry, but how are you going to cover all those checks you wrote?" Marlys asked, hesitation filling her voice. But she had a right to ask. After all, she did my books for me.

"It's covered. Don't worry." I didn't want to tell anyone that Detective Tate Wilson had floated me a loan. I wasn't sure why, but I just wasn't comfortable with that. It implied intimacy, which I wanted to believe we had shared—or at least were going to share—but it was all too new, to unsure, to talk about it.

"Okay," she said. Four-year-old Maribel, her youngest daughter, who had just started the Tots class, came up to me and tugged on my leg. "Jenny, can we do stensions today? I like stensions."

"Stensions? What is she talking about?" Marlys asked.

"You know, Mommy, stensions." Then Maribel lifted up

her right leg and tried to hold on to her foot and pull it into the air, all the while hopping all over the room, a small pink tornado in a leotard, tights, and dance shoes. Marlys and I both started laughing, and I said, "Sure, Marble," using her nickname, "it'll be an extension kind of day."

I was glad to teach, to get back to safety.

There had been far too little of that going on in my life the past few days. And with an unsolved murder hanging over my head, Taylee still missing, and a hard to explain relationship with a certain detective investigating that unsolved murder, I would be happy to do extensions until the chickens came home.

FOURTEEN

DANCE classes did not go well, particularly with the Seniors, as they were all fighting for the plum role—heh heh, get it, *plum*?—of the Sugar Plum Fairy. I wasn't promising it to anyone else, holding out in case Taylee was found, but still, I had to find a backup. Someone else needed to know the part. Marilyn Glass was, unfortunately, at dance, although Krystal did not show up, and so, she did nothing but glower in a corner and incessantly text message someone.

Ariel Fox was tall and pretty graceful, but she landed like an elephant. Loni Richards was pretty good, but very unreliable, and she missed more classes than she made. The rest of them simply didn't have the technical skill to pull off the role. But I started Ariel and Loni both learning the routine, wishing I had a bigger pool of talent to pull from.

Of course, that would mean more psycho moms. Just what I needed.

Classes ended at 9 p.m., and I was glad to see the last of the girls go. Amber packed up and left early because she had a hot date—of course—and James had to go home and make sure little Winkie hadn't piddled all over his expensive rugs.

When the last student left, I sighed with relief, and turned on my favorite CD, a mix of songs good for stretching. I did a series of exercises intended to relax my tense neck and shoulder muscles. It wasn't working, so I knew I needed to dance. It was the only thing that relieved my tension. I walked over to the stereo and rustled through my CD holder until I found the Pussycat Dolls' CD, and I stuck it in the player. I couldn't exactly use that music during class time—unless I wanted to have seventeen million parents trying to wring my neck—but I loved the sensual rhythm of the music, and it was very, very danceable. The exotic Middle Eastern rhythm of the song "Buttons" filled the room, and I began to stretch to the music, then began to dance full out. I did jeté turns as the Dolls sang about a man they wanted to loosen up their buttons, proving he was a real man. I felt my body move with the music and I lost myself, leaping and moving in time with the music. I did a series of pique turns and ran into a solid body mass, and almost screamed, except I recognized the shirt covering the muscular chest.

Detective Wilson had returned.

He watched me with a silky, sultry look on his face, and the song ended, neither of us saying anything, just staring at each other, his arms lightly around me, holding me just where I had landed, fresh from a turn.

"Well, I guess I should have locked the door," I said, breathless both from my dancing and the fact that I was now in the arms of the man I had naughty dreams about—or at least had since meeting him a few days before.

"Considering you were attacked just last night—something you forgot to tell me—I'd say the answer to that is yes."

"I figured the troops would let you know about it. It's not like you were so concerned you showed up or anything." The words came out before I realized what I was saying, and it was only then I fully realized how much it bothered me he had not come over to see if I was okay. I moved away from him and walked over to the stereo to turn it off.

"Jenny, I had a good reason for not being there, okay?" His lips tightened, and I could tell that he was bothered that—what? That I was bothered? And why wasn't he sharing his reason?

"No big deal. Marshal Fallon was there, watching me, of course, so he was able to chase her off, whoever she is."

"Considering what I saw in here today, it could be any one of these women."

"She was kind of big and very soft, not muscular at all. It was probably Emma. I don't know why she is trying to frame me, but there is no telling the mind of a psycho dance mom. She really wanted Ella to be the Sugar Plum Fairy, instead of a dancing buffoon."

Tate chuckled. "God, I love this case."

"You are not supposed to love murder cases."

"Thank you for that, Suzy Sunshine." The way he was looking at me made me squirm, and alternately, made me want to jump on him and hold him tight, never letting him go. But then I remembered his vague answer about being busy last night, when I was being attacked, and I wondered just what had kept him so enthralled. Another woman? I did not want this man to be playing me. I could feel it so bad it ached. But if my luck ran true to form, he might be. I had to protect myself.

"Well, I guess I should close up the studio. Did you just come by to make sure I hadn't left town?"

His mouth hardened. "No, I came to make sure you were okay, and taking care of yourself, which, obviously, you were not, considering the door was unlocked and you were dancing around without a care in the world."

"That is not fair. I have more cares than anyone would ever care to have," I nearly shouted. "I just needed a release. I needed to get rid of some of this tension."

"I could help you with that," he said, stepping closer, his voice low and scratchy. I took a step back and swallowed. It didn't seem to matter which way I turned with Tate Wilson. He was always getting the better of me.

But I was no longer sure of his interest in me, and whether it had to do with the case. Just this morning I'd been ready to pledge lifelong allegiance to him, but all it had taken was for him to clam up about his whereabouts the night before, and I started second-guessing myself.

Either I was very, very smart and cautious, or I was the world's biggest doehead. Experience told me it was the latter, but I wasn't going to examine that too closely tonight.

"Okay, thanks for coming to check on me. I'll close it up now, and get home. I'm very tired. It's been a trying day. Uh, thanks again for helping me out with the cookie-dough fiasco. I'll find a way to repay you." Maybe Mom and Dad could get a second mortgage on their house, and somehow I could explain how this was all necessary because of cookie dough.

He sensed that I was shooing him off, and his eyes narrowed, as he watched me closely. "Well, you were just all thankful earlier today. Now you are shutting me out like I'm yesterday's garbage. Which means one of two things. You just met the love of your life, and he's waiting for you at your apartment, or you are second-guessing everything because I was busy last night and I won't tell you where I was."

Damn him.

"Ah, it's the second, I see."

"Look, Tate, I'm a big girl. I haven't reached this age without running around the block a few times, and I guess . . . I guess I'm tired of getting hurt, plus I'm all caught up in something pretty bad right now."

"Yes, you are. But I'm still going to tell you that where I was has nothing to do with you, or with another woman. And that's all I'm going to say, because I don't really know you well enough. And if you can't accept that, we'll probably never know each other that well."

Could I accept that? I guess I didn't have a choice.

"Okay. I accept it. But I still need to lock up the studio and get home."

He sighed and asked what he could do to help. He helped me straighten up a bit and then watched as I gathered my coat and scarf, helping me with the coat and watching me wrap the scarf around my neck. He stood outside on the landing as I locked the dead bolt and then waited for me to pass him and walk down the stairs. I could feel his breath on my neck as I passed, and could feel the metal staircase vibrate with his heavy steps as he followed me down.

I reached my Bug and unlocked the door, then turned to tell him that I was going to start it and let it warm up. He caught me by surprise, pulling me close, and then kissing me deeply. I lost all thought of everything.

When he pulled away, finally, I was sure hours had passed—or was it just seconds? He gave me one more deep gaze and then told me to get in and start my car.

"I'll be following you home, so don't panic if you see headlights behind you."

"You're still following me," I said, sadness coloring my voice. I wasn't sad because he was following me, but because he was following me for the wrong reasons.

"I'm following you because someone is trying to frame you for murder, and you are in danger, not because I think that you are guilty, Jennifer T. Partridge." His voice was soft. "And right in the middle of a case is not a good time to get involved, despite what you've seen in movies and on television. Actually, you might have an idea, based on those movies, just what can happen when a police officer gets involved with . . ."

"A suspect?"

"No, someone integral to his case. I think you're a witness, and I think you're a potential victim, and that is why I will be watching you until I solve this case."

"Tate?"

"Yes?"

"Where's Taylee?"

He sighed. "I don't know, Jenny. But I intend to find out."

FIFTEEN

DREAMS had become nightmares.

No matter how good a dream started out, it inevitably deteriorated into shouting matches with psycho dance moms, or me going to jail for a variety of crimes, none of which I committed. I woke up Tuesday morning with my hair sticking up straight and fuzzy, and I assumed with big bags under my eyes. I'd showered and then collapsed into bed while my hair was still wet—not good. I had not slept well. I had no control over my dreams, and what was worse, I also had no control over my waking life.

I jumped out of bed and padded into the bathroom, avoiding the mirror, mostly because I was pretty sure of what I would see. I splashed water on my face, dried it with a towel, and then moisturized with the "miracle cream" yet another of my dance moms sold. So far, no miracles, but since they mostly supported me, I felt like I had to support them.

I needed to do something to try and solve my problem, but I didn't know what, especially since it had become pretty apparent someone either wanted me behind bars, or dead. I changed into my favorite pair of sweatpants, T-shirt, and jacket, and went back into the bathroom to run a comb through my unruly mop, wetting it and slicking it back and then pulling it into a tight ponytail. It would take another shower and tons of conditioner to make my hair behave after a night like last night—a night spent tossing and turning—and I needed to get proactive. I had the biggest performance of my life coming up—yikes, it was less than a week away!—and I could not afford to let it fail just because people were dying around me. Okay, one person, and a nasty one at that, but still . . .

A loud honk in front of my apartment building caught my attention, and I walked over to my window, looking out to see a big yellow school bus sitting in front of my house. Marlys. Every once in a while, especially when she knew I was down, Marlys would show up and take me for coffee and pastries. There was still one day until tuition was due, so Marlys would have to buy. She usually did anyway. Our favorite spot was Grounds for Coffee on 30th and Harrison. The upside was I got pastries and good coffee. The downside was Marlys drove a school bus, and since it was her break and she still had more driving to do, I had to drive my Bug.

A quick tap on my door told me Marlys was waiting. I opened up, and said, "This is a good morning for coffee and pastries. Especially pastries."

"Is there ever a bad morning for pastries?"

"No, but some are better than others, and this is a really, really good morning for pastries."

I gathered up my purse and keys, and we headed out the front door. I was careful to lock both the doorknob lock and also the dead bolt.

"Where's the Pepto Mobile?" Marlys asked, looking around.

"I had to park around the corner last night. There wasn't a space out front. I got home too late."

"Oh, hot date? A certain detective?"

"Marlys! I am not dating Detective Wilson. He's just investigating a murder in which I am the central suspect, and I . . ."

"You sound like a television show. Or your uptight aunt. Come on, Jenny, the guy is hot, and I haven't missed you two giving each other goo-goo eyes."

"Goo-goo eyes? Marlys, you are hanging around kids way too much."

"Look who's talking," she shot back, and then a real shot rang out.

"Holy shit," Marlys said, as we heard a crack and my apartment's front window shattered. I looked around frantically and grabbed her arm, pulling her toward the school bus where we could hunker for cover. I'd dropped my purse on the sidewalk but I wasn't going after it. I noticed that Marlys's purse was in the same place, right next to mine, both of our cell phones inside the respective purses. So much for calling for help. We leaned against the bus and I frantically turned my head left and right, trying to see where the shot had come from. I could see nothing. Until I spotted something that made my heart nearly stop.

Around the corner came two young men, dressed in suits, carrying their church books. No, no, no, no, no.

"No, no, no, no, no." I had to utter that aloud, as if to convince myself of how bad this situation was getting.

"Hiya, Jenny," Elder Martin yelled, waving his hand cheerily. Was near poisoning and stomach pumping not enough to keep these two missionaries away?

"Get over here, now," I hissed through clenched teeth, as the two drew nearer. "Quick."

I guess maybe that came off as my Linda Blair *Exorcist* impression because it resulted in both Elder Martin and Elder Tuatuola stopping short right where they were. Bad move. Another shot rang out, and the big Samoan elder moved quicker than I thought humanly possible, right into the school bus, since Marlys had left the door open.

Elder Martin stayed where he was, eyes wide, mouth agape. I would have thought, hailing from the South as he did, that he would have been a little more familiar with fly-ing bullets and their purpose. Didn't everyone hunt there? But no, he just stood there like one of those clowns at La-goon Amusement Park, mouth open wide, just waiting for someone to fill it with water so its balloon head could pop.

I did not want to see Elder Martin's head pop, so I glanced quickly both ways, then dashed over and grabbed him, pulling him into the big yellow school bus, Marlys following close behind. Two more sharp cracks and metal-lic pings followed, and Marlys jumped into the driver's seat and started up the bus, muttering something about los-ing her job and having to find some new friends who were more normal.

Elder Martin was hyperventilating on one of the front bus seats, and Elder Tuatuola was stretched out flat in the aisle of the floor of the bus, not moving. He was fast learn-ing that missionary work was a dangerous business, espe-cially when you were trying to convert Jenny T. Partridge.

Another shot rang out and shattered the rear bus win-dow and Marlys pulled out quickly into traffic.

"Can you call for help on your radio?" I asked Marlys.

"Broken. They've been promising to fix it all week."

Great. My life was such a joke.

"Put your head between your knees," I told Elder Martin, not sure that was going to work, but unsure what else to do.

"You alive down there, Elder T?" I asked. The big Samoan grunted.

"I think it's safe now. Just drive us to the police station, Marlys."

She was doing a lot of muttering as she navigated the big bus.

As usual, I was wrong. Another shot rang out and cracked the other back window, and I looked behind us to see that we were being chased by a Humvee. "You've got to be kidding me," I said.

"I good here on floor," muttered Elder Tuatuola.

"I . . . can . . . t . . . br . . . e . . . athe," Elder Martin rasped out.

"He needs a paper bag, Jenny," Marlys said over her shoulder, her face set and determined as she drove through the side streets of Ogden, trying to lose the silver Humvee hot on our tail. I knew, of course, that a school bus could not lose a Humvee. I suspected Marlys knew this, too, but it's not like we had options.

I scanned the aisles of the bus, and spotted a crumpled bag on one of the seats a few rows back. Some kid must have been too hungry to make it to school without eating his lunch, and I silently thanked him. I made my way toward the seat, trying to step around the prone Samoan. It was not easy. He was big. I snatched up the bag and turned back to the front, just as Marlys made a quick right turn. I tumbled forward into Elder Martin and knocked him flat on his back, me on top, breasts pressed against his chest, him staring up at me, his face turning purple as a man already struggling to breathe now had someone crushing him. Plus, a female someone, an event he had been expressly forbidden to even think about, let alone do while on his mission.

I quickly scrambled off of him and pulled him upright, shoving the paper bag into his face. "Breathe into this," I said, moving as far away from him as I could. I didn't want to be responsible if he had a heart attack and died. The Mormons were already mad at me over the cookie-dough incident.

Elder Martin breathed in and out of the bag. His breathing slowed as he regained control of his respiratory functions.

"Did bad sneells lke una fsh," he said, trying to speak while breathing into the bag.

"Huh?"

He took the bag away from his face. "I said, 'This bag smells like tuna fish.' "

"Beggars can't be choosers," I said. "Now put it up to your face and keep breathing."

"Dammit, I cannot lose these guys," Marlys said, apprehension tingeing her voice.

"Quick, pull into that alleyway and hide."

"Hide? You want me to *hide*? Did you somehow miss that we are driving a freaking school bus?" Marlys's voice was filled with tension as she tried to maneuver corner after corner, and I began to feel a little sick, my stomach churning with each turn. I glanced back every so often to see if the Humvee was still following us. About three blocks from the police station it veered off and disappeared.

"It's gone," I announced loudly. "They must know where we are headed."

"Yeah, to the depths of hell," Marlys muttered. She wasn't taking this very well. Most of the time, Marlys's life was pretty tame. She drove a school bus, raised her kids, and laughed at the psycho dance moms. She wasn't usually in the line of fire. To be honest, neither was I. But I'd had a few days to adjust to being attacked and all that.

The big yellow school bus slowed to a stop in the parking lot of the Ogden police station.

"Are you okay, Marlys?" I asked gently.

She didn't speak for a moment, and I felt movement and turned around to see the giant Samoan raise his head a tiny bit and look around. "It safe now?" he asked.

"Marlys?"

Elder Martin was still breathing into the paper bag, his eyes darting back and forth between me and Marlys.

"This is serious shit, Jenny," she finally said, a deep breath following her words, her body almost visibly collapsing, shoulders slumping. "I have kids. I have a husband. They need me. I can't afford to die."

Despite the fact I had no kids and certainly no husband, I really didn't want to die, either. I needed to do something to keep my friends safe, even if I couldn't keep myself safe.

There was a rap at the bus door and we all jumped, and then Marlys looked over and pulled the lever that allowed my favorite detective, Tate Wilson, into the large yellow bus, followed by a few uniforms.

"Well, this is quite a crew," he said, surveying the scene. "Who's the big guy on the ground? And why is he there? Do we need an ambulance? Is everyone okay?"

"I safe," Elder Tuatuola muttered. "I safe?"

"You can get up, big guy," Tate told him. "This is the police station."

Elder T rose up and brushed off his white shirt, which was now stained with all manner of little people gunk. I doubted it would ever come clean, but it was definitely better than a bloodstain. Elder Martin continued to breathe in and out into his tuna-flavored bag, his eyes traveling back and forth, surveying the scene. He had a weird look on his face, something akin to pleasure. Was he enjoying this?

"How'd you know?" I asked Tate, wondering why he was right there, always right there. Except for the other night, of course.

"Fallon. They were parked about a block away, since you weren't real excited about their presence. Once they heard the shots, they tried to catch up to you, but that bus was moving pretty fast. You training for the Indy 500?" He directed that last part to Marlys, who finally found her sense of humor and grinned.

"Did they see the Humvee? Did they get the plates?" I asked.

"Humvee?"

Of course not. Why would anything, ever, work in my favor?

"Yes, we were being chased by a big, silver Humvee. I did not see the plates."

"Can anyone else here verify that a vehicle was chasing you?"

"Uh, I was kinda busy," drawled Elder Martin, who was still holding his tuna bag, although he was not breathing into it anymore.

"I was driving. I looked into the rearview mirror and saw a flash of silver, but I was too worried about navigating turns in this big mother to tell what kind of vehicle it was," Marlys said.

"I see nothing," Elder T uttered in his deep voice.

"You sure there was a Humvee? Fallon didn't mention a Humvee." Tate gave me a studied look.

"But he heard the shots, right?"

"Yes, he heard the shots, and several neighbors called in reporting the altercation."

By this time, I was getting a little worked up. "Altercation? Some nut job shoots at me, my apartment, my friends, a school bus belonging to the Weber County School District, and two Mormon missionaries, and you call it an altercation? Doesn't an altercation imply that it's two people who know each other? I don't have a damn clue who's doing this. Do you?"

"Bad choice of words."

"Damn bad."

Tate ushered us all out of the school bus and inside the police station. Elders Martin and Tuatuola got downright perky as they were questioned, and I was starting to wonder about their motivations. Were they coming around because they wanted to convert me, or because their lives were so boring they wanted to live vicariously through me? None of that mattered, of course, when the same uptight, dark-suited man showed up. The one who came to my house before. He was seriously going to put me on some kind of list. I just knew it. He hustled the two missionaries off after Tate told them they could go, but the looks he gave me were even nastier than before.

"This is so unfair. I did not ask those missionaries to come back. You would think that stomach pumping would put them off a little."

"Maybe they crave the excitement," Tate said. "Mission work can't be that action packed."

"Unless you hang around me."

Marlys's supervisors had shown up at the police station, as her bus was currently being processed for evidence. Tate had assured them that Marlys had been quite heroic in saving the lives of not just one erstwhile dance teacher, but two Mormon missionaries, and I saw the two men's eyes light up as they considered the PR possibilities. Marlys would undoubtedly not be in trouble, the media would probably be alerted, and my life was going to get worse.

"I ask you this a lot, but here I go again," Tate said softly, after he pulled me away from the hullabaloo and bought me a bad cup of police station coffee. "Are you okay?"

"This is getting too serious. My friends are involved. I'm scared. I've been scared the whole time, but now other people are involved."

"I know."

"I don't know what to do."

"I do. You're my responsibility, and I'm going to make sure you are okay. Starting now, you have a twenty-four-hour police guard."

"Didn't I already have that, or at least a watchdog? Marshal Fallon? And fat lot of good that did me."

His face hardened. "It won't be them. It'll be me."

I gulped. "I'm not so sure that's a good idea. I think I'm more afraid of you than anything else."

"Then it's time you started living, Jenny T. Partridge."

I gulped again, and he laughed.

"Give me twenty minutes and I'll take you home. I think you need to cancel your dance classes for today."

"Can't do that. In just a little less than a week I have my first *Nutcracker* performance, and no Taylee, so I have to work with the two Seniors I have who are capable of pulling it off. Plus Wednesday is dress rehearsal, and Monica is coming tonight for the final fittings for costumes, and you have already seen what a nutbag she can be, and the buffoons look like crap, and since I gave Ella a role, and now her mom has hightailed off with her, I'm up a river without a paddle. I've got to fix windows, and . . ."

"All right, all right. I have no idea what half of what you just said meant, but I guess I'm going to dance class tonight."

* * *

TATE sent over someone the police department used to fix my windows, and then he took me to lunch. Good thing, since I never got my pastries and caffeine fix at Grounds for Coffee. Since we were down at the police station, he took me to a small Italian restaurant on Washington, Bocca D'Italia, and I had fettuccini alfredo. I also sampled some of Tate's lasagna, which was to die for. Good, carb-loaded food. I would make it through another day.

After we finished, he drove me down 25th to my building, and parked in the lot. "The dance moms will scream bloody murder if they don't have a place to park," I told him.

"The department will have my hide if this car gets dinged in that little alleyway," he countered. "And I will help you handle the psycho dance moms. I have a gun."

"You win."

He followed me up the stairs, and I self-consciously realized he was staring right at my butt. Great. At least I couldn't afford to buy a lot of food, otherwise it would be much wider. When we got to the top, I jostled my key in the lock, opened the door, and then turned to stare at Tate, who had a funny look on his face. "What?" I asked him.

"You go in. I'll be right there."

"Is something wrong? Did you see something bad? Is the Humvee parked here somewhere?" I scanned the parking lot but could see nothing out of place.

"I'll be right in, Jenny. I just need a minute."

"I don't understand. What's wrong? What do you see?"

He sighed loudly and then pulled me up against him, tightly, and I could feel his arousal pressing against my groin. It caused my heart to thump and moisture to pool in my nether regions, and I felt a flush rising from my crotch up to my face. "I think I understand now," I whispered.

"I hope so. It isn't easy to follow you up a flight of stairs and not react. I'm only human, and I'm incredibly attracted to you, crazy life and all."

"I think I understand now." I parroted my last words.

"Now, will you go inside?"

"Yes, I think I understand now."

He chuckled, a deep throaty sound.

I turned away and walked inside my studio, thinking how warm it had been in his arms—a little too warm, actually, except I wanted to heat it up with him even more—and how cold it felt in my studio now. Wait. Oh no. I breathed out and saw the cloud of fog that was becoming just a little too common. *Not again.*

Tate opened the door and stepped inside and looked around. "You saving on heat?"

"Stupid damn, damn furnace."

"I guess the answer to that is no."

"Marco is gone, and I don't know squat about furnaces, but it keeps going out. I don't want to have to call my dad again, but I can't teach dance when my studio feels like a refrigerator."

"I'll look at it."

"You know furnaces?"

"Pretty well. Better than most. My dad was an HVAC guy."

"I have no idea what that means, but if it has something to do with furnaces, I am forever in your debt."

"Heating, ventilation, air-conditioning."

"Heating. Heating is good. Let's go."

I led the way down the inner staircase and unlocked the door that connected my studio to Marco's store. I punched in the key code to keep the alarm from going off, and from there, we continued to the basement, but not before Tate glanced in at the darkened store that was filled with junk and priceless antiques. Only Marco and the truly gifted seemed to know which was which.

I flipped on a light in the cavernous basement, and the fluorescents flickered on, revealing more of Marco's priceless treasures and more than a little junk, and in the front, facing 25th Street, the huge, ancient furnace.

"Wow, that's old."

"Yes, it is," I answered. "Do you think you can fix it? I think my dad said it had something to do with a pilot light."

"I'll figure it out," he said, and then proceeded to tinker with the furnace until I heard a whoosh and a roar.

"Yea! You did it!" I considered doing a happy dance, but thought it might scare him off, and frankly, I didn't want that. I wanted him close.

Tate brushed off his hands and then looked around, his eyes focusing on an alcove that was bricked in, but that had once clearly been an opening.

"What's that?"

"An entrance to the tunnels."

"What tunnels?"

"You haven't heard about the tunnels of 25th Street?"

He shook his head.

"Back in the early 1900s, 25th Street was a pretty rough place. Rumor has it Al Capone said that it was too rough of a place for him to come. This building we're in used to be a bordello. I guess they had the tunnels to hide from the police, and to run their moonshine and illegal gambling. The tunnels run all through 25th Street."

"Wow, I'd never heard that before."

"Really? Everybody around here knows about the tunnels. I guess being from Brigham City, though, you wouldn't know. How long have you been here?"

"Oh, two years. I spent about seven years with the Las Vegas PD, before I realized I was more a small-town kinda guy, so I came back. Tried the Brigham City PD, but it was just a little *too* small. Ogden came calling, and I answered. So why are the tunnels blocked up?"

"Well, mostly because they are pretty ancient, and they don't meet earthquake codes. See that beam? That is for reinforcement. And they had to close off the tunnels."

"Damn, it would be interesting to go into those tunnels."

I shuddered as I considered going into one of those dark, small tunnels. "No thanks."

"Claustrophobia?"

"Yeah, along with a morbid fear of spiders and rodents."

"Still, it must be fascinating."

"I heard that some of the tunnel entrances are still open, but I never investigated more. No desire."

"Do most people know about their history?"

"No, and I'm not sharing it. Pyscho dance moms are psycho enough. They sure don't need to know that this building used to be a house of ill repute."

"Well, I'd love to explore those tunnels."

"When Marco gets back, I'll ask him where the openings are, and you can have fun. Just don't invite me along."

I started back up the stairs, and then stopped, a sudden rush of heat to my face reminding me what had happened when he had been walking behind me before. "Uh, you can go first."

That deep, sexy chuckle caused electrical pings in my body, and it was all I could do not to knock him to the floor and take advantage of him. Of course, the floor down here was dirty, and there were probably mice droppings and spiders and . . . Whew, that cooled me off.

And if that didn't work, there was the air in the building. When we reached the top floor, I sighed in relief to hear the noise of the furnace. It would be a bit before the studio warmed up, but we had come here straight from lunch, and so by the time the Tots filed in, it would be much warmer.

To me, anytime Tate Wilson was around, it was too hot for comfort.

$\mathcal{S}$IXTEEN

$\mathcal{S}$INCE I had my own version of *The Nutcracker*, I got to create roles for all of my dancers. This wasn't always wonderful, since many of my dancers were greatly dance-challenged, but somehow, I usually managed to find a way to make all of them look decent in one role or another. For example, my Tots were of the age where the cute factor was big. Dress them up in a pretty costume, curl and fluff up their hair, and it didn't much matter what they did on the floor. Everybody oohed and aahed over how cute they were. I'd made my Tots swan babies for the past two years and it brought in entire passels of families to see their little ones act cute. Probably one-third or less of the girls actually had any dance talent, but at that age, it didn't matter. Sometimes I longed to be that age again myself, where skill and talent were not a big factor, but being cute was. I could do cute. Really.

Today, I was trying to get a bunch of Tots to do the unthinkable—hold a leg extension without hopping off to Nevada. They would lift their chubby legs up, holding them high, and then hop, hop, hop until they looked like a bunch of mutant frogs instead of swan babies. Granted, real swans did not do leg extensions, but this was dance, and there was *not* going to be a passel of frogs performing in my *Nutcracker*.

Finding your center, an integral part of dance, was a feat too advanced for four- and five-year-olds. After Marlys's daughter Marble crashed into Abby Fredericks, and both of them ran to their mothers in tears, I decided to pull the leg extension from the choreography, going instead with a simple grapevine move.

Tate was in the back, sitting on a folding chair with all the other dance moms, who were supposed to be sitting in the waiting area and not watching class. I really had to enforce that rule again. I kept glancing back at him, and it was making me really nervous. He was deep in conversation with Marlys and Angie Jones, one of the other Tot moms, and I couldn't imagine what had them so engrossed except discussing just how strange I really was. I couldn't help it. I was an artist. We were supposed to be weird.

I finally got the swan babies working in unison— somewhat—and then it was time for the Minis and Smalls classes. Amber and James sauntered in at the same time, almost late, but not quite. Made it hard to complain. However, James was toting the rat under his arm, and today, the creature was wearing a sweater. A sweater!

"Hello, you ravenously beautiful creature," James said, smiling widely at me.

"Good try, Pied Piper. Get rid of it."

"Jennifer, but then I would be late for class, and who would teach the Smalls?"

"Me, as I always do. You came in today to help, remember? You can't help with a rat attached to your side. It's too distracting."

I really should just stop talking, you know, because the moment I said that, all the Tots spotted the little dog under James's arm, as did the incoming stream of Minis and Smalls, and soon it was a small dance riot, as everyone tried to pet the rat that James called a dog. Big problem was no one was dancing, and our performance was getting awfully close. Damn James.

"Phreee-wweeeet." A sharp whistle pierced the air and Amber clapped her hands and all the little girls scattered back to their proper positions. The Tots headed out the door, and the Smalls and Minis were on the floor stretching. How the hell did she do it? It was a good thing Amber was not a choreographer, or I would be out of a job—and a dance studio. While she was a fabulous dancer, she did not have the skill or artistic vision to create dances. Thank God for me.

Marlys lingered behind and I walked up to her and gave her a hug. "I'm sorry about the bus, Mar. I really am."

"It's cool. The news stations interviewed me, and now my bosses think I'm the neatest thing since sliced bread. Somehow, you always end up smelling like roses, Jenny. I don't know how you pull it off."

"I haven't pulled anything off. I have no clue who killed Sandra Epstein, and any minute now bullets could start flying again, so I'm not sure what you mean, but thanks for the vote of confidence."

"It's going to be okay, Jenn. Tate has everything under control."

Nothing like an hour of watching mutant frogs to put people on a first-name basis.

"And Jenny? This one's good. He's golden. Don't let him go."

With that, she grabbed Marble's arm and headed out the door. Great. She was all but planning the wedding.

"Jennifer, can I speak to you alone, please?"

"Only if you lose the rat."

James sighed deeply.

I ushered him into the office, while Amber continued to warm up the Smalls and Minis. I needed to run the Buffoon and Snowflake routines with them, but if I didn't listen to James now, he would drive me crazy with anguished sighs and tormented glances, so I knew I'd better get it over with.

After I shut the door, I leaned against the desk and folded my arms, waiting for James to speak.

"Now, Jennifer, please do not freak."

That was not a good start. This wasn't going to go well.

"James, just spill. What is it?"

He put the little dog down, and Winkie promptly wandered over to my garbage can and made good on his name, lifting his leg and going winkie on the floor.

"James!"

"Oh, bad dog. Bad, bad, awful, annoying, despicable little piece of hairless . . ."

"Uh, James? I thought you liked this dog."

"This creature is not a dog. It's a walking fleabag alarm clock, mother . . ."

"James! Then why do you have it?"

"Stupid Cullin. Stupid, stupid Cullin. He bought it for his wife, and she was repulsed by it, so he came by, and sweet-talked me, and got me into bed, and next thing I knew I had a dog and what the hell was I supposed to do?"

"Oh, James. You have got to stay away from him. When did this happen?"

"He says the same thing about you, Jennifer dear."

"That's just because I know what a two-timing weasel he really is. I don't care that he's gay, but I suspect his wife might! And he's not honest."

"A judgment that is easy for you to make, Jenn. You don't know what it's like to be a gay man in this culture. It's hard in any family, I suppose, but here in Utah, it's even worse."

"Fine, you're right. I don't know what it's like. But I do know that he is cheating on his wife, and apparently, with you—again—and I don't understand how you can . . ."

A sudden sharp rap on the door made us both jump. "Everything okay in there?" Tate called through the door.

"Yes, fine. Be out in just a minute," I called. Winkie chose that moment to lift his leg on the fake palm plant decorating my office.

"Winkie, no!" James and I hollered in unison, and the

dog stopped, turning to stare at both of us with a perplexed look on his face, leg still raised.

I sighed deeply. "James, you need to just say no to Cullin. He's bad news. He's playing on both teams. How do you think that is going to turn out for you?" *Urk.* I'd become my father.

"Not well. He's hard to say no to, but Jenny, I have to talk to you about something else. It's this . . ."

He reached into his pocket and pulled out a slightly bent lilac-colored envelope. While I knew James liked lilac, I had a terrible feeling in the pit of my stomach about this particular lilac-colored envelope. He extended it toward me, and I reached for it with trepidation, scared about just what I was going to find inside. I opened it up, and pulled out a folded card. The card matched the lilac hue of the envelope and featured a darker-colored purple ribbon tied on top. The front of the card featured the names "James" and "Jennifer" in elegant calligraphy handwriting. This was bad.

"What is this?"

"Jennifer, please, just read." James offered up one of his long-suffering sighs, and I fought the desire to wring my hands around his neck.

I opened up the card, and saw words that welcomed guests to an informal gathering at the Chez Panisse restaurant—James's uncle's restaurant—this Friday night. The same night that my annual *Nutcracker* production was scheduled to go on at the Eccles Center. This was an invitation to an engagement party. An engagement party for James—and me. Blood rushed to my head and spots swam before my eyes. How could it have gotten this far? How could this lily-livered coward standing in front of me have *allowed* it to get this far?

"Now Jennifer, before you get too worked up, I want you to know that I had nothing to do with this. My mother cooked it up all herself, and I told her it isn't going to happen, and that we aren't ready to even think about setting a date, but . . ."

More spots. Maybe some shooting flames. Could heads literally explode? Since all I could hear was a roaring noise in my head, but James appeared to be still blathering on, I was very worried that this might be true.

The office door opened and in came Monica, holding about fifteen shimmery peacock-colored costumes, trimmed with what appeared to be genuine ostrich feathers. Her timing, as always, was impeccable. And of course I could not ask her to wait, because she was nutty and flighty and might threaten to jump out of my two-story building if I got her even slightly upset. The relief crossing James's face told me he was well aware of this, and once again he was off the hook. But this time, not for long.

"James, as soon as these fittings are over, I am getting in my car and driving to your mother's house and setting her straight as to exactly who and what it is you are interested in, and also making sure she knows there will not now, nor will there ever be, a wedding between you and me."

Sheer terror crossed his features as he backed out, apparently trying to gauge just how serious I was. Unfortunately, he didn't seem to know me as well as he thought. This was messing with my livelihood. I wouldn't be a mustache for anyone if it stood in the way of my yearly *Nutcracker* performance, the only thing that kept me solvent the rest of the year. Could I be considered solvent? Probably not, but that was not the point. It kept me from being homeless and unemployed, and that was all I cared about.

"We'll chat after the fittings, okay?"

"I am not kidding, James. You have about two hours to fix this. That's it. That's all I'm giving you."

He chuckled weakly, his face pale and wan.

Monica stood holding the costumes, her big brown eyes traveling back and forth from James to me, and back again.

When he turned and disappeared, Monica moved forward and set the costumes on my desk, a few stray feathers floating up from the pile and hanging in the air like tiny turquoise birds.

"I have the rest of this stuff in my car. I'll go get it, and then we'll do fittings," she said, her voice calm and moderate, and, I thought, a bit smug. Could it be that she was enjoying this circus that had become my life?

"You seem remarkably calm and happy today, Monica. New man in your life? Win the lottery?"

"Prozac," she said with a straight face, and then she turned and walked out the door.

Maybe I should get myself some of that.

MONICA did a remarkable job on the costumes, and the fittings went smoothly. She stayed calm, cool, and collected throughout the entire thing, and I was starting to get worried. Nothing around Monica ever went smoothly. Usually there was a costume that was too big, or too small, and as soon as she realized she had changes to make, the hyperventilating and threats started up. Not this time. Everything fit, with only minor alterations, except for the Sugar Plum Fairy costume. The reason for that, of course, was obvious. It had been designed for Taylee, who was two inches shorter and much thinner than the other two Seniors who were currently vying for the role.

Things were going too well. I didn't even want to bring this up, but I had no choice. While making a costume smaller was no big deal, making it bigger was an entirely different thing. In other words, it didn't happen. We would have to start from scratch, and I would have to accept that Taylee was not going to be here to dance the role.

I closed my eyes and dove in, headfirst, waiting for the explosion. "Monica, I need a costume that fits these two," I said, indicating the two Seniors I was considering giving the Plum role to, as the girls sat next to each other on the hardwood floor. They were chatting idly, and you would hardly know their moms were bitter enemies, the result of a front-row-fifty feud a few years back. Both girls were pretty even tempered, and although talented, they had not picked up the sharp-edged ambitions that both of their mothers had—even though the ambitions were for them.

I waited for Monica's head to pop off.

"That's fine, Jenny. I ordered extra material for this costume, since you usually change your mind at least three times, so I should have it done by Thursday. That gives us time for any last-minute alterations."

Good God. Who was this person, and what had she done with the real Monica? I was totally puzzled. Surely this complete turnaround would require more than a simple antidepressant like Prozac. Knowing Monica, I would suspect she would require heavy-duty drugs like lithium, and maybe some electroshock treatments.

"Ooookay," I said warily.

Monica chuckled. "It's okay, Jenny. I've been doing some relaxation and yoga classes, and learning to meditate. I'm searching for inner peace, and I think I've found it. You should come with me to the classes. They are doing me so much good."

"Uh, just a few days ago you were locked in my bathroom here and threatening all manner of crazy things if I didn't let you have your way."

"These things take time. One does not heal from a life of torment overnight."

"Right." Was she implying I had been tormenting her? No matter. I wasn't going to ask. She'd offered to fix a costume without hysterics and a mini–nervous breakdown, so torment accusations or not, I was accepting her answer.

"I'll be back on Thursday. Should I just make it to fit both girls, or do you have one specifically in mind?"

"They are close to the same size, so just make one that will fit either of them." I didn't want to admit to it, but I was still holding out hope that Taylee would be found, and not just for my dance, of course. I wanted her to be safe. And well. With arms and legs unhurt, so she could dance.

Was it really that much to ask? Don't answer that.

Seventeen

When classes were over, I gave James a look that said "time to come clean," and he reluctantly walked in my direction. "I'm going now. I'm headed to my mother's house, with the express purpose of breaking her already fragile heart, so don't say another word."

"Don't lay the guilt trip on me, James. You created this, now you get to fix it. Your mom will be fine. If she hadn't taken it so far, I might have allowed you to use me for a while longer, but it's gone off the edge. It's too much, and you know it."

With another long-suffering sigh—one that would make my mother proud—James headed to the front door and pushed his way out. All the dancers were gone, and now it was just Tate and I left in the studio. He'd watched the entire exchange between James and me with interest, and now he headed toward me, that sexy half smile on his face. My imagination ran wild as he reached for me, and then the front door opened and Marshal Fallon walked in, followed by the marshal I didn't know, but who had complimented my agility when I was assaulted.

"Fallon," Tate said, nodding his head. I detected a distinct chill between the two men that had not been there before. They had been buddy-buddy just a few days ago. What had happened?

"Wilson," the other man answered, also nodding his head. Men were weird. They resolved problems in the strangest ways. I'd seen best friends beat the heck out of each other, and ten minutes later they were best friends again. As opposed to women, who usually destroyed reputations by talking behind each other's back and held grudges for years. Hmm. Maybe there was something to be said for beating the heck out of each other.

At any rate, I wasn't sure what was up with these two, but their officer-ly camaraderie had taken a hit of one kind or another.

"Why are you here?"

"I have something I need to ask Ms. Partridge."

"And what would that be?"

"Well, if I needed you to run interference, then I would let you handle it. But I have this under control, and this is a matter of the United States Marshals Office, so if I can just take Ms. Partridge somewhere private . . ."

"Whoa, whoa, whoa, you aren't taking her anywhere," Tate said with a growl. "She's staying where I can see her."

"Are you implying that I can't be trusted to keep Ms. Partridge safe?"

"Well, you haven't exactly done a bang-up job of it so far."

"Okay, you two, knock it off," I said, although I was enjoying the show. "I'm sure both of you are equally endowed, and I don't really enjoy pissing matches, so does someone want to share with me just what the hell is going on here? Just a few days ago you were both pretty chummy, and now you are bickering like teenage boys over a girl." *Ulp.* No, it couldn't be that.

Both men looked at me expectantly, waiting for me to

keep talking, which of course I usually did, and Tate had an amused look on his face, but I'd decided now was probably a good time to shut up. Some lessons took me awhile, but you can't say I was totally incapable of learning from my mistakes. I was just slower than others.

Since I was not talking, and the two men practiced silent-but-deadly on just about every occasion, we all stood there staring at each other, quiet filling the room like the icy air that had been all too common in my studio the past few days.

"Look, Wilson, I just need to speak to Jenny alone for a moment." One point for Tate, since Fallon spoke first—if anyone was keeping score. I was pretty sure both men were, based on their behavior tonight.

"There's nothing you need to say to her that can't be said in front of me," Wilson volleyed back. "I have jurisdiction on this case."

"Please tell me you aren't going to throw jurisdiction in my face? I thought we were cooperating together to find a desperate young girl."

"Desperate young girl? Good one, but maybe you ought to see if first you can keep a grown woman safe. You didn't even manage to do that."

I sighed heavily, channeling my mother. "Okay, okay, Marshal Fallon, you have five minutes. In my office. Tate, do you really think I'm not safe just ten feet from you, with another officer of the law?" Tate tightened his jaw and a muscle pulsed on the right side of his cheek. He was not enjoying this.

"Fine, five minutes. No longer."

Fallon followed me into my office and I heard the other marshal ask Tate how he thought the Utah Jazz were going to fare this year, before I closed the door on their conversation.

"You don't have much time, so let's get going. What do you want?"

Fallon hesitated for a moment, and then a look I wasn't able to identify crossed his face. Finally, he spoke. "Look,

I'm really sorry about what happened to you. Twice on my watch you've almost gotten hurt, and I started thinking about it, and I realized that it's because I've been looking at this all wrong. I've been viewing you, at the least, as a witness, and at the most, as a suspect, and the truth is you are just an innocent bystander who got caught up in something really, really bad."

What the hell? "Ooookay," I said slowly, drawing out my words. "Thanks for the . . . apology?" Where the hell was this one going?

"Look, Jenny, I've spent ten years doing this job, and the end outcome on a missing child is rarely good. It hardens you, and makes you look at everyone around you differently. Especially when those people are directly involved—however they are involved—in a crime."

His words sunk in slowly, and four of them stuck out in my mind like neon glowing from the windows of a 7-Eleven. End. Outcome. Rarely. Good. Taylee's odds of being recovered alive were not good. I guess I'd never really let myself think she might be dead. I just kept thinking she was alive somewhere, and that she would be returned safely, and hopefully in time to perform in the lead role of my *Nutcracker* performance.

Spots started swimming before my eyes and I felt all woozy, and the next thing I knew there were shouting voices and loud arguments and lights that were entirely too bright. I slowly came to, aware that my head was throbbing and I was feeling pretty sick.

"What the hell did you do to her?" Tate asked, his voice sounding ferocious and wild, and most of all, protective. If I wasn't all oogie feeling I might have been warmed by it. As it was, I needed a bucket or wastebasket—fast.

"I didn't do anything. We were just talking and then she keeled over, and I caught her before she hit the ground. She passed out. I think she got really upset when I mentioned that Taylee might not be safe."

"Well, surely she figured that from the beginning,"

Marshal John Doe said, very unhelpfully, I might add. Since I didn't know his name, he was John Doe to me.

"Jenny's a little different that way," Tate said, his voice calmer, I supposed, because he had determined that Fallon had not tried to manhandle me.

"Hellllooo," I said from my position on the floor, as I tried to sit up. Since the world spun alarmingly, I quickly lay back down. "I'm alive down here, and I can hear you. I may not be able to move my body, but my brain is working."

All three men knelt down toward me and I suddenly felt like some sort of virgin sacrifice or participant in a weird religious ritual. I forced myself to sit up. "I'm fine. Get up. No need to worry." Slowly I regained my balance and equilibrium and my stomach stopped threatening to spill its contents. The three men stood up and Tate reached down a strong hand and pulled me up. His clasp was warm and firm, and I felt bubbles of excitement in my stomach that had only a little to do with the nausea I'd been feeling earlier.

He led me over to my office desk chair and helped me settle into it. I watched the three men staring at me attentively, and wondered—not the for the first time of course—just how this had all come about. "So you all think Taylee is dead, don't you?" Saying the cold, cruel words made me blanch but I'd already done too much running from reality. It was time to face up to this ugly situation, and the truth was, odds were against Taylee's survival. This wasn't about a stupid dance performance, or even my yearly income. This was about a little girl who was missing, possibly dead, and she had no one here to defend her. It was time for me to step up to the plate.

"We don't know that, obviously. We actually have two cases here, I guess. One is a murder, and one a missing person," Tate said as though he knew Taylee were alive, but his face told another story. He wasn't holding on to any extreme hope that she was alive.

"We need to find her, Jenny, which is why we have been following you and watching you so closely," Fallon said. "With her mother dead, you're the closest thing she would have to a mother or mother figure. We figure if she's going to go to someone for help, it would be you." The thought of me as a mother figure to anyone was ludicrous at best, but now wasn't the time to mention that.

"But thinking she will come to someone for help seems to imply that you don't think she was taken."

"We don't really know. But all indications lead us to believe she happened upon the crime shortly after it happened, and was either removed from the scene or ran."

I sucked in my breath. What kind of trauma would that do to a young girl, seeing her mother's dead body on the floor, and then realizing the murderer was still close? Poor Taylee.

"What evidence do you have that supports that?" I asked Fallon.

He shook his head, slowly, and tightened his lips. "I can't tell you that. I'm sorry. Just believe me when I say that we know Taylee was alive shortly after her mother was murdered."

"Witness protection, right?" The time had passed for the cloak-and-dagger routine. I'd decided that I needed to do whatever I could to find Taylee, if she was still alive. "I can't tell you" worked for the old Jenny T. Partridge, but not this one. Fallon blanched as I said the words, and the other marshal's eyes got wide. Bingo. Wow, I never thought life would be like the movies, but it was certainly turning out that way right now. "Yet you can't find her. And you are scared she might be dead. Well, you marshals don't have anything on the dance-mom rumor mill. I'm going to find Taylee. I'll do whatever I have to. Put up posters around town, call press conferences . . ." Something suddenly occurred to me. While Sandra's murder had made the local news, there had been no pictures displayed, and none of the television stations had mentioned her missing daughter. Why was that?

"You can't do that, Jenny," Marshal Fallon said quietly.

"You have a hat on this whole thing, don't you?" I said, wonderment filling my voice.

"A hat?" Marshal John Doe asked.

"She means a lid," said Tate, who had apparently decided to become my interpreter.

"Whatever," I said, my irritation rising. "Meanwhile, no one is out looking for a scared, desperate little girl. You're doing nothing to find her, because she's in witness protection, and you're afraid that . . . Oh." Damn, I hated it when I figured things out after I spoke. The only person they were trying to protect was Taylee. They thought she'd be safe here in Ogden, Utah, with a new life, and a new name, but death had come calling for her mother and possibly had taken her, too, in the wake. I hoped not. God, I hoped not.

"So the person you hid her from originally might find her if you put her picture in the papers, or in the news, right?"

Fallon nodded.

"Isn't it possible that that person only wanted her nasty mother, Sandra, and now that that threat is gone, Taylee will be safe?"

He shook his head. Damn.

"Right now, you're the best hope we have, Jenny. So we're sticking close to you," Marshal Fallon said. Tate's face tightened at those words. Apparently, he didn't want Andrew Fallon sticking close to me at all. As for me, if I didn't have the very sexy Tate Wilson dogging my every step, I certainly would have considered tangoing with super handsome Andrew Fallon. Of course, it's not like I had some commitment or understanding with Tate. Those dinners did not count, because he was just trying to keep me where he could see me, and it was just easier that way. All in all, while I knew he found me attractive, that was hardly enough to build a lifetime on, or even to, say, rule out every other guy.

"Are you sure I didn't hit my head?" I asked Andrew Fallon, and he grinned at me, an ear-to-ear smile, dimples accentuated, that made my heart do a little flutter. That smile almost said, "I know what you're thinking!" I felt a rosy, hot flush climb up my chest and into my face.

Most days I climbed out of bed knowing that everything would pretty much be the same. Every day. While I didn't consider my regular life boring by any means, this type of thing never happened to me. The scary part was that I was confused, tired, worried, more than a little desperate, terribly poor, and also, really getting addicted to the excitement.

Now, in addition to a carb addiction, I apparently craved adrenaline.

Eighteen

Tate insisted on escorting me home, and Andrew Fallon didn't say much, other than, "You know where to find me, Jenny. I'll be a lot closer just in case anything happens."

That whole "cement balloon" cliché was really appropriate here, because Tate did not like that at all. I could tell because his lips were clinched together tight, sort of like Grandma Gilly's always got whenever she saw me coming. Break a few holy statues, flood the bathroom once or twice, and you were branded for life.

"You seem kinda pissed," I said after a few minutes of frosty silence. "I don't get you men. Just a few days ago, you and Marshal Fallon were buddy-buddy and practically at the ball-scratching, beer-drinking phase of guy relationships. Now you can barely look at him without spitting nails. Care to tell me what's up with that?"

"No," he said grimly, not even cracking a smile at my little joke. Hmmph. We rode a little further in silence, and then I was forced to say something else, because the quiet was getting to me and I did not need time alone with my own crazy thoughts. That always got me in trouble.

"So, what do you think you should do next to find Taylee?"

"Dunno."

Mr. Morose was starting to piss me off. I hadn't exactly asked to be put in this position. I started stewing, and my stomach churned, and just about that time, Tate pulled in front of my apartment building. Lights pulled in behind us, and I assumed that it was Fallon, staying close as he had promised. Surely Tate could not be angry about that? Surely he realized that we did not have some huge commitment that required me not to even look at extremely handsome U.S. marshals without getting slightly weak-kneed? Surely I was totally insane to even think that this was bothering Tate at all?

He opened his door and got out, and I did the same, a light honk from the car behind us indicating Fallon's acknowledgment that I was headed into my apartment.

Tate followed me closely—a little too close—and I put the key in the lock and turned it, then removed it and inserted the dead bolt key, Tate standing right behind me the entire time, almost pressed up against me, causing me all kinds of emotional turmoil and mixed sexual feelings.

After I got the dead bolt open, I reached for the knob and slightly turned it, determined to get rid of Tate Wilson and collapse inside of my apartment, surrounded by all my confusion, attraction, and misguided lust. It didn't work that way.

Tate was pretty quick on the draw, pushing the door open and propelling me inside, moving us both out around it and then shutting it tight. He pushed my back up against the door, one hand around my waist, almost cupping my butt, the other on my shoulder, pushing me back gently, but firmly. He leaned in and put his mouth on mine, softly at first, little feathery kisses, followed by firmer, stronger pressure. The hand around my waist moved up, trailing over my rib cage until it stopped just below my left breast, teasing me. Torturing me, really.

He continued to kiss me, and I found myself unable to move, to protest—which I definitely should have been doing. His tongue drove hungrily into my mouth and I was hit with the sudden impulsive urge to just rip off my clothes—and his, too—and drag him to the floor. But I couldn't. Because he stopped, breath ragged, and pulled away from me, running his right hand through his hair as he paced toward the living room.

I tried to catch my breath, leaning against the door, wondering what I'd done wrong, and hating myself for my constant self-doubt. Why did it have to be about me? Maybe it was his issue.

"Maybe you should go now," I said, my voice high and faltering.

"Is that what you want? You want me to go?"

"I have no idea what I want, because I have no idea what you want. You're driving me crazy. Half the time I think you're interested in me for reasons other than the fact I am tied to one of your cases by a dead psycho mom and her missing daughter, and the rest of the time I think you are just playing me, trying to get close to me because I can help you solve your case. I don't know which one of those things is worse."

For the first time in quite a while, he smiled and then chuckled.

"The fact I might want something more from you than just information scares you?"

"It terrifies me."

"Why?"

"I'm not entirely sure. But what I want to know *now* is what the hell was your problem tonight? Why are you acting mad at me?"

He sighed, and that hand went through his hair again, leaving it rumpled and terribly attractive in a way that made me want to smooth it out and groom it for him. This was bad.

"I'm mad because we've done a pretty crappy job of keeping you safe, and I feel responsible. And I feel bad that

I have to admit that for a time there—a short time—I really thought you were involved, and that means my senses are off and . . ."

"You did? You really did think I might have killed Sandra Epstein?" The tears that stung my eyes surprised me. I guess they surprised him, too, because he took one look at me and pulled me into his arms, holding me tight.

"I think it's because you have my senses reeling. I don't know what to think. I seem to be losing balance here. And I'm mad that Fallon didn't do a very good job keeping you safe. And that now he's playing up to you to try and get you on his side so that he can get what he wants."

I let a few more self-pity tears trickle down my face and then I pulled away from him. "This whole situation just keeps getting crazier and crazier."

"Don't fall for his lines, Jenny. He only has one purpose. He wants to find Taylee."

"Maybe that should be your only purpose, too."

Tate shook his head. "You don't understand, and I can't enlighten you, but just remember this. Don't trust Fallon. He's not a bad guy, but he's a Fed with an agenda, and that makes him dangerous to you."

I wanted to think he was jealous. That he wanted me looking in no other man's direction, but that really didn't make sense. Plus things like that did not happen to me.

"Tell me this. Why were you all friendly with him when this all started out, and now you seem to hate him?"

"Maybe I don't like the way he looks at you now."

While this was a flattering thought, and I certainly wished I could evoke that kind of reaction from men, I was a realist. "Liar. What is it really?"

"I'm not lying. I don't."

"Fine, maybe a small bit of that is true, but that's not the majority of it, and I want to know what you mean."

He shrugged his shoulders, then turned away. "Let's order a pizza." He walked into my living room and plopped down on the overstuffed couch, the only furniture I had in the room besides the beanbag chair. "Ooomph," he said as he sunk deeply into the old couch.

He looked kind of funny sitting there, sunken into the couch, knees sticking up high in the air. I fought back a giggle and reminded myself that I was still kind of mad at him for his erratic behavior at the studio and on the way home. And also terribly confused with how quick he seemed to turn on and off the charm and attraction.

"I really think you should go."

"I'm not going. I told you I'm sticking close to you until we figure this thing out."

My home phone rang and I walked over to it, wondering why these psycho dance moms would not stop calling me late at night. I pulled the handset off the cordless base and checked the number, only to feel all the blood drain from my face and I gestured wildly to Tate, who struggled to get up out of the couch, which was eating him like a giant Venus flytrap eats a bug. I couldn't wait for him to get there, because in just one more ring the call would go to voice mail, so I clicked the On button and said a breathy "Hello?"

There was silence on the other end, and then light breathing, and I said again, "Hello? Taylee is that you?"

Hearing the name I uttered, Tate shot up out of the couch like he'd been projectile vomited, and headed toward me. In just a few steps he reached me. "Is she answering?"

I shook my head. "Hello? Taylee, are you there? This is Jenny. Are you okay? Please answer me. I'm so worried about you." I heard a sigh on the other end, and then a voice whispered, "No. No, I'm not okay. I'm scared, and I don't know what to do and . . ." And with that, the line went dead.

NINETEEN

ALL sorts of techy people were wandering around my house, and I feared the old people upstairs would think I was having a late-night weekday party and call the police. Never mind that half the force of Ogden City and the regional office of the United States Marshals Service were already in my apartment. At least they wouldn't have to go far to answer the call. Of course, the old people were probably all looking out their windows and could see all the police cars, so they might just call for information. Or to find out if that weird young dance teacher was actually a serial killer. "I knew something was off when she kept selling all those Books of Mormon," they would tell their neighbors. Who would tell their friends. Who would tell their relatives. Who would tell . . . My phone rang and everyone around jumped to attention, signaling me to pick up the handset but not to answer yet until they had a clear connection. Or something like that. It was kind of conveyed to me in a weird U.S.-marshal sign language, so I hoped I was getting it right. Whatever they had done had something to do with tapping my phone, which I had reluctantly agreed to, although my reason for objecting was sketchy. I knew that if they recorded my calls, it would just offer up definitive proof about how pathetic my life really was.

I looked at the caller ID and shook my head. Auntie Vi. I knew it wouldn't take long.

"It's not her."

"Answer it please, so we can test how this thing is working," said the techno-nerd who had hooked up the whoosie-whatsie thing to trace the calls that came into my phone.

"I . . ."

Tate gave me a look and I reluctantly answered it. They had disconnected my voice mail, so the phone would just ring and ring and ring, and Auntie Vi would not give up. She, of all people, knew I did not have a life.

"Hello, Auntie Vi."

"Jennifer, I am absolutely appalled at your behavior." The guy wearing the headset gave me a funny look.

"What behavior?"

"Nana's heart is not that great, you know, and hearing this news is surely going to kill her!"

"It's just the cops trying to find Taylee, Auntie." Tate shook his head at me, so I stopped talking, remembering they weren't saying too much about the missing girl, and they sure as hell didn't want to get Ogden's biggest gossip going.

"That is *not* what I am talking about, Jennifer."

"Then what are you talking about?"

"Works great," mouthed the guy with the headset, giving me the okay to disconnect, but unfortunately I did not get it in time.

"What is Nana going to say, and your poor father, and his poor heart. If it isn't bad now, it will be by the time you get done. And whatever will I do? I'll not be able to go out in public in this town again, once word gets out that my niece is a lesbian."

Lesbian. *Lesbian.* Blood rushed to my head and I screamed out the name of the man I was going to kill. *"James!"*

I spent something like forty minutes reassuring Auntie Vi that I was not a lesbian, while the officers and Tate kept giving me anxious looks to remind me that Taylee might call back. I had call waiting, so I had to stop this rumor from going any further, now. At nearly eleven thirty, my aunt declared herself ready for bed and at least partially believed that I had not stayed single for so long simply because it was illegal for me to marry my same-sex partner. I almost told her that I was having wild sex fantasies about the officer who was investigating my case, and was also somewhat attracted to the U.S. marshal who was pretty much parked outside my door, but that would bring with it a whole set of other problems, so I decided that would not be a wise move.

I hung up the phone exhausted, and Tate steered me toward the bed, assuring me that he would sleep on the couch, and a whole army of other people would remain—at least somewhat discreetly—outside, in case a call came in from Taylee in the middle of the night.

"You don't want to sleep on that couch. It is not comfortable," I told him.

"Like you, it appears to be quite hungry."

I giggled, remembering the way he had struggled to get up when the phone rang.

"I'll be fine on the couch. Just be alert if the phone rings and I bring it to you. We have to be ready to trace the call in case Taylee calls back, and you need to keep her on the line."

"I don't do middle-of-the-night alert very well." At this point he had me inside my bedroom door and was pushing me toward my bed. I'd had men anxious to get me there before, but usually they were wanting to join me, and not headed out to a man-eating couch.

"I'll help you," he said, his voice a low growl as he unzipped my sweat-suit jacket, then helped me take my arms out of it and dropped it to the floor. He pulled down the covers while I watched him, wondering just how far he would go—would he strip me completely naked? Did I care? Did I have enough energy to even respond to him, should he make love to me? Nope. He set me on the side of the bed and undid my sneakers, then pulled them off, laughing aloud at the socks I wore, which, as usual, were mostly holes. I gasped as he scooped me up into his arms and plopped me into my bed, pulling the covers up to my stomach, and then running a hand down my bare throat to my breast, which was covered by a thin spandex dance cami, with built-in bra. In other words, there wasn't a lot of material between his fingers and my breasts and I shuddered, wanting to feel his skin on my skin. And a few more things.

"Goodnight, Jenny T. Partridge," he whispered. "Have sweet dreams. Hopefully of you and me together, here in this bed. When this case is over, that's where I intend to be. No matter what you think of me, the truth is I want you. And I intend to *have* you. This isn't all about the case. It is about you and me."

Then he leaned down gently and kissed me, and I shivered with desire. I would never sleep. Never. That's the last thing I remember thinking.

I woke up the next morning with a strange sense of apprehension. I supposed it could have been attributed to the man who was hopefully still alive on my couch, having made it through the night without being swallowed. But I knew it was something more. Something important. Something . . .

Tuition! Tuition was due today. Today, I would eat, and not on someone else's charity. Today I would eat and put gas in my car and buy a few groceries and pay rent and utilities and then . . . it would all be gone again. Oh well. At least I had today.

I rose from bed and was appalled to see I was still wearing the dance cami and gaucho pants I had worn to dance and then gone to bed in. Good thing dance clothes were comfortable, or it would have been a long night. Of course, I supposed what I wore to teach in was a little skimpy and to a man like, say, Tate, it probably looked like pajamas. What would he know? He always had to wear a suit. I padded into my bathroom and shut the door and locked it, aware that I had company, although I had not heard much from the other room. I suffered my usual morning fright at the state of my hair, and then turned on the shower, stripping off my clothes and stepping under the hot spray of water. I turned on the waterproof radio my mother had given me last Christmas—a silly gift, perhaps, but I was seriously addicted to music, so I was thrilled—and sang along with the latest tunes while I rubbed at my face. I turned and wet my hair, reaching down for my shampoo to lather it over my head.

After I rinsed the shampoo, I poured a good-sized portion of conditioner into my hand—one of my few dance dads sold the latest lines to beauty suppliers and gave me deep discounts, so I could afford the best—and I rubbed it in, leaving it to soak while I shaved my legs. I was almost ready to wash it out when I heard a man's voice call my name, close, really close, and I screamed.

"Jenny, it's a pay-phone call. I'm sorry to scare you, but we really need you to answer this call."

I put aside my modesty, even though I was shaking like a leaf, and turned off the shower radio, pulling the curtain back just far enough to poke my head out and see Tate standing there with the phone, which he quickly handed to me. "Hello?" I said, trying not to think about the fact I was separated from him by only a thin, nearly sheer shower curtain.

"Jenn, please don't be mad. Please, please don't be mad. Things got way out of hand, and before I knew it . . ."

James.

I shook my head at Tate to let him know it was not Taylee, and then spoke into the phone. "This is not a good time. I am in the shower. My hair is full of conditioner, and I am seriously, lividly, angrily pissed off at you!"

"Jenny . . ."

"Not now, James. It's about time you stopped thinking about yourself, and considered the people around you, and how your actions impact them. Do you have any idea what you have done to my reputation? Do you have any idea what this will do to my business? Did you even consider how much explaining and placating and guilt-visiting I am going to have to do with my mother?"

"Jenny . . ."

"No, I don't want to hear your excuses. You are not going to ruin my life, James. I love you, but it's time to grow up. Time to accept who you are, and tell your mother the truth. Time to think about someone else." I finally slowed down and took a breath.

"Are you done?"

"No . . . well, maybe yes. Yes, I think I am." I felt empowered. I felt strong. I felt . . . naked. I had been so caught up in my tirade that I forgot all about Tate Wilson, but he had not forgotten about me. He was watching me with that sexy half smile on his face, and I followed his eyes down a little to see that the shower curtain had slipped and exposed one of my breasts, nipple and all.

I hastily pulled it back in place, my face flaming, and then heard James say, "Jennifer, you will never get how hard this is. I like men. This world does not like men who like other men, at least sexually. I will never belong."

I sighed, and spoke gently into the phone. "Well, I like you, and I don't care if you want to sleep with Detective Wilson. I still care about you. But you can't go around putting your issues on me. You have to tell your mom the truth." Tate looked up from the spot he had been staring at longingly, waiting for my now-hidden nipple to reappear, and alarm spread across his face. It was only fair, but I still felt a little bit sorry for him.

"I know. I know. I'm sorry, Jenn. I'm really, truly sorry." James paused for a moment, and then said, "So do you think I stand a chance with the yummy detective?"

"You'll have to ask him that yourself. Bye, James. Tell

your mother the truth. Hey, why are you calling me from a pay phone?"

"Lost my phone. Third one this month."

"You're worse than I am."

I disconnected the phone and gave Tate a look. "I need to wash this conditioner out of my hair."

"I'd offer to help you, but I'm on duty. And it's killing me." His eyes went down to where my breasts were now hidden—at least as hidden as they could be behind a sheer shower curtain.

"I'll be fine. And James is wondering if you are available."

"You are not a nice woman."

"Paybacks are a bitch."

"What are you paying me back for?"

"You saw my nipple."

"You showed it to me."

"Not on purpose."

"James is not my type. I like your nipple. I can't wait to see more."

"How did you get in here? The door was locked."

"I'm a cop. I have my ways."

"Isn't that called breaking and entering?"

"I was already in. B&E doesn't count on a bathroom door, when you've been given open access to a house . . . and the contents . . ." He started to walk toward the shower and my heart raced in double time, until we heard a voice call from the other room. It stopped him cold, so he gave me a sexy grin full of promise and then left the bathroom. I wasn't sure it would be safe to ever listen to my shower radio again. Unless Tate was in here with me. I got all tingly thinking about that possibility, and I didn't even dare wash my own body, afraid I'd run out of the shower and the bathroom and drag Tate back in there with me, lathering him up and washing him all over until he . . . *Ack!* I turned the water on full blast cold and then yelped as the chilling spray hit me.

I heard the door swing open and Tate yelled, "What's wrong?"

"Um, cold shower."

He chuckled loudly and then I heard the door shut.

My life got weirder and weirder every day.

TWENTY

AFTER I got dressed, and blew my hair dry, taking special care with my makeup and trying to get the frizzies completely out of my mop, I walked into my kitchen, which had been appropriated by the police. Andrew Fallon was there, along with Marshal Doe and Tate. All the phone-call tracking equipment was spread across my table. Fallon and Doe were talking quietly, while Tate stood back a bit. They all looked over when I entered. None looked all that excited to see me, including Tate, until Fallon and Doe pasted on huge smiles. I felt like I was being played. Why did Tate look so distant?

"I have a solo lesson, so I'll be going now," I told them. Little Tiajuana Stone was just five, and solo competition season was more than four months away, but she needed all the help she could get. Plus her mom was one of the psychoest psycho moms, but she had a lot of money, of which I was in short supply. Oh, and today tuition was due! I was in a real hurry to get to my studio.

"You sure you don't want to stay here, in case Taylee

calls again?" Fallon asked gently. I thought I liked the old, diffident, definitely uninterested Fallon better.

"No, Taylee knows how to reach me. She knows my hours. She knows when I'm at the studio, and when I'm here. She wouldn't call when I'm not here. She also knows my cell phone number. And I need to go to Monica's house to pick up my costumes after the solo lesson. I have a lot to do."

"Fine, well, we will have someone monitoring your home phone for calls."

Apparently, judging by the look on his face, Marshal John Doe got the honor of sitting and watching my phone, which undoubtedly would ring off the hook all day with calls from psycho dance moms, who wouldn't be happy my voice mail had been disconnected and they had no way to vent to me.

I got ready to leave, sneaking a few furtive glances at Tate, who remained remote and distant, as though we had never met, and then I realized I didn't have my cell phone, which some days would be a blessing. But, considering the circumstances I knew I needed it. I had to search for it, because, as usual, it was not where it should be, in my purse, in the pocket made specifically for cell phones. I bought this purse just for that reason, but it didn't seem to matter. The phone never made it into the pocket. I was hopeless. It took me at least five minutes to find it. It was in a pocket all right, just not the one in which it belonged. It was in the pocket of the sweat-suit jacket I had been wearing the night before. A jacket that was lying by the side of my bed. The one that Tate had taken off me the night before. Last night, I had been too exhausted to even think about responding. Today, every sexual part I had was tingling. And he was acting like he'd never seen me before. Great.

I set the phone to vibrate. "I'll check each caller to make sure it's not Taylee. If it is, I'll answer."

"We need to get a tracker on that phone, too, and . . ."

I sighed loudly, and Fallon stopped speaking.

"Have you not learned that my life is a joke? You really want to listen to all the psycho dance moms and also my weird family? Be my guest. Really, just walk all over my civil rights, because I'm sure I don't deserve to have them, based on the fact that I'm a slightly eccentric, redheaded dance teacher who was just trying to raise some money!"

"Maybe you didn't sleep very well last night," Fallon suggested. His voice was calm. Gentle. Grating on my nerves like a shovel on cement.

My cell phone chose that moment to ring, and I looked at the ID, seeing that Tiajuana's mom was calling, probably to confirm that I would be there for her daughter's lesson. I didn't answer. There were three cops staring at me, and for heck's sake, I hadn't missed a solo lesson before. After four rings it stopped, and I'm sure she left a message. This would go on all day. Before it was over, the voice mailbox would be full and there would be no more venting. That was one upside.

A very distant Tate—where was the man who had just an hour before been gazing longingly at my nipple?— asked me to please check my e-mail to see if I had any more messages. Before this was over I was going to be really computer proficient. Really. Okay, maybe not, but at least I was doing it without help.

Marshal Fallon excused himself and left my apartment, perhaps concerned I was going to explode and things might get messy. I turned the computer on and listened to the soft whirring as it started up. When it was ready, I logged on to AOL, proud I could do it without any help or instruction. After the deep male voice told me, "You've got mail," I clicked on the mailbox and read the list of correspondence, Tate looking over my shoulder, but not getting too close or commenting. Again I wondered what had happened to cause this distance. I'd probably obsess about it all day. Damn. I did not get men. But it made me mad. Really mad. I felt used.

I sighed lightly, hoping he wouldn't hear, and then perused my mail. I had a lot of spam and more requests for me to help Nigerians move large sums of money out of their country and into my bank account with no strings attached—and yet another e-mail from my cousin Kim, this one titled "Eternal Mate Fireside you would love, bring cute Det.!"—but nothing else. I signed off just as Fallon walked back into my apartment from outside, where, I had learned, they had one of those fancy surveillance vans set up. You know, the ones they have on TV, with all the electronic equipment, and headphones, and bells and whistles. I really wanted to see inside that van, but was afraid to ask.

He carried in his hands some papers, and he gave them to Tate, then turned to me and smiled. My stomach did flip-flops. I was a hussy. All it took was for Detective Wilson to go distant on me and I was all over the next hot man. Please. This was not my life. Any minute now I was going to wake up in a movie. "Were you out there all night? Are you tired?"

Tate snorted. I ignored him. He deserved whatever he got.

"No, I was off duty and went home. We trade off shifts. Nobody can work that many hours straight."

"Yeah, I guess that doesn't make a lot of sense. So does Marshal John Doe take over when you are off, or are you guys partners?" Good God, was I really flirting? Or just trying to make Tate jealous? What really scared me was I didn't know the answer.

"Marshal John Doe?"

"Uh, him," I said, indicating the man whose name I did not know. "Nobody ever told me who he was."

"Jenny, you are a crack-up," Fallon said, a genuine smile lighting up his incredibly handsome face. *Help me!*

"I'm Marshal John Smith," the other marshal said, a confused look on his face. Now that was funny. John Doe or John Smith. Sevens. Or was it sixes? I could never remember.

"Let's get back to the case here, please. I'm guessing we are nowhere on those two strange anonymous e-mails that Jenny got," Tate said, no hint of a smile or any amusement at all on his face. "No way to trace them?"

"Nope, they were sent from an Ogden Public Library

computer from a Hotmail account, which was set up with false information," Fallon answered. He didn't look as grumpy as Tate. "Whoever did this knew what they were doing, or at the least had received some lessons in remaining anonymous."

"Like someone who had been in witness protection for a while?" I asked without realizing that I had stumbled onto something. "Even a young someone like Taylee, who obviously knows she's in danger. I'm guessing you primed her pretty well."

Tate and the two marshals all turned to stare at me. Fallon didn't look as happy now. I didn't care. At least I didn't think I did.

"I'm not as dumb as I seem," I said in explanation. "Taylee is alive, and she's hiding out because she doesn't know who the bad guys are and who the good guys are. Even with you. She's not sure you can keep her safe. That's hard enough to know when you're an adult." I wasn't trying to drive home a point, or even thinking about the cookie dough that showed up without warning in my fridge, the assault outside my door, or the Humvee full of snipers (okay, maybe it had just seemed like a lot of people), but all three officers looked chagrined. Even Tate, who was looking angry, chagrined, distant, and hot all at the same time.

I continued. "About the only thing Taylee is sure of is me. Poor girl. She's probably not sure I can keep her safe. I guess I get that. But she's just a little girl, and she's out there somewhere. Alone. How is she surviving? We have to find her. And I'm not kidding when I say 'we.' Because the truth is, as much as I would like to believe it's my charming personality and ravishing good looks that have you all hovering around, if you thought you could find her without me, none of you would be here."

There was no response, even from Tate, and even though I knew he couldn't really show interest in me, outside this case, for right now, it hurt. And the truth was, he had shown interest. Even Fallon had seen it. And now he was acting like he'd never seen me before—or my nipple—outside of this case.

"You need me, because you don't know where she is, or where to look, or basically anything at all. Admit it."

"We don't know," Fallon admitted, a crestfallen look covering his handsome face.

"Well, I think I do."

"Huh?" Fallon said, giving me a hard look, his eyebrows getting closer to his eyes as he glared at me in consternation.

"See, ever since I met her, Taylee has been like a little adult. She was so young, and yet she would do her own hair and her makeup. At dance competitions, when other moms hover and fuss, Sandra was missing half the time, and obnoxious the other half when she was there, but she never, ever took care of Taylee. Ever. It was more like Taylee was taking care of *her*."

"Yes, we got the same impression, when we would . . . uh . . ." Marshal Smith shut up, especially after the glacier stare he got from Marshal Fallon. What a sucky job they had, working in a field you couldn't talk about, on a case that was top secret. Why the heck would anyone pick this line of work? Thinking of my job, and all those psycho dance moms, I decided that was not a question I wanted to be asking.

"Yeah, yeah, right. You know nothing. Anyway, Taylee is very self-sufficient. She's been taking care of herself for a very long time. And so she is going to be okay. For now. But she knows that eventually she is going to have to surface. That's why she is contacting me. She's trying to find a safe avenue."

"That's good, Jenny," said Tate, admiration filling his voice. I was still kind of peeved with him, so I chose not to acknowledge him.

"At any rate, I better not lose my cell phone in the next little while. Hmm, where is my cell phone?" Damn, I had just had it! I reached over to the side table in my entryway, and grabbed my purse, rummaging through it until I came up successful. Apparently, I had stuck it in there without realizing it, just moments before. I did that a lot.

"Okay, I have a solo lesson to teach, so I'm outta here."

"I'm coming with you," Tate said, the look on his face something between consternation and anger. Perhaps he realized he was no longer my favorite Ogden police officer. Despite the fact I knew my anger was not logical, I couldn't help it. I wanted him to speak up about his interest, and he hadn't. He couldn't. And to me, that spoke volumes.

"Not necessary. I'll be fine."

"No, you won't."

"Yes, I will."

"Jenny . . ."

I turned and glared at him. "I will be fine. I can take care of myself. You go ahead and investigate your case. Do your job. Find Taylee."

His face hardened, as though I'd implied he wasn't doing his job, but I didn't care. I was flying high on what was possibly PMS and too little sleep, and the need for some really good potato salad.

I gave a nonchalant wave and headed out the door, hoping that Detective Tate Wilson was not following. Of course, he was. Things like this never happened when I *wanted* to be followed.

Why couldn't my life go the way it did for the heroines in movies?

"You aren't leaving without me."

I whirled around and glared at him. "I'll be fine. I know I need to be cautious now, and I will be, but I do not need a babysitter."

"You're really mad at me."

"No, I'm not. I just have a life, and I have to live it. I have a solo lesson to teach, and then I need to go pick up costumes, and I don't have time to waste, okay?"

"I'm not letting you out of my sight."

I gave a sigh of disgust and turned and walked away, but I knew he was following me. I didn't care. I wanted to get to my solo lesson, and away from all this chaos, and the confusing sexual chemistry between me and Tate.

I unlocked my Bug and jumped inside, starting it up and fighting the desire to just take off, because I knew the car would do its stutter-and-stall routine and I'd end up looking like an idiot. I waited a minute, and watched as Tate pulled his car up directly behind mine and waited. Great. I had a cop on my tail.

I put the car into drive and moved forward, Tate following closely as I edged out into traffic, which, of course, was pretty nonexistent. It was, after all, just a bit after 9 a.m. on a weekday morning.

I was determined to ignore the man following me, mostly because he seemed to be doing some ignoring of his own, in regard to me, at least in front of other people, but it wasn't easy. You're supposed to watch your rearview mirror all the time, but I was trying to pretend I didn't see or care that there was a very hot man following me closely.

I reached the studio and parked in my usual spot, continuing to ignore the man who parked in my lot and watched me closely, then followed me up the metal stairs to the glass door with the "Jenny T. Partridge Dance Academy" decal on it. My dad grumped all the time about the door being glass, and letting all kinds of cold air in, but it was a dance studio. I wanted people to see what was happening inside, to want to come in and participate. This, of course, was sheer vanity on my part. In order to come in and see what was happening, they would have to climb the metallic stairs. So far, no one ever had wandered in after hearing the music. Even in the summer, when I opened all the windows. But someday it might happen.

Camari Stone was waiting there with her daughter, Tiajuana Jacqui. Camari did not fit her exotic name. She wore a simple V-neck cotton sweater, covered with a coat that was probably new once—twelve years before. She had on sweatpants that matched the black stripe in the V-neck, or at least had probably matched it once, and worn, scuffed tennis shoes, and her dirty blond hair was pulled back into a ponytail.

"Hi Jenny, Tiajuana is ready to go, aren't you, Teej?"

Tiajuana said, "I am ready to go, Jenny." She sounded thirty-six, like her mother. She was five. And unlike her mother, she was wearing a brand-new knee-length coat, with beautiful white fur trim. Underneath, I'm sure, she was wearing the latest in dancewear, purchased in Park City, an upscale resort not far from Ogden. Camari hoped, I'm sure, that other dancers would not have the same clothes, but the dance world is small. And competition tough. And forty minutes was not that far to drive when you were trying to best the other psycho dance moms.

Camari turned toward Detective Wilson and raised her eyebrows, but didn't say anything. As long as he wasn't in the way of her daughter's solo lesson, she probably wouldn't complain. For Camari, it was all about dance—her daughter's dance, to be specific. I'd been around her long enough to know one thing—there is an interesting dichotomy between moms whose daughters love dance, and who want to support their children, and those who are just plain freaking nuts. Camari was nuts. She would probably go out there and do the damned solo herself, except there was no division in youth competition dance for thirty-six-year-old soloists. I guess they figured by the time you reached eighteen or so, you either realized you didn't have a future in dance or you moved on to professional companies and whatnot. Camari talked incessantly about her days dancing with a local franchise dance team, and then her high school drill team, but beyond that, her resume was kinda slim. Then along came Tiajuana.

Tate followed us in as I opened the studio and quickly set Tiajuana into action, so I could get this solo lesson done, collect my twenty dollars, and get on my way to pick up costumes from Monica.

Tate watched with great interest as both Teej and her overachieving mother did the movements I'd choreographed for the solo. On the five-year-old, they were cute and spotlighted her dance skill, which was just about, oh, below average for a child of that age. Still, kids that age were so cute most people weren't too critical of their skills. On the mother, well, let's not go there.

After we finished up, Camari informed me that "they" needed at least one more lesson that week.

"Busy week, Camari. I have the *Nutcracker* performance coming up, so we're just going to have to settle for once a week, okay? At least until competition season. You are aware that it's about four months away?"

"That's barely enough time to prepare, Jenny!" Camari said, shock tingeing her voice.

"It's enough, Camari. She's five."

She gave me a look and then turned and stomped off, Teej scrambling to follow in her mother's wake, one shoe still untied and her dance shoes left on the floor. Worst of all, I realized just as the door thumped behind them that she had not even paid me. Great.

My life was great, all right. Great big mess.

"That was interesting," Tate commented from the chair where he sat.

"Thanks. We're glad we can amuse you."

"Who is the 'we' you're talking about? You've been hanging around the psycho moms too long."

"Oh, drop it, Detective Wilson."

He stood up and headed toward me, and a brief moment of panic flowed through me. Then I remembered how angry I was, and the panic fled and irritation replaced it. Mostly. Okay, there was a tiny bit of hormonally charged panic, but he was hot, you know.

Tate had an intense, purposeful look in his eye, but I still remembered how it hurt to have him hide his interest—if that was what he was doing. Why was I so unclear on this? I turned away from him and walked away toward my office, trying for nonchalance. I heard him behind me and turned to tell him to back off when a deafening roar erupted from behind me, in the stairwell. I turned to the noise, confused, and then a whoosh of air told me that Tate was right there beside me. He grabbed my hand and pulled me toward the door, even as I was headed to the stairwell to investigate. "Come on, we have to get out of here, now," he said, yanking me through the door and down the metal stairwell, our footsteps making a clanging, metallic noise. He pulled me out into the snow a short way from the building. We heard another loud boom and black smoke started filtering out the door, still slightly ajar. The smoke stopped when the door closed with a slight "smack" noise, and I screamed. Tate pulled me into his arms as I watched, silently and helplessly, as my life, my studio, and my dreams all went up in smoke. Literally.

TWENTY-ONE

DESPITE my fear of total decimation, the truth was not quite so bleak. Everything in both my studio and Jack and Marco's store smelled pretty bad, and there was an ugly sooty covering to all the walls and floors, but there had been no real fire, and nothing had been destroyed. Nothing, that is, but the entrance to the tunnel that had been walled off. Someone had placed a small but potent bomb there, and it had effectively cleared all the cement that had been shored up there years before, when the building owners were trying to meet·earthquake codes.

Luckily, the Ogden Fire Department had not come in with blazing hoses. A quick investigation showed the damage done by the bomb was minimal. Since they investigated first, before shooting water out of the enormous hoses, the studio, and all of the priceless antiques below it, were not waterlogged and ruined. Thank God.

Now the police were trying to figure out why someone would want to blow open the tunnel, and who would do such a thing. The only person I had let into the building that morning had been Camari and her daughter, and so I was more than a little worried. I couldn't see what Camari would have to do with such a horrible event, and she certainly couldn't know how to make a bomb—could she?—but the police told me they would have to question her. I told them to get my twenty bucks while they were at it, but they just gave me a funny look.

Camari was nuts, but not bomb-making, tunnel-blowing nuts. Was she?

After all of the hullabaloo settled down, and Tate called in the Disaster Cleanup Company, who promised to get rid of all the soot and most of the smell, he pulled me away from the studio, and put me into his car. I was too drained to argue.

"Guess I'll cancel dance tonight," I said dully, after I heard his car door shut with a snick. He started up the car and moved away. He'd given the key to the studio and the key to my car to one of the uniforms and instructed him to watch the cleaners carefully, then lock things up and bring the key to my apartment, along with my car. I stared out the window, not looking at him. "I certainly can't afford to cancel dance tonight, and God knows these girls need the practice, but hey, the gods are telling me to cancel dance, and I guess it is about time I started listening. Of course the gods aren't going to have to listen to the psycho dance moms who are pissed off that I'm shorting their darling daughters one dance lesson, but hey, such is life. It happens. It's the way things go. It's . . ."

"Are you okay?"

"Sure, fine, just fine. Oh, hey, I need to go pick up costumes at Monica's house, although I'm sure the way things are going I will have no need for them. Since you have kidnapped me and are driving, can you take me there?"

Tate chuckled. "You are not fine. You are in shock. The only place I am taking you is to your home."

"No, I really need to go to Monica's and get my costumes." The despair and wooziness was starting to wear off, at least slightly. I was going to pick up my costumes. I *was*. "If you don't take me, I will walk."

"Jenny, do you ever just back off and let someone help you, or just listen to their advice?"

"Sometimes. I'm sure I do. I'm sure I have. Really." I listened all the time. I just didn't agree, usually. "I'm not trying to be stubborn, but the truth is, I am. I'm very stubborn, and I'm independent, and I have a lot at stake here. I know someone is trying to kill me, or hurt me, or at the least frame me and scare the hell out of me, but I don't know who that is. And so I have to keep on going, because I am not going to let this destroy me. Now if you don't . . ."

"Stop."

"I can't. I have to explain why . . ."

"Jenny, I'll take you to Monica's to get your costumes. Why don't you call Marlys and ask her to call and cancel dance."

"You and Marlys are tight now, huh? Fine, I'll call." I reached for my purse, only to realize that I'd left it behind in my studio. No phone. "Ah, no phone. Oh well. What else is new?"

Tate pulled his phone out of the hip holder where he kept it, dialed a number, and instructed whoever answered on the other end to find my purse and retrieve my phone, keeping it where they could see it in case Taylee called. They were to bring both my purse and phone to the apartment, when they brought my keys and my car. I was starting to feel like my life had shattered into a million pieces, and Detective Tate Wilson was being forced to try to pick them all up. After he hung up, he handed the phone over to me.

I dialed Marlys's number and she answered, "Hello?" I told her to call the team moms and have them call all their team members and tell them there had been a mishap at the studio, and there would be no dance tonight. Instead, I would reschedule for tomorrow night, which was normally one of the Golden Agers nights, but they were just going to have to wait.

"Why are you calling on Tate's phone?" she asked me, after she'd assured me that she would take care of getting the word out.

"How'd you know it was Tate's phone?"

"It came up on the caller ID, and so I . . ." her voice trailed off. I was kind of technologically impaired, but one thing I did know was phones. At least I knew how to destroy and lose them. But I'd had enough of them to know a few things, and one of those was that caller ID registered only if you had that person's phone number registered in your phone address book. Which meant that . . .

"Why do you have Tate's number programmed into your phone?" I asked Marlys, hoping that it wasn't jealously that was coloring my voice, and rather just confusion and some other emotions I could not identify.

There was silence, and then she sighed. "Because you are in deep shit here, Jenny, and as someone who really cares about you, I intend to make sure you get out of this okay. And Tate is one of the good guys, so I am trying to help him help *you* stay safe."

Why did I suddenly feel like I was in kindergarten, and as helpless as a newborn kitten?

"Just call the moms, Marlys. Thanks for doing that. I'll see you tomorrow."

"Okay, Jenny, I will."

I clicked the disconnect button and was so surprised when the phone's bells pealed that I dropped it on the floor under my feet, and had to reach over to pick it up. As I grabbed it, I accidentally hit the On button. I'd intended to hand it over to Tate, but the voice I heard coming from the phone stopped me cold. "Hello, hello? Tate, what are you doing? Why aren't you answering? Tate, are you there? I hate these phones. I really do. Tate, can you hear me?"

It was Alissa's voice on the phone, and followed so closely by the revelation that Marlys had Tate's number in her phone, I was entirely unsure what to think. Were all of my friends really his friends, too, or was he trying to take over my friends and my life? Now that was a crazy thought. Damned crazy. A more likely reason was that they all thought I was totally incapable of taking care of myself, and so they were treating me like a child. I imagined three-way conversations that started with, "Whatever are we going to do about Jenny?"

"Why are you calling Tate, Alissa?" I said calmly into the phone, although I was boiling inside.

"Jenny?"

"Bingo."

"You sound different. A little stressed, and maybe kind of angry. Are you okay?"

"Why are you calling Tate, Alissa?"

"Because I've been calling your phone for more than two hours, after I heard about the explosion, and you weren't answering. And I'm damned worried about you, and now I'm wondering why you would even ask. I work for the cops, and we have all of their cell phone numbers."

It made sense. I knew it, but suddenly I was becoming Queen Paranoia. My entire life was being hit from all directions, and everything was turned upside down. So I was paranoid. Could anyone really blame me?

"I'm sorry, Alissa. I'm a little on edge. I'm okay, and it'll all work out. Everything's going to be fine."

"Jenny, who are you trying to convince? Me or you?"

"Maybe both of us. At least no one got hurt."

"Okay, I'm on break at work, so I have to go, but I have been worried sick. I'm glad you're okay. Call me tonight."

She disconnected and I handed Tate's phone back to him. He tucked it back into the holder and gave me a sideways glance, before turning back to watch the road.

"You're acting really weird," he said.

"Well, if I had my cell phone here, I'd just go through and give you all the numbers I have programmed in it. That would make things easier for you, wouldn't it?"

His jaw tightened and his lips thinned, and I immediately regretted my words. But, like all spoken words, I couldn't take them back, and it did seem like all my friends were suddenly turning to him, whether it was for me, or about me.

"Where are we going, anyway?" he asked, his voice tight and controlled, and I realized he needed directions to

Monica's house. I gave him the address and then stared out the window as we drove, me not really seeing the familiar landscape, but rather indulging in a self-pity party.

Tate pulled up in front of Monica's house and turned to me, reaching out with one hand and placing it gently on my shoulder. I shrugged him off and opened the car door. Pity party was over. I could not give into my self-indulgent tendency to cry right now. I had to stay tough.

I walked up to Monica's front door, and Tate followed. As I attempted to knock, the door swung in slightly. It was not shut tight, which was strange considering it was December 1, and remarkably cold.

I turned to Tate, alarm bells ringing in my ears—God, I hoped that was imaginary—and I could see from his face he was just as concerned. He motioned me back with his left hand, and drew his gun from the holster on his side, then moved to the door and yelled, "Monica, are you in there? Monica?" There was no answer. He yelled again, then pushed the door open and carefully went inside, using all those cop stances you see on television. Technically, I supposed, the real cops had invented the moves, and the TV cops just copied them, but . . . "Jenny!" Tate hissed, apparently for the second time.

"What?" I whispered.

"Go get in my car, lock the doors, and wait."

"Shouldn't you call for backup?" I asked, my voice still a whisper.

"This is not television."

I thought about that one for a moment. "You're right, it's not television, which means we have no idea what's going to happen. If it were television, what was going to happen would be scripted and you would know whether or not to . . ."

"Oh God, all right. I'll call for backup. You are very annoying, you know?"

We weren't really whispering anymore, so I put a finger to my mouth in a "shhh" sign and he shook his head as he called for a patrol unit to come assist. It was just minutes later when a police car drove up and two uniformed officers jumped out and joined Tate. They also motioned me to get back. Geez, I wasn't that dumb.

"My car, now. Lock the doors," Tate ordered. Another patrol car pulled up and the cop got out and ran excitedly to the door, only to be told by Tate that he got to babysit me. I couldn't blame him for being disappointed.

Tate and the other two officers slowly entered the house, doing the evasive cop moves again, while the third uniformed officer escorted me back to Tate's car and told me to get in.

I slammed the door shut, feeling peevish, although not sure why. I was pretty worried about Monica, because she was just a little bit bonkers.

It was only a few minutes before Tate and the two officers came out the front door, guns holstered.

I opened the car door and almost ran to Tate. "Is Monica okay? Is she in there?"

"No sign of her," he said, his expression strained, his voice taut. "Place is a mess. Looks like someone has torn it up, looking for something. Or someone."

"Place is a mess?" I asked.

"Yes, trashed."

"Can I see?"

"Yeah, sure."

Tate led me back through Monica's front door and I carefully surveyed her house. Colorful fabrics of all texture and length covered every inch of furniture. There were feathers on the living room side table—black. My ostrich feathers. Sequins scattered over the carpet and led, almost like a trail, to the kitchen. Spools of thread could be seen scattered all across the floor, and a tape measure was wrapped around the neck of a sewing mannequin. Wrapped tightly. Damn, she'd done it again.

I knew that the mannequin's name was Jenny.

"This is not trashed," I announced.

"Huh?" Tate asked.

"This is how Monica's house looks right before a costume

deadline. She has about six breakdowns and tizzy fits before she finishes up. It's just her way. And that," I said, pointing to the mannequin, "is me. She calls it Jenny. I see today I have been strangled. Last time I had pins poking in my eyes." I walked over to the mannequin, turned it around, and pointed out a gash in the back. "One year it was scissors in the back."

The three uniformed officers had come back into the house and were listening to the conversation with great interest.

Tate came close to me. "Are you telling me that she physically threatens you, and you didn't tell me this? You said she was nuts, but you didn't mention that she was *this* nuts. I thought you just meant like one of your other psycho moms. This is lunacy. She is fucking batwing crazy."

I shrugged. "She's a genius when it comes to costumes."

Tate pulled out his phone and hit a speed-dial number. "I need an ATL on one Monica . . ." He covered the phone with his hand. "What's her last name?"

"No, no, no. You can't do this. She probably drank a pint of vodka and is sleeping it off in the house, somewhere." I'd worked at the sheriff's office long enough to know that ATL meant attempt to locate, and generally it was used on a suspect.

"There is no one in this house. Now what is her last name?"

"Tate, please. I need these costumes. I can't afford to have her arrested, or worse, in the loony farm, this close to my performance."

"Tell me her name, and I'll cancel the ATL for now."

"Fine. Monica Finch."

He spoke back into the phone. "I need a BCI search on one Monica Finch, approximately thirty to thirty-two years old, blond hair, blue eyes. Petite build. I have no social or DL number. Cancel the ATL for now, but call me back as soon as you have anything on her."

He hung up the phone and turned to me. "I'd like you to

think about something. Someone has been murdered, and the murder is tied to you. They used poisoned cookie dough, and then snuck into your house and put some dough in your freezer. Someone has also tried to attack you outside your house—and you told us you were sure it was a woman—and also, someone tried to shoot at you and run you off the road. Now a bomb has gone off at your studio. And you want me to believe that a woman who is obviously absolutely crazy, and who has a mannequin she calls Jenny and regularly strangles that mannequin, or stabs it, is not something I should worry about?" His voice rose with each sentence. I guess the wackiness of my life was starting to get to him. I could understand that. It got to me, too, most of the time.

"Look, Monica has been doing this for years. It's like her ritual. She acts like she can do it all, then, as the pressure builds and deadlines come close, she gets a little . . . strange. This is how she releases steam."

"By strangling you."

"It's not me. It's just a mannequin she calls Jenny. And one she regularly tries to kill, but of course it can't really die, because it's not real."

"Well, I almost shot that mannequin myself, when I ordered it to hit the floor and it didn't obey!" Tate said, almost yelling.

I couldn't help it. A small guffaw escaped out of my mouth, and I clapped my hand over it, not wanting to let the laughter boil over, but I couldn't stop it. I threw back my head and laughed.

At first, Tate looked pretty mad, but then his lips started to quirk up in twitches, until finally he was laughing with me.

It probably wasn't that funny, but the stress was getting to both of us, and it felt good to relieve some of it with a little laughter. The three officers just watched us.

"What are you people doing here?"

We turned to see Monica standing there, in the doorway,

dressed from head to toe in bright red sequins. She had on sequined Dorothy high-heeled shoes, red fishnet stockings, and a tight-fitting sequin dress. A red feather boa was wrapped around her neck, and she had on a sequin cap, her blond hair sticking out in tufts around it. In her left hand she held one of those long cigarette filters old movie actresses used to carry, and in her right was a martini glass. Her eyes were glazed, and she was swaying slightly. Yep, she was on one of her benders. Guess my extra costumes were going to be late.

The three uniformed officers put their hands back to their guns, almost in unison, but Tate gave them a signal that must have meant "don't pull them" because they moved their hands back to their sides.

"Where were you, Monica?" I asked gently, using my "Monica's a lunatic again" voice. "We came over, and the door was ajar, so we were worried something had happened to you. We've been looking for you."

"Oh, I was out back on the porch swing. It's a lovely day today."

It was freaking forty degrees. Lovely, all right. "And look at you, all dressed up to enjoy it," I said, placating her the way I always did when she went completely over the edge. So much for that meditation. I knew there was a reason I never took that up.

"Oh, this. It's just shumthing I threw together. I'm good at that. Did you know that, Jenny?"

"Yes, Monica. I knew that. Let's get you into bed."

I took her arm and led her into her bedroom.

"But I'm nawt tired. And I have to finish your costumes."

"Tomorrow, Monica. Tomorrow."

Monica's bedroom was in the same state as the rest of her house, and I knew when I came back tomorrow it would all be spotless and shipshape, and she would be normal—as normal as she gets, anyway—with no indication she had gone off the deep end. And the Jenny mannequin would be back in the closet.

I pulled down the covers for her, and she kicked off the Dorothy shoes, one of them hitting a mirror just above her dresser, shattering it. "Great. Sheven years bad luck. Just great."

"That's just a silly superstition, Monica. Everything will be fine."

"Sheven years. Sheven years. Sheven years," she muttered rhythmically as she curled up into a ball in her bed, still wearing the feather boa and sequin dress, along with the fishnet stockings. I pulled the boa off her and tucked her in, covering her with the blankets.

Almost immediately she stopped muttering, closed her eyes, and passed out.

Tate was watching the entire exchange from the doorway, and he shook his head. He pulled his oft-used phone out of its holder and called dispatch to let them know that Monica was no longer missing.

I shut the door as I walked out of her room, and Tate followed me. The three officers asked Tate if he wanted them to do anything. He asked one of them to watch the house and make sure she didn't leave—I was pretty damn sure she wasn't going anywhere in the state she was in—and he walked me to his car. On the way there, his cell phone rang and he answered it.

"Right. Right. Got it. Okay. No, I'll get back to you."

He didn't say anything as he opened the passenger door for me, and then I watched as he briskly walked around the front of the car and got in his side. He put the key in the ignition and gave a wave to the two uniformed officers who were also leaving. But he didn't start the car.

"Are you going to tell me, or do I have to beg you? It's something bad, isn't it?"

I had seen the look on his face during the phone call, and I knew it wasn't good. *Please God, don't let it be Taylee.*

"As far as we can tell, there is no such person as Monica Finch. No driver's license, no state ID, no nothing. Of course, we don't have a Social Security number, or even a birth date, but usually we can pull up something. Not this time."

"Great. Sandra Epstein isn't Sandra Epstein, Monica Finch isn't Monica Finch, Camari Stone is the freaking Unabomber. I need a drink."

TWENTY-TWO

LIFE had become a wild ride, even crazier than usual. All around me were whacked-out women, who, I had to admit, I'd always known were slightly crazy, but not this bad. No, never this bad.

Cops were now watching the homes of Epstein, Anderson, Stone, and Finch. They knew where Epstein was. Her whereabouts would never again be in question, but of course they were looking for Taylee. Emma Anderson had skipped town after she lied about me giving Sandra the cookie dough. Camari Stone had not been seen since her daughter's solo lesson. She was wanted for questioning in the placement of the bomb. Monica was passed out in her bed, so they couldn't exactly interrogate her.

That left Krystal Glass, and even though it was a long shot, it was all we had. If nothing else, she always had her nose in everyone else's business, so she might have heard something that could help. I gave Tate instructions on how to get to her store, located just across the way from my studio on 25th Street. Marshal Fallon, he told me tersely, was going to join us there, and the other marshal, whom I would forever think of as Marshal Doe, would be manning my home phone. My cell phone had been recovered from the studio and Fallon would be bringing it with him, in case Taylee tried to make contact.

Tate pulled into a spot down the street from Krystal Klear Designs and just sat there for a moment.

"Who was Sandra Epstein, really? What was her name before they put her into protective custody?" I asked.

"I don't know." His answer surprised me.

"You don't know?"

"No. So far that information has not been shared with me. The Witness Protection Program only works because of the complete and utter secrecy involved. The more people that know something, the quicker it gets out. That works in all aspects of life, not just witness protection. But so far, Fallon hasn't found it necessary to tell me." I heard the tension in his voice, and the estrangement between the two men became more understandable. It probably had never been about me at all. It was probably about the fact that Fallon had information that Tate needed to solve this case, and he wasn't willing to give it up.

A strange sense of disappointment flooded my body. It had been nice, in a weird way, to think someone cared enough about me to be territorial. But who was I kidding? Sexually, Tate was obviously attracted to me—and vice versa—but that didn't mean it went any further than that.

I tried to ignore the pang in my heart and stomach.

"Why did you suddenly get so quiet?" he asked.

"No reason. Just thinking. Trying to figure this out."

"Well, let's go talk to Krystal Glass."

KRYSTAL'S shop was enough to give a normal person a pounding migraine, because the moment you walked into the store you were hit with millions of glittering crystal mobiles, flashing in your eyes. There was a soft clinking noise, as some of the mobiles spun around, twirling in the light breeze that had entered when we came through the door.

The crystal mobiles were quite beautiful, and handmade, but very expensive, and frankly, I didn't have time or energy for such things. Krystal claimed crystals were healing. She even spouted off information about "chakras" and a bunch of other stuff I couldn't remember and didn't really want to know.

"Well, hello, Jenny," Krystal said, as she walked out of her back room to see who had entered her store. "Detective." She nodded her head at Tate in greeting.

"Mrs. Glass, I have a few questions for you, if you would be so kind as to answer them."

"Of course," she said, her voice young and girlish and . . . flirty. Great. "Ask away."

"Did you know much about Sandra Epstein? Have any real doings with her during dance?"

A shadow crossed Krystal's face and her light flirty air disappeared. "No, I did not. She was a vile and nasty woman, and I don't befriend that type of person. Her energy was terrible. She let off an aroma that was evil, and I couldn't even stand to be around her."

"An aroma?"

"I am sensitive to auras and smells, Detective. What ordinary people do not see or smell, I can feel with an intensity that is sometimes painful."

If Tate wasn't looking directly into Krystal Glass's eyes, I knew he would be rolling his own, because she was so over the top. I, of course, was used to her.

"So, besides this evil aroma, did you know much about her?"

"Well, she thought her daughter was God's gift to dance. But then, of course, so did Jenny." She glared at me. I glared back. Why was she talking about Taylee in the past tense, as though she no longer existed? Could Krystal really have had something to do with this?

"Anyway, she didn't get close to any of us, so of course I can't say I knew much about her personal life. I could just sense that she was not right in the head, and not a good person, and she knew I could tell, so she stayed away from me."

"So you never had much personal information about her, and didn't know much about her habits and her activities?"

"I knew absolutely nothing, other than the fact she would sometimes show up and support her daughter, but most of the time she did not. I would never treat my own daughter like she did Taylee. I do everything for Marilyn. She is my life. It was almost like Taylee was raising Sandra."

As much as I disliked Krystal, I had made the same analogy to describe Sandra and Taylee's relationship.

"If you think of anything else, please call me," Tate said, pulling out a card and handing it to her.

"Of course, Detective," she said, her voice simpering and flirty all over again. She made me nauseous.

"Where do you want me to put these, Krystal?" Marvin Glass said, coming out of the back of the store carrying three mobiles.

"Marvin, I believe I already told you where to put them," Krystal said, her voice high and edgy.

"Yeah, well, I'm not really willing to stick them up my ass, so do you have a different location where I can hang them?"

Krystal gasped and Tate's eyes got big, and I covered my mouth, trying not to laugh. I'd met Marvin Glass only once or twice, but I had great empathy for him, living his life in the same house as Krystal and her brutish, sullen daughter Marilyn.

"Well, thanks for the help," Tate said, and we walked out of the store, leaving Krystal yelling at her hapless husband. Her voice grew louder the farther away we got.

"Marriage troubles," Tate said, after we got into the car.

"Yeah, well, wouldn't you have troubles, trying to live with her? And her daughter is worse. I feel for Marvin. I'd be on the first quick boat to China."

"Slow boat to China."

"Huh?"

"Never mind. So, they were having marriage troubles.

So do lots of other couples," Tate said, obviously just running through facts and not really talking to me. "But marriage troubles. Still, there is no real connection to Epstein, except Krystal couldn't stand her. If we are suspecting everyone who couldn't stand Epstein, the list would be really long."

"Yeah, although Krystal really wanted her sad-sack daughter Marilyn to be the Sugar Plum Fairy, instead of Taylee. Of course, Emma Anderson also wanted Ella to have the role. And she's tied to this more deeply than Krystal."

"We've tracked her cell phone, and her credit cards, and nothing has shown up. No charges. Her ex-husband has no idea where Emma is, and he doesn't seem to care, even though it means his daughter is also missing."

"She'd be hard to miss," I said unkindly, then immediately felt the backlash of regret. Oh well. So I wasn't the nicest person in the world, especially after the week I was having. At least my failure to be a decent human being wouldn't grossly disappoint all my loved ones. They already had me figured out.

"This would all be easier if Fallon would just tell me who the hell Epstein really was," Tate muttered, anger crossing his handsome features. He drove up 25th toward my apartment. "I think it's time maybe he answered some questions."

FALLON was not at the apartment when we arrived, but after Tate called him, it didn't take him long to arrive.

"Did you find something?" he asked, his face all angles and innocence, with no sign he was hiding secrets, which we all knew he was. It was his job.

"We have no less than four suspects in Sandra's murder, none of which have a real strong motive. We need to know who she was and why she was in protective custody. That, to me, seems like a much stronger motive than issues over whose daughter is better at dancing."

"I can't share that, and you know it," Fallon countered.

"Epstein's dead."

"Taylee might not be, and until we know for sure, this information cannot get out."

The two men glared at each other, and Tate's cell phone went off. "Hello? When? How many? Okay, I'll be there in ten." He hung up and turned back toward Fallon.

"I have to go handle something. You need to watch her." He pointed to me, and anger sparked in my chest. Watch her? Like I was a dog or a two-year-old or something? And the fact that he was willing to leave me alone with Fallon, even with Marshal John Doe as a chaperone, rankled, too, because it just emphasized the conclusion I'd already reached. Tate wasn't mad at Fallon because of me. He was mad because Fallon wouldn't talk about Sandra and Taylee, and who they really were.

"I'll be back soon, Jenny."

"Whatever. I'll be fine. We'll be fine, won't we Marshal Fallon?"

"Andrew," he reminded me.

"Andrew," I said, copying Krystal Glass's simpering flirty voice and smile. I didn't do flirty, but I was seriously pissed at Detective Tate Wilson.

He gave me a hard look, which I ignored, and then he left. My stomach rumbled, and I put a hand to it. Somehow, it never lost track of time, even when I didn't have money or food or any of that.

"You're hungry. Me, too. Famished, actually." He stood up and walked over to Marshal John Doe, and asked him to go pick us up some sandwiches from the small deli just around the corner. "What kind do you want, Jenny?"

"Turkey, avocado, swiss, lettuce, mayo, tomato, and olives." I could save half of it until tomorrow, when, hopefully, I would collect tuition.

"Right, and I'll take a roast beef on sourdough, mayo, mustard, extra Swiss cheese, and chips. Lays. You want chips, Jenny?"

"Are you serious? If it involves potatoes, I'm in."

He chuckled. Doe glared and then left.

"So, how are you doing?" he asked gently. This side of Marshal Fallon made me seriously uneasy. I knew he was playing me, knew he wanted information and wouldn't hesitate to sacrifice me if it meant getting Taylee back, and yet . . . I was strangely attracted. Of course, that meant he was bad for me, because that had always been the case.

"I'm okay, except somebody is really trying to keep me from putting on this performance of *The Nutcracker*, and without it, my whole studio is going to go belly-up. After the cookie-dough fiasco, it's already in extreme danger. If I can't pay . . ." I stopped short, realizing I had nearly given out information that I really didn't want out. I did not trust this man. "Anyway, it sure seems like someone is targeting me, even if this is all about Taylee. And I don't understand why you won't just tell me what is going on. Who is she? Her mother is dead. I am not going to scream her identity from the rooftops, but considering that my life has been put in extreme danger, I think I have a right to know."

"Jenny," he said, moving closer to me, "I really can't tell you. I know that's putting you in jeopardy and so I intend to stay close and keep you safe, but that doesn't extend itself to violating the oath I took to protect Taylee and her mother. Sandra might be dead, but if Taylee is still alive, I have to find her so that she can help us put this sick bastard away."

"What sick bastard? The one who is doing all this?"

"Of course," he answered smoothly, but for just a moment there I had caught a glimpse of something else and it told me that he wasn't talking about my case at all, but the one that had put Taylee and her mother Sandra into this situation in the first place.

I backed away from him, even less willing to trust him than I had been before.

"I scare you, don't I?" His voice was low and modulated, and damn him, pretty sexy. His eyes were a darker green than I'd ever seen on a human being, and they were almost mesmerizing. But I was not going to be swayed by those eyes, oh no. I backed up a little, and swallowed hard.

"Of course not. Why would you think that?"

"Because I see it on your face. The fact that I can't tell you what I know makes you wonder if you can trust me, because you think I have an ulterior motive. I guess I understand that, because I do have an ulterior motive, and it's directly related to finding Taylee and keeping her safe. But that doesn't mean I'm going to put you in danger." He moved a little closer until we were almost eye to eye and I could smell his breath, a mixture of spearmint and a vague hint of morning coffee.

"Trust me, Jenny."

"Not a chance in hell," came a voice from behind us and he whirled around to see Alissa standing there. We had both been so intent on . . . what? Anyway, we hadn't heard her come in. "Do not trust this man, Jenny. His only interest in you is this case. You'd have to be an idiot to fall for that line."

Who was she calling an idiot? Oh yeah, me. I should be offended. But I was still trying to shake off the almost intoxicating effect of those green eyes, and so I decided to ignore it.

Andrew looked pretty pissed at Alissa. "You don't know me, and you don't know my intentions."

"I know cops. I work with them every day, and you are no different from the rest of them, and honestly, a little worse. You are ruthless and single-minded, and you want to move up the ladder, which makes you more than a little dangerous. Your job keeps you on the edge, in between the lines of truth and lies, and you get mixed up about the boundaries of decent human behavior. Well, guess what? Jenny is my friend, and I'm going to protect her, and I won't let you put her in danger."

"Wow," I said. I was pretty stunned by Alissa's speech. She grabbed my hand and pulled me toward my bedroom.

"I need to talk to Jenny in private. Girl stuff. Don't get any ideas and follow."

She pulled me into the bedroom and slammed the door shut.

"You know, any minute I'm going to wake up and learn that this has all been a bad dream, and everything will be back to normal."

"Don't count on it. This is no bad dream. It is a nightmare, but you are fully awake, and all of these things are happening."

She pulled the laptop case she had been carrying off her arm and put it down on my bed, then motioned me to sit down. She pulled the laptop out and then a clear cord that I knew was a modem cord, and looked around. "Don't you have a phone line in here?"

"Nope. Sorry."

She sighed, and then jumped as a sharp rap sounded at the door. "Sandwiches are here," Andrew announced through the door. "Guess you're going to have to share with your friend."

"We'll be out in a minute," I called.

Alissa stood and quietly walked to the door and put her ear to it, then pulled it open quickly to find Andrew standing there, ear to the door, just like she had been. He had the grace to look somewhat abashed, and I almost laughed as the two confronted each other. "Go away. Do not eavesdrop. This is not your business. I need to talk to Jenny about . . . about . . . dance." *Urk.* She should have done better than that. By now it was probably pretty apparent to everyone that while Alissa was my friend, she was not a part of my strange dance world.

Andrew smiled smugly and folded his arms, keeping his gaze on her. Alissa stood about two inches shorter than he, and yet she had a more commanding presence. While I could tell Andrew did not find her abhorrent, he did not seem to be falling for her intoxicating beauty. She was wearing a tight-fitting T-shirt and even tighter jeans, and stylish boots on her feet. She didn't need makeup, because of her natural beauty.

Most men would be a puddle right about now. He was holding firm. I suspected Alissa might have finally met her match.

Finally, he broke the gaze. "Fine. But Jenny's sandwich is going to get soggy."

He turned and walked away, and Alissa shut the door, but still stood there. She waited a moment and then whipped it open again, and I heard a chuckle from down the hallway where Andrew stood. She glared at his back until he was gone, then shut the door. She walked to my bureau, grabbed a pair of my leg warmers out of the top drawer, and shoved them under the crack of the door.

She booted up her laptop computer and said, "Well, let's hope someone has a wireless connection close we can tap into, because I have something I need to show you."

Her laptop whirred and clicked and then came on, and began searching for a connection. "Bingo!" she said, after it announced a wireless connection had been found.

She quickly pulled up Internet Explorer and typed in a URL. Up came a news story about someone named Bugliosi. Vincent Bulgiosi, to be exact.

CRIME KING HENCHMAN ACCEPTS
MANSLAUGHTER PLEA,
THEN DISAPPEARS

read the headline. Mob. Interesting. Mob? I started to get a bad feeling in my stomach as I read the story, which was really familiar, mostly because I'd watched a lot of television and movies. I'd seen this scenario in movies hundreds of times: Mob henchman performs hit on target, and is identified by a witness who then has to be moved into witness protection to be kept safe. Only in this case the witness was apparently a young girl and her mother.

> The young witness, who is not being identified by name due to her age, told police that she was having dinner with her mother and her mother's friend

when her father entered the room and shot the friend, Sal Minnelli, four times in the chest. He then turned the gun on the mother.

I looked up at Alissa. "What makes you think this is Sandra and Taylee? And Sandra Epstein was alive and well, or at least well enough to move to Utah. Until recently . . ."

"Keep reading," she said, pointing to the next paragraph in the story. This was starting to annoy me. I didn't know why she couldn't just tell me what the story said.

The young witness told police that Minnelli was not her mother's boyfriend, but was, instead, the witness's dancing instructor, and they were celebrating her recent acceptance into the U.S. Ballet Theatre Young Dancers program.

Teresa Bugliosi was treated at a local hospital, and a complete recovery is expected.

Blood drained from my face. Taylee had been classically trained, and she had impeccable technique. It sure seemed like this fit here. And getting shot would make anyone bitter and ugly. Perhaps that is why Sandra had become so nasty. Bugliosi would be their real last name. But what was Taylee's first, if she was, indeed, this girl? And how had her father found her clear out here? Since it appeared to be a crime of passion—although how anyone could be passionate about the recently deceased Sandra Epstein was beyond me—then why would the mob be involved, anyway? And wasn't her father in jail?

I asked Alissa that question, and she clicked the Scroll button on the laptop screen, and I read further.

Vincent Bugliosi pleaded guilty to a lesser charge of involuntary manslaughter. According to an anonymous source associated with the case, the plea was in exchange for Bugliosi's agreement to cooperate

> with authorities on indicting his boss, Victor "Big Rock" Provenzano. Shortly after his court appearance, Bugliosi disappeared; he was likely placed into the Witness Protection Program.

I looked up at Alissa. "This stupid reporter just put someone's life in extreme danger."

"Yes," she agreed, but said nothing further, apparently waiting for me to put the pieces together. Who did she think I was? Nancy Drew?

"How can this have anything to do with Taylee and Sandra? They were out here alone. There is no husband. And if her father shot her ballet instructor, I wouldn't think Taylee would want anything to do with him. In fact, it seems like he would want her dead, because . . ." Oh God. He was in witness protection, too, apparently somewhere else. What if he had escaped and come to find Taylee, and killed Sandra?

"This is making no sense," I muttered. "Why don't you just tell me what you think, because my head is starting to hurt."

"Well, I don't exactly know, Jenny. I'm trying to figure it out, just like you. But here's what I think. I think that Bugliosi is a bad guy who thought he was killing his wife's lover, and both Sandra and Taylee could convict him. They were eyewitnesses. But the feds needed Bugliosi to testify against his boss, Provenzano, so they gave him a light sentence in exchange for what he knew, and moved him into witness protection. Then they did the same for Sandra and Taylee, because they needed them as leverage to keep him in line. If this is them, then Sandra could have been killed to send Bugliosi a message: Shut up, or Taylee will die, too."

This was giving me a headache.

There was a knock on the door to my bedroom, and Alissa clicked off the story we had been reading. She stood and opened the door to see Andrew and Tate standing there.

"What are you two up to?" Tate asked, looking first at me and then at Alissa.

"Nothing," Alissa said quickly.

"You better not be up to something, Alissa, because if you are . . ."

"What? What, Tate, you threatening me?"

"Because you are not a cop yet, and you are meddling in something that doesn't concern you, and if you fuck it up, then I can make sure you *never* get to be a cop."

Apparently, the fact that Alissa had higher aspirations than dispatcher was known in the department, and even worse, Tate was using them against her. She glared at him, and loaded up her laptop into its case, silent and brooding. And when did Tate show back up again, anyway? Where was he going when he did disappear? When had my life turned into one big question mark?

She finished packing it up, and then hefted it over her shoulder and walked to the door, where both Tate and Andrew stood, blocking her way.

"Please move."

"Alissa, stay out of this," Tate warned again.

"Get out of my way," she hissed.

They both moved, and she turned to me. "Be careful, Jenny, because it's pretty obvious that these two can't keep you safe, despite all their bravado and tough-guy stances. Watch your back."

She left, and both men stared at me. Then they moved into the room. This was not good. "What were you two doing?" Tate asked.

I had to think quick, and I couldn't think of anything that got rid of a man faster than talking about a woman's monthly functions, so I started rambling.

"Well, Alissa found this article on how to effectively ward off PMS, which is a real problem for me, mostly because of my diet and the fact that I really, really like sugar and chocolate, and so she was showing it to me. It also talked about how you could have lighter periods if you . . ."

"Whoa, whoa, I have a sandwich to eat," Andrew said, the first one to back off and leave the room. Tate stood his ground.

"Anyway, this article was really clear that if you bleed through more than one pad a day . . ."

"Enough, Jenny. You weren't reading an article on periods or PMS. I've known Alissa a long time. And she was up to something."

"You are not a very nice person, you know that?" I answered.

"Huh?" He even looked a little bit hurt, but I was going to say what I was thinking.

"What you did to Alissa. That was not nice. She is a smart person, and she'll make a great cop, and you basically treated her like she was just a stupid woman—a dispatcher. I remember how you guys treated the dispatchers from when I worked there. You'd be dead on the side of the road without them, but you treat them like garbage. I can't believe I ever thought you were a good guy." I'd gotten a little caught up in my speech and now felt close to tears, almost believing my words. Wait. I did believe my words. What Tate had just done to Alissa was awful, and it showed me a side of him I did not like.

"You're right."

It was my turn to say, "Huh?"

"You're right. What I just did to Alissa was crappy, and I felt like shit doing it, but neither one of you knows what you are messing with here. It's dangerous stuff. I can barely keep you safe, and I'm not doing a very good job of that. If Alissa keeps digging, she is going to catch the notice of some very bad people, and then what?"

"You don't really even know that, do you? You told me you didn't know who Sandra and Taylee really were."

He pursed his lips, and that told me all I needed to know. Apparently, he had been given the go-ahead and knew the secret identities of the dead Sandra and her missing daughter. Perhaps that was even why he'd been called away just a short while ago.

With the way he was acting, I knew that if they figured out that Alissa knew the identities of Taylee and Sandra, things could get really bad for her at the sheriff's office. I didn't know how much pull Fallon had, or if he would use it, but if they did find out, what would happen to her? Could they get her fired, or threaten her to keep her quiet? How would it affect her dream of becoming a cop? Personally, I thought she'd done a great job investigating, but my opinion didn't hold a lot of weight, and sometimes the egos of men were pretty fragile. More than one career had been toppled because someone pissed off the wrong person.

She needed to keep quiet about her discovery, and so I had to warn her. She'd been saving my behind for a long time. It was my turn to help her out. Where the hell was my phone? Oh yeah, in my purse sitting on the kitchen table. Now, how was I going to get away from Tate and Andrew long enough to call her?

"Oh, I feel my period coming on. And I'm completely out of tampons. I need to run to the store, unless you want to do it for me?"

"Uh, no thanks, but I'll drive you there."

I'd become a virtual prisoner of Tate Wilson, and even though he was hot, I was getting a little tired of it. Every step I made that he did not approve of required manipulation on my part. Oh well. Manipulate I would.

Tate told Andrew where we were going, tripping over the word "tampon" and using "personal products" instead, which caused Andrew's face to go all slack jawed and red, and he turned back to Marshal John Doe and continued to eat his sandwich. My stomach growled hungrily at the sight of the food, and I sighed. Alissa had to come before my stomach.

WHEN we drove up to the convenience store on 36th Street, Tate told me to hurry. To my chagrin, he opened his door and got out of the car, determined to come in with me. But I was one step ahead of him. I'd picked the store for three reasons. One, it was close to my house; two, it was small, and I knew Tate would figure he could keep an eye on me easily, without standing too close; three, the women's restroom had two doors. One that opened into the store, and one that opened into a back lot. The restrooms had originally been one of those outside entrance ones, but when the place was remodeled, the new owner wanted customers inside the store, so he had put a door that led to the bathrooms from the inside. While the outside entrance was no longer used, it still worked.

I paid for the small package of tampons with my debit card, and the $3.79 purchase pretty much cleaned me out. I really needed to be able to collect tuition. I also needed my studio, and the performance ahead, but first I had to think of Alissa. I had to warn her. The other stuff would wait.

After I signed the slip the man gave me, I excused myself to the bathroom, explaining that it was an emergency. Tate blanched a bit, for the first time, and then nodded uncomfortably.

By the time he figured it out, I'd be long gone.

As usual, I had not thought things through very well. I had no car, and I had to move fast or Tate would spot me. Plus, he was a cop and he could call in reinforcements. I was sort of a fugitive.

I headed north, and east, jumping a small fence that led to the cemetery grounds of Leavitt Mortuary. I traipsed through the graveyard, trying not to tread on anyone's gravestone, because that wouldn't be very nice. Plus I was a little bit nervous about graveyards, even in the middle of the day. I passed the frozen fountain, all the time staring behind me at the convenience store, and Tate's parked car. It was still there, but I knew I didn't have much time.

Reaching the main building, I turned again and saw Tate run out of the store and jump into his car. Time had run out.

I had to hide and hide fast, so I ducked into the first door I found open. Unfortunately, it was being used. A whole room of old people turned to stare at me as the funeral director at the front of the room stopped in the middle of his speech.

"Sorry I'm late," I mouthed to one of the old people,

like I knew her, and she just shrugged her shoulders and turned back forward. The director continued with his eulogy. Apparently Mike Towers had been a good man, a kind man, and one with a great sense of humor.

His unexpected death, at the age of ninety-six, was a terrible burden to bear.

Unexpected death at ninety-six? Surely that was all you *could* expect at that age.

I kept turning nervously to stare at the door, sure that any moment now Tate would be coming in. A red and blue flashing reflected into the room, and I knew I was in deep trouble. I stood up and quietly headed for another room off the side of the small chapel where I had ended up. This room must be for families or something, because it was small, and another door led to what appeared to be an office. Maybe the funeral director's office. I found a set of stairs and traipsed down them, until I was in what could only be the bowels of hell. Or the morgue. Take your pick. Death was everywhere here. I could feel it. I could smell it. I couldn't see it, but I couldn't see air either, and I still knew that existed.

I felt myself begin to hyperventilate, and I reached into my purse and grabbed my phone. "Get. Me. Out. Of. Here." Marlys asked where I was, and told me she'd be right there.

TWENTY-THREE

I felt sorry for Marlys, because she was always bailing me out. Usually that involved psycho dance moms and their crazy maneuvers, but things had changed in my life since Sandra Epstein had been murdered, and the stakes were up.

I knew Marlys well enough to know that she walked into the funeral home like she owned it, following my instructions about where to find me, and when I heard her walk down the stairs, I've never been so relieved in my life.

She carried a big bag, and didn't say much, just handed me a scarf and a trench coat, made me put on some old lady shoes, and told me to hunch over. Then she led me up the stairs, out of the funeral home, right past an officer who was parked in the lot of the mortuary, and into her car. We drove off, and I breathed a sigh of relief as we headed toward South Ogden, where Marlys lived. "I have to call Alissa," I said, pulling off the scarf and trench coat and pulling my tennies out of the bag where I had stuffed them when I put on the old lady shoes. I dug deeper to find my phone, but as usual, I could not come up with it. "Dammit, where is that phone?"

Marlys just shook her head, picked up her own cell phone, and called my number. Sometimes I would find it that way, but today wasn't going to be one of those days. There was no responsive ring. The last time I'd used it, I'd been cowering in the basement of Leavitt Mortuary. *Damn.* This was not good.

"I think I left it in the mortuary. I took it out to call you, and that's the last I saw it. Call it one more time. Maybe we just didn't hear it ring." Marlys shook her head, but dialed the phone again and let it ring.

When she said, "Hello, Tate," I almost passed out. She reached out the phone to me. "He wants to talk to you."

"Hello," I said tentatively.

"Not nice, Jenny. Using women's reproductive issues to escape."

"You might want to ask yourself *why* it was necessary for me to escape," I countered.

"I'm trying to keep you safe."

"Are you? Or do you have some other motive?"

"What would that be?"

"You tell me."

"I'll let you know if Taylee calls," he said, and disconnected. Wait a minute. He was answering my phone. Surely he had to play by my rules. I called back, and he answered. "Yes, Marlys."

"This is not your friend Marlys. And you are answering my phone, so you have to play by my rules." It was worth a try.

"Nope."

"I got tired of being followed. A girl needs downtime."

"And a girl needed to call her friend, Alissa, too, and warn her."

I was quiet for a minute. I must be pretty transparent, or he wouldn't have known that was exactly what I was doing.

I sucked at this stealth stuff.

"I want my phone back."

"Come get it."

"Are you going to arrest me?"

"Why, did you rob a bank?"

I tried to think if he had any real reason to arrest me, and couldn't come up with anything. "Fine, I'll meet you at my studio in thirty minutes. Bring my phone."

He hung up without answering.

MARLYS let me use her phone to call Alissa, but I had to leave a message on her voice mail, because she wasn't answering. "Liss, be careful, okay? I really think you could get into trouble if they figure out you think you know who Sandra and Taylee really are. Don't let anyone know, or your dreams might be over, and you won't ever get to be a cop. Or worse. Just keep it quiet, okay?"

Usually, I was the one Alissa was trying to keep out of trouble. It was strange to have the tables turned.

"So why did you escape from Tate, anyway?" Marlys asked me after I hung up. She hadn't said much, and I sensed disapproval emanating from her, even though she had come to my rescue.

"Don't you think it's kind of weird I *needed* to escape from him, Mar? I mean, really, think about it. I couldn't even make a private phone call. And he's not as wonderful as you think. I needed to call Alissa without him listening, and he wouldn't let me out of his sight. And why is it you are taking his side in this, anyway?"

"Are there sides to be taken?"

"Yes. No. There might be."

Marlys finally laughed, and the mood lightened up a bit. "Jenny, Tate is just trying to keep you safe. If I seem like I'm taking his side, it's because I'm worried about you."

"Marlys, how do you know he's trying to keep me safe?" I asked, as Marlys pulled her car into the parking lot of the dance studio. She drove a Subaru wagon, just right for the busy soccer/dance mom, and entirely too practical for me.

"He's a good guy, Jenny, and have you somehow missed he's entirely all fired up for you?"

I blushed, and felt my face get warm. "He's not hot for me. If he wants anything, it's just sex, and I don't have enough time and energy to comply. And he's trying to find Taylee, and so far, I'm the only lead he has. I don't trust him or Andrew."

"Andrew?" she asked, as we got out of the car. I glanced up at the studio door. My heart dropped. There was yellow police tape in front of the door, and some piece of paper stuck on it. I vaulted up the stairs two at a time, and read the notice on my door. What it told me was something I did not want to hear. My building was closed—closed?—by order of the fire marshal. This could not be happening. I had a performance. I needed to collect tuition. My building couldn't be closed. "Let me use your phone," I ordered Marlys, and she handed it over.

I called the number listed on the notice and a chirpy young voice answered, "Ogden City Offices, Fire Marshal McGowan's office. How can I help you?"

"Yes, someone has put a 'closed' notice on the door of my studio. I realize there was a bomb that went off in here, but the damage was minimal, and I really don't . . ."

"Hold, please."

Soon I was listening to elevator music, and watching as Detective Tate Wilson pulled up. He got out of the driver's side of his car, and U.S. Marshal Andrew Fallon exited out the passenger side.

They walked up the stairs and Marlys greeted them, giving Fallon a sideways glance. She hadn't really met him yet. I didn't feel like proper introductions were necessary, anyway, since this wasn't really a social situation.

"My building is closed," I said to both men, as I held the cell phone to my ear, waiting for the receptionist to get back to me.

"I can see that," Andrew replied.

"Does it say what for?"

"No, it just says closed by order of the fire marshal."

There was a voice in my ear and I jumped, and put a finger up to indicate I needed to take this call . . . Oh boy, did I. "Thank you for holding, can I help you?" the same chirpy voice said.

"Yes, as I just explained, someone has put a 'closed' notice on the door of my dance studio, and as I need to open up and get ready for a performance that I have coming up, I really need to find out . . ."

"Hold, please." Elevator music in the ear again.

"Wow, she's getting pretty mad. Her face is turning red," Tate said, smiling.

"Yeah, it practically matches her hair." Andrew had to get his shot in, too.

"You two are a regular laughfest," I said, holding the grating music away from my ear.

Tate grinned and my heart did a little beat-skipping thing.

"Thank you for holding, can I help you please?"

"Are you really going to make me explain this again? I need to find out who put a 'closed' notice on my building, and I've already explained that twice, and now . . ."

"Hold please." This time, I couldn't hear the elevator music over the roar in my ears, and I chucked the phone out and over the stairway and it hit the parking lot and shattered into pieces. Have I mentioned I'm hard on phones?

"Gonna be hard for Taylee to contact you on that phone," Tate commented drily.

"Well, she kept putting me on hold and this is a serious situation. I need to get into my building. I can only cancel dance for one night. We have to practice tomorrow. I have a performance on Friday. And I don't have time for this."

"No reason to worry, because Taylee won't be trying to contact you on that phone, now will she, Jenny? After all, it belonged to me!" Marlys said, with more than a little bit of irony and anger. Oops. I had just destroyed Marlys's phone, which was unforgivable, especially since she had rescued me from the mortuary, not to mention all the other things she did for me daily.

"I'm sorry, Mar, I sort of forgot, what with all the things that have happened. Can you forgive me? I'll buy you a new one."

"No, you won't, Jenny, because you don't have a pot to piss in!"

Boy, Marlys was steamed. And what kind of saying was that, anyway? A pot to piss in? That gave me some seriously warped mental images.

"Mar, I really am sorry, and I will pull whatever funds I have to from the *Nutcracker* proceeds to buy you a new phone. Please don't be mad at me. I'm just so upset about my building being closed. It makes absolutely no sense that it's closed! It was just a little bomb."

"Well, since the entryway to the tunnel was blown open, the building no longer meets earthquake codes. That's probably why they closed it," Tate said.

My eyes narrowed. "You seem to know an awful lot about this," I said through grated teeth.

"Common sense," he said.

"Or a desire to make sure I don't put on my performance?"

"Uh, Jenn, you're getting a little irrational here," Marlys interjected. "First you destroy my phone, then you accuse Tate of . . . well, whatever it is you are accusing him of. What possible reason could Tate have for not wanting you to put on your performance?"

I tried to think of one, but came up blank. Yes, I owed him money for the cookie-dough loan he had floated me, but he assured me that was being taken care of, and that he believed the owner of the cookie-dough company would come through. Still, he hadn't even known the tunnels existed until I showed them to him, so . . . When it hit me, it was almost physical, and it also made me a little weak-kneed. Was it possible he wanted to keep me in debt to him in order to control me? But why? What possible reason could a man have to keep a woman in control . . . except sex. Or housecleaning, but Tate wasn't that deluded. Even the biggest lunk in the world wouldn't want me as a housecleaner.

So, sex? Of all the sexist, raunchy, nasty, and frighteningly appealing things . . . I needed more sleep. Tate blowing up my studio so he could keep me as a sex slave? I needed more than sleep. I needed medication. And why wouldn't he want me as a sex slave, huh?

"Why are you suddenly glaring at me like I'm a can of bad tuna fish?" he asked.

"I'm not glaring."

"Actually, yes, you are," Marlys interjected unhelpfully. If I didn't need her so bad, she would find herself out of one jack-of-all-trades job. Oh, and now I owed her a phone.

I decided to ignore all the whack jobs standing behind me, especially the one living inside my brain (*sex slave, Jenny? Good God!*) and turned to look at the door. Technically, there was no lock on the door. And technically, I still had the key. What was a piece of paper, really? I mean, how serious could they really be, with some yellow tape and a piece of paper?

"I can tell you are thinking about just ignoring the order, and I want to point out that you have an entire passel full of psycho dance moms who are not going to want to endanger their darling daughters," Tate Wilson said, right into my ear. I could feel his warm breath on my neck, and a shiver wracked my body from head to toe. I hated that he could do that to me. I really did. And, of course, I couldn't help but wonder what else he could do to me.

"So, what exactly do you suggest?"

"Well, I have some contacts at the office of the fire marshal, and I can give them a call. Probably, you are going to have to get an engineer in here, and have them determine whether or not the building is safe."

"Engineer? But that would cost money. And you already know I don't have any. And I don't even own this building. I rent it, but Jack and Marco are in Mexico fishing, so I can't even get ahold of them. Oh God, why me?" I felt like someone had just drained all the blood out of my body, and I supposed, in a way, they had. My lifeblood. I was fighting a battle I couldn't win. Without being conscious of it, I slowly sank to the ground, my butt pressing against the cold, hard metal of the balcony entrance to my studio. It really would be easier to just give up. I was hardly a raging success at this, and now someone was making it nearly impossible just to get through a day—alive. Maybe it was time to give up this dream and join the real world. Maybe 7-Eleven was hiring.

"Jenny, are you okay?" Marlys asked.

"Hell, what do you think, Mar? The one thing I count on all year, the one money-earning performance I do, the one thing that keeps me barely bobbing afloat the rest of the year is now in danger, because my studio is shut down. I can't practice with the girls. Without practice, and with a new Sugar Plum Fairy who desperately needs the practice, I'm screwed. Up shit creek without a sail."

There was a moment of silence, during which I considered the fact that while most of the time I appeared mostly eccentric, today I must seem just plain nuts, and then Tate said, "I'm sure there must be something you can do."

Before I could think of a good retort to that, I heard a honk and I looked down to see Auntie Vi's 2006 Cadillac cruise into my parking lot. Great. This was all I needed.

Auntie slowly got out of her car and made a production of telling her yapping dogs to quiet down and "wait for Mommy like good little poo-poo dogs." As usual, Auntie's voice carried like thunder during a storm.

Yikes.

She slowly walked toward us, and no one spoke as she headed up the stairs, grasping at the handrail as she stomped up. She was at least a hundred pounds overweight, and each step she took shook the metal staircase with a pounding metallic thrum, which made me feel as though she was telegraphing a message to me with each step. "When. I. Reach. The. Top. You. Will. Be. Sorry. You. Were. Ever. Born. In. This. Family." Or something like that.

When she finally reached the summit of the stairs, she was breathing heavy. Sweat beaded on her forehead, and I could hear each exhalation as she struggled to regain both her breath and her composure.

I waited for the axe to fall.

After a moment, when she could finally speak, she opened her mouth, and I almost found myself physically cringing. My butt had gone numb, both from sitting on the hard metal latticework balcony and from the cold. I didn't care anymore. Numb was good. Numb might get me through this extremely dark day.

"Jennifer, I came . . ." Huff, huff. "I came because . . ." Huff, huff. "I came because I have an idea. I heard your studio was closed, and I know you need a place to practice." Huff, huff, huff. "I called my bishop, and he was very, very kind and he agreed that as long as your dances meet the church's standards," huff, huff, huff, "you are welcome to use our ward house to practice, and get ready for your *Nutcracker* performance. They have the basketball court in the cultural hall. So it will be the hardwood floors you need. He assures me that he and his wife buy tickets every year, and they are not willing to ruin family tradition. They will do whatever they have to do to help." She took a couple of deep breaths and then looked at me expectantly.

I was floored. I shouldn't have been. Of course she knew my studio was shut down. She had too much time on her hands, and she knew everything that happened in Ogden, especially when it involved someone she was related to, in any way.

But this? To have gone out on a limb and found me a place to practice—a place with the very essential hardwood floors that dancers need, mind you—was beyond belief to me. Of course, immediately the wheels started spinning in my head. What would be required of me in return? Would I have to give my firstborn child, should there even ever *be* a firstborn child, to the Mormon Church, in exchange for this . . . gift?

I didn't know what to say.

"She's thrilled," Marlys said, apparently deciding I needed some help. Damn her. She was right, as usual.

"We'll be there tonight at six for a group practice. Will that work?"

"Yes, dear, of course. I already told you that I had it all cleared. Do you know where it is?"

This last comment was delivered sweetly, without a hint of malice, at least in her voice, but I'd known Auntie Vi for a lot of years. She knew damn well I did not know where her particular ward house was, mostly because there was a Mormon church on every corner in Utah. Sometimes two, right across the street from each other. With the plethora of ward houses available, I had no idea which particular one was Auntie's.

My savior was quickly turning into my Judas. Wow. I was pretty sure I got that right. I actually referenced the Bible correctly. That was really amazing, wasn't it? I couldn't believe . . .

"Jenny? Jenny! Are you okay?"

"Nope, not okay. Definitely have had enough of this crazy turn my life is taking."

"Yes, dear, I understand," Auntie Vi said. "I hear Telegenix is hiring. Kim works there, and she just got her second raise. Eight-fifty an hour to start, Jennifer. You can't beat that. And they are so willing to work with you when you have your babies. Why, they told Kim that since she's already been there three years, she can get three months paid maternity leave and then come back part-time. They would welcome her back with open arms. What a family-friendly organization that is!"

"Uh, Auntie Vi? Kim's not married. Pretty sure she doesn't even have a boyfriend. Isn't it a little odd she's asking about maternity leave?"

"Planning for the future, Jennifer. Something you have never bothered to do."

I felt my blood begin to boil, but refused to let my temper get the best of me. I'd already destroyed Marlys's cell phone. Who knew what I'd decimate if I let Auntie Vi get me in a dither, and then, of course, she might rescind her offer of the church to practice in.

I really needed my girls to practice. I rose from the hard, cold metal and winced as my butt started to come back to life.

"Where's your church, Auntie?"

She gave me the address, and Marlys, ever ready, pulled out her pen and wrote it down, then copied it again and handed it to me.

"Well, you better get going, Auntie Vi. Here, let me help you down those metal stairs."

I reached out my arm and grabbed hers, firmly. I knew she wouldn't willingly walk away from the Jenny T. Partridge Disaster Show, but I wasn't in the mood to perform for her today.

I led her down the stairs, and heard the metallic tromp and reverberation as Marlys, Tate, and Andrew followed behind. Auntie was getting older and arthritic, so it took us a bit of time to get down the stairs. I started to feel like I was descending Mount Everest, until we finally reached the bottom, and I escorted my aunt to her car, making sure she got in and drove away.

Then I turned back to my little entourage. Gee, what fun my life had become.

"I'll start calling all the dance moms, and make sure they call a few, too," Marlys said. "I'll also let Amber and James know. Six o'clock, right?"

I nodded, and she turned to leave, then stopped. "Wait. You came with me. You don't have a ride."

"Yes, she does," Tate said, uttering the first words he'd spoken since Auntie Vi appeared. He and Andrew had watched the entire proceedings with great interest, and more than a hint of amusement. If a woman wasn't dead, and a little girl missing, I would have suspected them of setting this whole thing up, just because they were bored. Of course, they'd never met before it happened, and the bomb thing was kind of out of whack for law-abiding police officers. And the attacks on me, of course.

"Jenny, I'll make sure everyone brings their tuition

checks tonight, so we can get that money in the bank. Nobody gets in the door until tuition is paid," Marlys said.

"You won't let them in if they don't pay tuition?" Tate asked. "Wouldn't some of them just not come, or go home? People practice all kinds of avoidance in order not to pay things. It's why there are so many warrants issued."

"These are psycho dance moms. Not paying means your daughter doesn't dance, no one sees her huge potential, and the world comes to an end. They'd rob banks before they'd let that happen," I explained.

Tate just shook his head, and Andrew smiled. Not at Tate, of course, but at me. Yowza.

I suddenly realized I didn't know when we would get back in the studio, and this might be our last practice. "We're going to have to make it a dress rehearsal, Marlys. So make sure everyone brings their costumes."

"Okay, I will. Well, I'm off." She gave me a glance as if to say, "If you want to go with me, you'd better come now."

"Really, Marlys, if you would just drop me off at . . ." Where? The cops were staked out at my house, waiting for Taylee to call or for the bad guys to attack me again. Even if I didn't ride there with them, they'd be there right behind me. My studio was closed, by order of the fire marshal. The only place I could feasibly go was my parents' house. And I wasn't in the mood for that. My mom was kind of a "delicate flower" type. She didn't handle adversity or conflict well, and bodily harm sent her over the moon. She'd probably resort to wringing her hands and crying tears that leaked sneakily out of the corners of her eyes, trying all the while to pretend like absolutely nothing was wrong. I wasn't feeling strong enough to deal with that. And it was easier for my mom if she didn't have to confront the way I'd turned out.

"We'll take Jenny home," Tate said, his voice insistent and firm.

"Well, okay. Jenny?"

"Okay." I had to agree, because Marlys needed to get

going and call all those moms and get them directions to the ward house where we would be practicing. It was going to take a while. I had no choice but to let her go. She didn't have time to deal with me.

Marlys left, and we loaded up into Tate's car, me in the backseat. Andrew slid in next to me, and Tate turned to glare at him. One point for Andrew. He ignored Tate's nasty look.

"Actually, I need to go back to Monica's, to make sure she is awake and alert now, and finishing up my costumes."

"She's not there," Tate said roughly.

"What?" Alarm filled me. No costumes? Or something worse? Had she been kidnapped, too? "Where is she? What's going on? What aren't you telling me?"

"Monica had four warrants out for her arrest, so we went to her house to take her in," Andrew said, his voice gentle and placating.

I wanted to hit him. I was getting more irrational by the minute. "Warrants for what? This better be good. I need costumes. I have a performance. Did you miss that somewhere along the line?" I was starting to sound strident, and I certainly wasn't being logical. I didn't care.

"She had two counts of felony embezzlement and one for felony evading. And her name is not Monica. It's Karen Littlefield. She's been living here in Utah under an assumed name, and since she had no Social Security number, she could only work for people like, well, you. People who wouldn't ask for specifics like references."

"Oh no. Wow, that explains a lot, like why she is seriously nuts, but oh no. How could you? How could you arrest her? You knew I needed those costumes. You knew I have this performance, and my whole life is riding on it . . ." Sneaky tears leaked out the corners of my eyes, and I tried to wipe them away, but they kept coming. I was becoming my mother. Or maybe my cousin Kim, wishing for something that had no hope of ever happening. Planning for something that just plain was not going to work out, ever.

When Tate spoke, his words filled me with a bunch of emotions I had absolutely no hope of ever putting ID tags on. "Jenny? We didn't arrest her. Monica, er, Karen was gone when we got there. Somehow she got away."

TWENTY-FOUR

SOMETIMES, in life, you spent all your time building fences, only to have the wicked winds keep blowing them down. Sometimes, you needed to just admit that too many things were going wrong, and the wind was blowing too hard, and it just wasn't going to work to rebuild the fence that day. Maybe next week.

While I was no philosopher, I knew enough to realize this time was one of *those* times.

Monica/Karen was gone, on the lam, and I had all the costumes but the most important one—the one the Sugar Plum Fairy wore. Last year's costume had met with an unfortunate pink juice incident, and so was not usable.

My studio was closed—by order of the *fire marshal*, no less—and I was going to have to practice in the gymnasium of a Mormon ward house, where my aunt and her bishop would undoubtedly sit watching, making sure I wasn't violating any principles of morality or decency.

If I didn't do the performance, I would lose the huge deposit I'd paid the Eccles Center to rent it. That deposit money had come from my father's retirement fund, and I'd promised to pay it back.

In addition to that, most of Ogden was probably now convinced I was a lesbian, because I didn't really trust James's dedication to righting this wrong, and therefore outing himself, so my reputation was probably already shattered.

Considering all this, and even weighing in my dad's retirement money, how could I do it? How could I put this show on? Too many things were working against me. It had to be a sign that it was time to give up. Surely, that was what God was trying to tell me. Either that, or "Get your ass to a church, Jennifer." I wasn't too good at listening to God, or anyone for that matter.

But I was pretty desperate right now. Very desperate.

We pulled up in front of my apartment building, and I quickly opened my car door and got out, before Andrew and Tate could fight for the right to show me whose penis was bigger.

I walked swiftly to my door and opened it, striding through and waving at Marshal John Doe—who was reading *People* magazine at my kitchen table—as I headed to my bedroom. Once there, I shut the door securely and locked it, then threw myself face-first onto my bed, and just laid there. What the hell was I supposed to do? This was getting too hard.

"Jenny, are you okay?" Tate called to me through the door.

"No, not really. I just need a few minutes alone, okay?"

There was a pause, and then he spoke. "Okay, but I want you to think about something. Right about now, I know you are thinking of giving up, and I understand that. But I've gotten to know you pretty well over the past few days, and I just have to tell you this. You aren't a quitter. You keep going no matter what. You get upset, and mad, and feisty, and you cry easily, but you don't quit. And you can't quit now. You can make this work. I've never seen someone so gifted at just making things work. It's almost magical. You can't quit."

I heard his footsteps as he walked away from the door and his words sunk into me, making me feel both warm and slightly nauseous at the same time. He was wrong. I'd quit everything in my life. I'd quit cheerleading in the eighth grade, because the other girls were poor dancers with weaker toe touches, and also mean and spiteful. I'd quit catechism classes because I always fell asleep in the first ten minutes. I'd quit the sheriff's office, and every other mundane job I'd ever held because I didn't play well with other grown-ups.

I was the queen of quitters. I was really good at it. The only thing I hadn't ever quit was dancing. I'd dance in the morning, and I'd dance in the night, and I'd teach other people to dance as long as I lived, or could walk, or until I danced right off the edge.

I sighed and sat up, the realization that Tate had been at least somewhat right hitting me squarely between the eyes. I would not quit on this performance, and I would not quit on my students or my studio, no matter how bad things got.

At six o'clock I stood in front of the Latter-day Saints Ward Building on Madison and watched as the bishop unlocked the door, Auntie Vi standing next to him, beaming, and opening her arm as an open invitation to all my students to come inside the bosom of the church.

Since most of them had more than a passing acquaintance with an LDS ward house, all of which were pretty much built from the same plan, they ran haphazardly to the gymnasium, like lab rats to the cheese, and sat down on the floor, pulling off sweatpants and shirts and pulling dance shoes out of bags.

The lights turned on in the rapidly brightening gym, and the bishop came out beaming at all the little dancers. Then the smile slowly left his face as he watched the girls, ranging in age from four to sixteen, as they stripped down and got ready to dance, pulling on costumes and plumage, and helping each other fasten hairpieces and tighten straps.

He blushed and turned away, and looked at my aunt with alarm on his face. "Here, Bishop Wendt, let's just go to the kitchen and get you a nice glass of water while the girls get ready to dance." She ushered him out, and I gave her a look of thanks. She smiled, and then turned away, and I didn't miss the smug look on her face. Damn, now I was going to owe her big-time, even more than I did for procuring the building.

James and Amber walked in together, again just a little bit late, but not enough for scolding, and soon music was playing loudly from the big boom box I'd brought. James didn't get too close to me. He was probably afraid if he did I would reach out and wrap my hands around his neck. I almost had to shout directions to him.

We had to practice each number at least three times, and run walk-ons and walk-offs for each routine, as well as the finale, which featured the whole company.

Three hours flew by as I yelled at the girls, and made more than one cry, and we finally got the whole thing looking . . . passable. Not great. The Sugar Plum Fairies were decidedly lacking. Both Ariel and Loni had the technical skills to pull the role off, but they didn't have the heart and passion for dance that Taylee had stored deep in her soul. That, and they didn't have a costume, either. With all the other girls decked in feathers and shimmer, and multicolored materials of shine and gleam, they stood out even more in their everyday dance clothes.

Around eight thirty I dismissed all the little dancers, and gave them the notes with instructions neatly typed up on them, provided by Marlys, of course. What would I do without her? I said a quick prayer I'd never find out, before I remembered that God was mad at me.

After the little ones left, I said good-bye to James and Amber—James practically ran out before the words "you can go" were out of my mouth. Then I ran the Seniors through the climactic Sugar Plum Fairy dance, one that only the more mature advanced dancers had the skill to pull off, choreographed to a great upbeat jazzy version of

"Dance of the Sugar Plum Fairy" from Rudy and the Surf Kings.

I still hadn't decided who would dance the role—Loni or Ariel—and they were both starting to get a little anxious. I'm sure most of that came from the fact both of their mothers were sitting in chairs, watching me like vultures, and projecting all kinds of angst at their progeny. We had two performances—a matinee and evening—so I decided to give each of them a performance. I'd held off as long as I could, but it was time to accept that Taylee would not be here.

Krystal Glass had arrived about five minutes before, and she was glowering at me from the corner, as though trying to burn holes in my body with her laser-beam eyes. Marilyn sat on the floor, part of the corp that would dance backup to the lead dancers. As usual, Marilyn was not happy to be here. As usual, her mother had made her come.

Both of the lucky Sugar Plum Fairy psycho moms beamed as I made my announcement, and then Ariel's mom started to glower as she considered that her daughter was given the matinee and Loni would be dancing the evening performance. I decided to hustle everybody out of there before things got ugly. Krystal's look grew even darker, and she snapped at Marilyn to get up and go get in the car.

"I'm going to ride with Aileen, Mom, okay, because I have homework." She knew her mother well. Krystal always berated me for at least twenty minutes.

"Fine," Krystal told her, then turned and headed toward me.

I decided to cut her off at the pass. "Look, I know what you're trying to do, and it isn't going to work. Just go home, Krystal, and stop trying."

She stopped about a foot away, a puzzled look on her face. "You know?"

"Yes, I know. Now, please, let me get this mess cleaned up and go home."

She backed up, which surprised me, and I saw a look of fear in her eyes, then she turned and moved quickly out the door of the gymnasium.

That was a weird reaction. Usually, she would spend at least twenty minutes arguing with me, then ordering me to fix things, then yelling because I wouldn't.

I knew this was not the last I would hear of this, but I shrugged it off for tonight.

The bishop had left Auntie Vi with the key and had headed home an hour before, apparently so flustered by the ease with which young dancers disrobed, he had to rest. Since she was looking very tired and drained, I told her I would lock up and bring the key to her home.

"I'm not sure that's a good idea, Jenny."

"I promise to just finish gathering up the things left behind, and then I'll lock up and bring the key, Auntie Vi."

I swept my hand over the sea of dance shoes, jackets, pants, and a few unmentionables like panties and bras that had been left behind by my dancers, and she blanched a bit and decided to take me up on my offer.

"You'll be careful, right?" She had to be considering all the things that had happened to me lately, and I couldn't blame her for being worried. But Tate Wilson stood right next to me, and he assured her that he wasn't going anywhere. He'd help make sure the place got locked up tight.

After she left, I began picking up the items, and soon my arms were full, and I wasn't even halfway through. "I need a bag or something," I said, looking around.

"There's probably one in the kitchen. Let me go see," Tate said, and he walked out of the gym and across the hall to the kitchen, and I saw the remnants of light as he began rustling around. In almost all Mormon churches, the kitchen was located directly across from the gymnasium, for ease in serving food for functions. Functions like Mormon weddings, like the one James's family had been planning for me until he convinced them I was a lesbian.

I sighed heavily, put the clothes I'd been carrying on the floor, and reached down to just build a big pile of abandoned dance paraphernalia. The fact that Tate knew exactly where to find the kitchen also had me wondering. Of course, I wasn't Mormon, and I knew how to find an LDS ward house kitchen myself, but I was seriously addicted to funeral potatoes. Was he Mormon? Did it matter?

A sound from the other end of the gymnasium caught my attention, and I looked up to see a shadowy figure disappear through the door. The gym was located smack dab in the middle of the building, and so there were entrances on both sides. Tate had gone out the one closest to the kitchen. The other entrance led to areas of the church with which I was not familiar. I didn't really know who had headed out the door, but my first thought was one of the dancers hadn't been picked up, and was off playing in the dark recesses of the building. Since I was responsible for all of them, I sighed.

"Hey, who is that? Who's there?" There was no answer. I headed toward the door, but stopped in the entrance, not willing to go into the darkened hallway. While I did not want to be responsible for one of my dancers being locked up tight in a Mormon church overnight, I'd also seen enough teen horror flicks to know that if you wandered into a darkened hallway, you were gonna get killed. The only surer way to get killed was to have sex, but since Detective Tate Wilson was in the church kitchen on the other side of the gym, and we hadn't exactly "progressed" to that stage anyway, I figured I was safe there.

I decided to get Tate, and his gun, and then we'd go looking for whoever was still roaming the church.

I turned to go back into the gymnasium but before I could take a step, hands grabbed me and a rough cloth was shoved over my nose, filling my head with an acrid smell. I became too dizzy to stand and I felt hands on my arms, pulling at me roughly, dragging me. And I saw a head full of big blond hair. Krystal Glass had never left the building.

Then the world went black.

Twenty-Five

I awoke to the same utter darkness I'd collapsed in. My head hurt, and I was woozy, my throat dry and aching. My hands were bound behind me, and flashes of memory ran through my head.

Someone had dragged me out of the church—or at least I assumed I had been taken from the church—although I did not know where I was now. I vaguely remembered blond hair and thinking, "Krystal." I moved around restlessly, disturbed to realize I was bound at my feet as well as my hands. My hands were asleep, and so I rolled over onto my side, trying to wiggle them awake. My cheek pressed into a soft blanket, but not soft enough, for I was lying on a hard cement floor. Where was I?

I heard a rustling noise and my heart began to pound, nearly jumping from my chest, and the soft noise grew closer. If it was a person, they had a very soft step, and even a child would make more noise than that, so the alternative had to be some sort of creature, and that made me even more anxious.

A squeaking sound told me rodent, and I scrambled and kicked, trying unsuccessfully to sit up, as the creature drew nearer. Panic pulsed through my veins, and I tried to contain it, but I couldn't. The thought of a mouse, or worse, a rat, nudging at me, running over me, possibly biting me, was more than I could handle.

I started thrashing and kicking and a scream of sheer terror involuntarily erupted from my throat.

I heard another noise, this one from farther away, and then a light flashed on, down what appeared to be a long tunnel. Tunnel? Good God, I was in the tunnels underneath 25th Street.

The bomb that had opened the entrance to my building had been no mistake. Someone wanted a place to put me, a place where no one would look. I couldn't think of a better place. I was going to die here, and whoever had done it was apparently headed toward me.

"Well, well, well," came a voice I recognized. Krystal Glass. One of the psycho-est of the psycho moms. Apparently, I had not realized that soon enough to save myself. "You're awake. What the hell are you screaming about, anyway? I didn't realize how much sound echoes in these tunnels. You really need to be quiet."

"Krystal?"

"Yes, it's me. And before you get all huffy and puffy, you need to think about all the attempts I made to get you to stop snooping. You brought this on yourself. I had no choice but to bring you here, especially after you threatened me. You just don't take advice or warnings very well, Jenny. You're too stubborn for your own good." Krystal's voice didn't sound good. It sounded, in fact, a lot more psycho than usual. Which could explain why she thought I was snooping, when I thought I was just living my life.

"Krystal, why did you do this? Why did you kidnap me? I don't understand why you would resort to this. You psycho moms are crazy." Hmm. That probably wasn't something I should have said.

I couldn't see her face, because her flashlight was pretty

much shining right in my eyes. The bright beam hurt and I blinked.

"I'm not crazy, Jenny. Just determined. I'll do whatever I have to in order to keep what's mine. When you said you knew what I was doing, I knew I had to take action." I heard an edge to her voice that told me I was in deep trouble.

"What are you talking about?" Then my own words, spoken to Krystal in the church gymnasium, flooded back to me.

"Look, I know what you're trying to do, and it isn't going to work. Just go home, Krystal, and stop trying."

Of course, I'd meant she was trying to get Marilyn the lead role. She'd thought I meant I knew what she was up to, and now because of that miscommunication between a scatterbrain and a psycho I was probably going to die.

"I don't know how you figured me out, because I had such a great plan, but it doesn't matter. I've handled it. Now I just need to shut you up, on the off chance someone hears your silly screams."

She reached down and pulled me to a sitting position, and every muscle in my body protested. My feet were hopelessly asleep, but the change in position sent some blood running back into them and soon I felt the pinpricks of agony that meant some of my circulation was being restored.

"My feet are asleep. Can't you untie them, please?"

"No, sorry. You might get away. You're pretty agile, and I'm not stupid. I can stand you up for a minute, though, and let you hop around."

Great.

She hefted me up, and I tottered, and then stood, trying not to cry out as my feet came back to life.

"These knots are too tight. Can't you just loosen them?"

"Sheesh, you are too damn much trouble. If I didn't need you, I'd just end it all right now."

She needed me? Why? A surge of relief shot through me. I wasn't going to die—yet. She let go of my arm, which caused me to teeter a bit, as she bent down to loosen the binds on my feet.

At this point, I had to make a decision. I could knock her over and try to render her helpless, but then my feet would still be bound, and since my hands were tied, too, I'd be stuck there with her until she woke up.

"Krystal, why did you bring me here?" I asked again. She was down at my feet, the flashlight on the floor, illuminating the ropes that bound me. She struggled to get them free, and I could see the sharp outlines of her face as she looked up at me.

"Stop asking questions. And by the way, I wouldn't try anything if I were you. I have a gun."

She pulled a small handgun out of her jacket pocket, and waved it at me. In the dim light I couldn't tell what kind it was—like I even knew the different kinds of guns—but I figured it was real.

She shoved it back into her pocket and went back to work on the ropes. "And also, you should consider that since you are bound, if you hit me or try to disable me, you're going to be in a world of hurt, because you won't get away." I didn't bother to tell her I'd already figured that out.

Just then, we both heard a noise coming from behind us. Krystal stood and turned in that direction, whipping the flashlight up and flashing it up the long, dark tunnel, trying to illuminate whatever had made the noise.

"I think there are rats in here," I said.

"If that was a rat, it's a big one."

Kinda like you, I thought, but I didn't say it aloud. I had no desire to make my situation worse.

Dismissing the noise, Krystal turned back to me and bent back down to the ropes. "I tied these too good. I can't get them loosened." She struggled with them for a few more minutes, then gave a disgusted sigh, picked up the flashlight, and stood.

"Sorry, no can do. Now back down on the ground. And I need to put this gag in your mouth." She pulled a bandana out of her pocket and waved it around. She pushed me back down to the ground.

"Wait! Don't do that, please. I won't scream. Where are we anyway?" I was desperate to keep her from putting that gag in my mouth.

"We're in the tunnels under 25th Street," she answered, without hesitation. Just as I'd thought. "This particular one runs between Marco's store and mine. They are supposed to be closed off, but I needed a place to hide a body, so I cleared mine out a while back. It's not like the city inspects them on a regular basis. I figured I could just hide the body, and then close mine back off, and no one would be the wiser."

"Why would you want to kill me? I know I didn't give Marilyn a great part in *The Nutcracker*, but to kill for that . . ."

"Not you, you simpering idiot. Although this has ended up to be a great place for you. I meant Sandra Epstein."

"So you did kill her."

"Damn straight. She was sleeping with my husband. Can you believe it? That ugly cow thought she could take what was mine. First her daughter gets all the dancing roles that Marilyn should have, and then she just walks in and takes my husband."

I found it a little hard to comprehend. Krystal's mild-mannered husband sleeping with the harsh, strange, possibly chemically dependant Sandra Epstein? "Are you sure? I mean Sandra was hardly a femme fatale or anything like that." Was this what Sandra had been up to all those times she left Taylee unsupervised? I'd assumed she was drugged or drinking, but an affair . . . It was possible. Maybe when Taylee said her mother was sleeping a lot, she didn't mean alone.

"Marvin is weak. She tempted him, and he gave in. Marilyn is just like him. If it weren't for me, those two would collapse and never get anywhere in life."

"But you didn't bring Sandra's body here."

"Well, things didn't go exactly as I'd planned. I figured out I could use arsenic and then bring her here. If by some strange chance she was found, down the road, and an autopsy done, they'd probably discover the arsenic, and since you had a beef with her, they'd look at you first. The cookie-dough poisoning was a perfect idea. Sandra never even suspected it. And everybody eats frozen cookie dough. It's too hard to resist. And I have easy access to arsenic, and nobody else does anymore. I use it with my crystal designs. No reason anyone would even question me buying it, because I've been doing it for years."

It occurred to me at this point that things were playing out here just like they did on television. She was telling me all the details of the crime, tying up the loose ends, because shortly after that she intended to kill me. Kill me. *Ulp.* Maybe this was information I did not need to know. It didn't matter. She kept talking.

"But it didn't go exactly right. I let myself into her house, and was about to haul her out when I heard a noise. I turned to see Taylee watching me. Then she ran. She ran fast. And I can't find her. I figured you would lead me to her. And I had to set you up to look guilty so no one would come looking at me. Or at least somewhat guilty. That one backfired, though. After I snuck the cookie dough into your house, I figured the police would focus on you. But you have way too many enemies! I mean, after you got attacked in front of your house, it looked like you were the victim. You really need to be nicer to people, Jenny. Of course, now it doesn't matter. But you do seem to have a lot of people out to get you. That's going to work out good for me."

"How did you get the cookie dough into my house?"

"Piece of cake. My brother Jake is a locksmith—when he works, which isn't often, but he's been useful for me. I fund his little business, and he turns the other way when I need to use the equipment. And your building just isn't all that secure."

"So now, you're just going to kill me?"

"No, of course not! Well, I mean not yet. I need to find

Taylee. She can put me away. And the best way to find her is through you. That child is addicted to dance. She can't not perform. Sooner or later, she's going to find you."

"This isn't going to work, Krystal. What makes you think Taylee will find me? Where could you put me to make that happen? This plan has some pretty major flaws . . ." I stopped talking as I realized I was trying to talk her into killing me right now. Best to keep my mouth shut.

"I don't know how I'll do it, but I'll figure it out. Now, let's get this gag on you." She reached out toward me and then I heard a scuttling noise to my right and I turned to look. Krystal heard the same thing, and she turned, just as someone rushed her and knocked the flashlight out of her hands. She screamed, fear, rage, and frustration all rolled into one primal yell, and I heard her fall heavily onto the floor. Then there was quiet, and I pushed myself against the wall, knowing I was trapped, my feet and hands tied. The flashlight had survived the fall, and I could see two small shapes hovering over Krystal, and then they stood and headed toward me, and I fought back a scream.

"Jenny, it's me. It's Taylee."

T WENTY-SIX

"T AYLEE? Is it really you?"

"Yeah," she said.

"Who is with you, Taylee?" I asked.

"It's me," said a familiar voice, and then Marilyn, Krystal's daughter, stepped forward.

"Marilyn? What are you two doing here?"

Marilyn flipped on a bright flashlight and I blinked at the sudden harsh light. I could see Krystal's still form on the floor behind us. She wasn't moving, but I wasn't going to take my eyes off her for long.

"I've been staying here," Taylee said. "Some of the time, anyway. The rest of the time I was at Marilyn's. She came to give me some food, and we had to hide when Krystal showed up with you. We saw it all. We heard what she said, too."

"I found the tunnel a while back, and knew my mom was not up to any good," Marilyn said harshly, anger filling her voice. "When Taylee told me what happened, and how she saw my mom at her house, I was determined to keep her safe."

"Why didn't you go to the police, Marilyn? I understand she's your mother, but the cops . . . Well, they would have arrested her, and they would have kept Taylee safe."

"No. No, they wouldn't, Jenny," Taylee said. "I know what they'll do. They'll move me. I'll have to go somewhere else, and this time I'll be all alone. I won't even have my mom. So Marilyn was trying to help me stay here, and out of sight. Because I wanted to stay here—with you. But I couldn't even get close to you. The cops were always there. I even sent you e-mails, but you didn't answer them. I didn't dare give too much information, but I thought you'd know it was me." She was giving me too much credit. But she was just a little girl, and I could hear the fear and concern in her voice, and knew that even though Sandra Epstein hadn't been much of a mother, she had been the only one that Taylee had. Once she was gone, I became her only hope.

This whole thing was mind-boggling. The killer's daughter was helping the victim's daughter. And I didn't even know they were friends.

"Nobody should have to do what they don't want to do," Marilyn said, determination filling her voice. "Nobody should have to move, or run away, or even *dance* if they don't want to."

"I don't want to leave, Jenny," Taylee said. "I want to stay here with you. And I want to dance here."

"But Krystal killed your mother, Taylee. She told me that. All you had to do was tell the police that you saw her there, and then . . ."

My voice trailed off. All she had to do was tell the police what she saw. She'd done that before. And then everything she knew in life had been taken from her, and she'd been whisked away to a new location, given a new name, told to forget the person she was before had even ever existed, except when they needed her to testify against her father.

Why would this be any different for her?

"Oh, what a mess this is," I said. "Can you guys please untie me so we can get out of here?"

"Okay," Marilyn said, and she bent down and had the ropes off my hands and feet in less than a minute.

"How did you do that? I mean, that was quick. Your mom tied them, and she couldn't even get them off."

"I'm good with my hands. I like hanging out with my dad. We hunt and shoot and tie knots and do that kind of stuff. I'm not a dancer. I hate dance. But *she* won't listen." As if in response, Krystal groaned heavily. Marilyn didn't seem too concerned that her mother was lying there unconscious on the floor of the cold, dark tunnel. In fact, she was pretty much ignoring her.

"We need to get out of here before she wakes up," I said, urgency filling me. "We need to go to the police with this, Taylee. They'll arrest Krystal, and you won't have to hide from her, I promise."

Taylee shook her head sadly. "No, Jenny, I need you to fix this. I need you to make it so I can stay here. I know what's going to happen. Marshal Fallon will make me leave. They will whisk me away somewhere. I want to stay here. I want to dance with you. I want to be the Sugar Plum Fairy, like we planned. I want that."

I did, too. "I'll make it work, Taylee. I promise I'll make it work."

I hoped I could keep that promise.

The girls stood on both sides of me and helped me to my feet. Krystal groaned again and urgency filled me. "We have to go, girls. Fast. Marilyn, I know she's your mother, but we'll send help down. We'll send someone for her."

"I don't care. She's a murderer. When things didn't go her way, she killed someone else's mom. How can someone do that?" There was a catch in Marilyn's voice, and I wondered how I had not seen the real child inside the sullen, unhappy girl that stood in my dance studio and refused to jeté. "But they'll put her away, and then Dad and I will be able to camp and hunt and fish in peace."

We turned toward the small light that I knew was the opening to Krystal's shop, when she suddenly shot bolt upright and jumped to her feet, catching all of us by surprise.

Leveling the gun at the three of us, she ordered us to move back into the tunnels.

"I've heard enough. Betrayed by my own daughter. Betrayed. I can't believe it." I wondered if she had been faking unconsciousness, but she touched her head gingerly and then shook it gently. She probably hadn't been unconscious, but had needed time to regroup, so she faked it, so she could take us by surprise. "Move."

She gestured back in the direction we had just come from.

"I've done everything for you, Marilyn. Everything. And this is the thanks I get? You helping them to put me away for good? I did everything for you. Give me that damn flashlight."

"No," Marilyn said. "I hate you! You've ruined my life, and you're a killer, and now you're going to . . . what are you going to do? Would you kill me? Would you kill your own daughter, too?"

"Just walk. And give me the flashlight." She reached out her hand, and then Marilyn flipped off the light and threw it as far as she could into the tunnel. We heard a thump as it landed, and a tinkling crash. I'd heard the indecision in Krystal's voice, and guessed that Marilyn had, too. Could she really kill her own daughter?

It was totally dark, except for the faint beam of light coming from the opening into Krystal's store, and I could see nothing else in the utter darkness in front of us. Taylee had grabbed my hand tightly when Krystal first ordered us back into the blackness of the tunnel.

I heard a shuffling noise and realized that Krystal was headed back to her building and out of the tunnel. "Now I will just have to close up the tunnel and no one will be the wiser. See, Jenny? You were wrong. My plan did work. I did get Taylee here, and no one will ever know. Since you've disappeared, I'll just write a note saying you couldn't live with the guilt, and you kidnapped my daughter and Taylee, and ran off. They'll look for you forever, and no one will ever find you."

I heard Marilyn gasp and then begin to cry, as she realized how willingly her mother would abandon her, mostly because she didn't live up to Krystal's ideals. "Oh, stuff it, Marilyn. You never really loved me anyway. You preferred your father, and his stupid idea of fun."

This was one harsh woman. And totally insane. More so than any psycho mom I had ever encountered.

Marilyn continued to cry and Krystal continued to berate her, her voice fading as she neared the opening of the tunnel. "Don't move, or I'll shoot and end it all fast." She was going to willingly let us die of starvation, dehydration, and exposure in the cold temperatures of the dank tunnel.

We heard her closing off the tunnel and then it was completely black. "I don't want to die," Marilyn cried. Taylee just clutched my hand tightly.

"We aren't going to," I assured them both.

"You're right, Jenny," Taylee said. "Because I've been staying here. And we can get out on your side."

T WENTY-SEVEN

SOMEONE had set off a bomb in my building, but it had apparently not been Krystal. Had it been her, she would have known that the entrance to my building was now opened, and we were not exactly stuck in here.

No psycho dance mom was going to do me in. I felt determination fill me, and I began to grope my way along the tunnel wall, pulling Taylee with me. "Grab Marilyn's hand and follow me." I shivered, and realized my head was aching and I felt as though I was inside a tunnel . . . eh, well, I *was* inside a tunnel, but it felt that way in my head. The shivering also made me realize I had been fairly unaware of the frigid temperatures during the time all of these crazy events had been happening. The headache was probably a result of the chloroform, but the shivering . . . It was very, very cold in here, and if I could see anything at all, I knew I would see my breath. As it was, I couldn't even see my fingers in front of my face, but I could feel my way forward, and I kept moving, edging us in the direction away from Krystal's shop and toward my building.

Marilyn sobbed softly as we moved, and Taylee clasped my hand tightly. A sudden softness under my foot, and a nasty squeal, made me step back and scream, and the two girls echoed my sounds. I waited a moment for my heart to calm down, and then told the girls, "Just a mouse. I stepped on a mouse." A big mouse. Possibly three or four feet long. Maybe eight. *Stop it, Jenny. Get in control!*

I started moving again, stepping forward gingerly, not wanting to step on another rodent. We made our way slowly through the tunnel, until I found an opening, jagged and small, but big enough that one of the girls could get through it. It wouldn't work for me, of course.

"You're going to have to go through," I told Taylee. Marilyn was still sobbing, and her emotional condition let me know she would be unable to help herself or us at all.

"But I can't see, Jenny," Taylee protested. "What is in there?"

"It's the opening to the basement of the studio, Taylee. You know, right below Jack's store? It's where the furnace is."

I stuck my head through the opening and could make out the faint, small blue and yellow glow of the pilot light of the furnace. Thank God it hadn't gone out again.

"See that light? That's the pilot light of the furnace. Immediately to the left of that is a light switch, on the wall. All you have to do is find that switch and turn on the light."

"I'm afraid of the dark," Taylee whispered.

"Me, too," Marilyn said, through guttural, phlegm-clogged sobs.

"You're afraid of the dark, and you were staying down here?"

"Well, I only stayed here twice, and I had a big flashlight and lots of books, and blankets, and I could go through the opening into Mrs. Glass's shop to go to the bathroom . . ."

"Okay, look, girls, we have to get out of here, or we will die. I don't want to die, and neither do you. So let's just focus here, and pretend it's not dark in there. Taylee, please go through and find the light. Once you find the light, it will all be better."

I could feel her shaking, her hand jerking in mine. I didn't blame her. The whole situation had been terrifying. But we were close. Really close to being safe. We just had to get into the other building, or Taylee did, and find her way upstairs and call for help. And then we would all be safe.

"Okay, I'll try," she said softly, letting go of my hand. I couldn't see her, but I could hear the noise as she felt the opening and moved into it.

"Ouch, it's too small. I can't get through."

"Please try, Taylee. Please."

I heard grunting and a few cries of pain, and then a loud thunk. I felt around with my hands, and knew that Taylee had gotten through the opening. "Taylee, are you okay?"

"Yes, I'm here. I'm trying to find the light."

The sudden illumination when the bulb switched on was as breathtaking and heartwarming as any vision from God could ever have been. But it didn't last. I watched as Taylee tromped up the steps and tried to open the door to go into the store, so she could call for help.

It wouldn't budge. She was out of the tunnel, but could go no farther than the top of the stairs.

$\mathcal{T}$WENTY-EIGHT

$\mathcal{A}$s much as I wanted to think there was a way out of this, I wasn't seeing it. Unless Tate made the connection—and how he could I didn't know—between my disappearance, Krystal, her shop, and the tunnels, we were stuck in here. I didn't know for how long.

"Can you find a hammer or something, Taylee?" It was freezing in the tunnel, and I intended to smash the opening wider so that Marilyn and I could get through, and at least move into the warmer basement.

"I'll see," she said, but her voice was devoid of emotion. It sounded like she had given up. Marilyn was still crying. "I found one." She handed the ball-peen hammer through the opening and I took it and began to smash at the cement, shattering small chunks of it as I tried to make the opening bigger, wincing with each strike. I turned my face to avoid the flying chunks, and told Marilyn to move a step back so no shards would hit and wound her.

I was determinedly smashing away, when Marilyn's hand clutched at me and grabbed, urgently pulling at me, and I turned to see a light moving toward us from the other end of the tunnel.

I stopped, and listened.

"What are you doing?" Krystal's voice was harsh and angry. "I came back for my Marilyn. I just wanted to scare her, so she would realize how much I do for her, and how much she needs me. But what are you doing?"

I didn't answer. I should have known she wouldn't leave Marilyn behind. She had too much invested in her. She must have gone back into her shop, grabbed another flashlight, and then came back for what she felt belonged to her.

"Answer me, Jenny T. Partridge! What are you doing?"

I turned and smashed hard a few more times, making the opening big enough for Marilyn, and I grabbed her and shoved her through. I tried to follow, ignoring the thump, thump of Krystal's footsteps as she raced toward us, the new flashlight she had found reflecting off the walls of the tunnel in a crazy pattern. I went butt first so I could see what she was doing, and about halfway through I realized I was stuck. Too many funeral potatoes and French fries and extra dishes of ice cream had done me in. Krystal was only ten feet away, and I started planning my eulogy—would I be able to transmit my wishes to my parents? Did dead spirits really stay around and give people directions, like they did on television?—when I felt tugging on my arms and legs, and with an oomph, my body was pulled free of the cement and I tumbled onto the ground in the basement.

Krystal stuck her head in the opening and then her hand, with the gun, and ordered us to get back into the tunnel.

Moving faster than I would have thought possible, Taylee picked up the hammer I had dropped and brought it down hard on Krystal's hand. Krystal screamed in pain and let go of the gun, which tumbled to the ground. She collapsed, halfway in and halfway out of the opening, her hand obviously shattered.

At the same time, we heard a pounding on the door of the basement, then a gunshot, and the door opened.

Detective Tate Wilson came through, gun drawn, followed closely by Marshal Andrew Fallon and Marshal John Doe.

The cavalry had arrived, but I knew the truth. We had saved ourselves.

Twenty-Nine

The events that had started what felt like weeks before—but what had actually been just days—were finally over. Those events, we also discovered, were not all closely connected.

Everyone involved denied planting the bomb that had ultimately saved my life, Taylee's life, and probably Marilyn's, because her mother would never again try to force her to be something she was not. Even though Krystal had come back for Marilyn, she had already done a lot of damage to the girl's psyche. I supposed it might help a little for Marilyn to know that her mother had ultimately not left her to die, but the fact remained that the girl believed she had, at least for a while. The mysterious car chase with the Hummer also was not solved, as Krystal denied all involvement.

Emma Anderson came forward after the events hit the local news, and turned herself in to the police. She'd been holed up in a condo in Park City, owned by a family friend, while she waited for the real killer to be caught. She'd been terrified that Ella would be taken from her, and although she figured eventually the real killer would be found, she didn't want to spend the time waiting in jail. She admitted that after the police questioned her, and before they came to talk to me, she realized she would be the main suspect. She was too embarrassed to admit she didn't have Sandra Epstein's cookie dough anymore, because she had eaten it. Plus, she wasn't sure they would believe her. Since she was already pretty mad at me, for not giving into her demands, fingering me was just the next natural step—at least to her.

Tate relayed her sincere apology to me, and then threw in a kicker. "She hopes that you won't take this out on little Ella, and will let her come back to dance. She thinks she has great potential to be a Sugar Plum Fairy."

He told me this while we sat at Rooster's and I ate my fill of Pacific Coast bisque.

"I think not," I said, shaking my head. "I never want to see either Anderson again."

"Can't say I blame you."

It had been two days since I'd been trapped in the tunnel and thought I was going to die, and we had already put on the matinee production of *The Nutcracker*, with Taylee in the lead role, and a very sad Loni and Ariel dancing in the corps.

Even without a week of practice, Taylee was picture-perfect. There were several spots where she simply chore-ographed her own moves, and while I was very attached to my version, I was overjoyed to see what talent and skill she had.

"And Monica? Where is she?"

Just saying her name gave me a sour feeling. I'd been forced to use a simple pink leotard and tutu for the lead role, and expected it would detract from the performance. I'd spent the night before putting rhinestones on it, Taylee by my side, helping, and was surprised to discover that the simplicity deeply complemented the rest of the costumes and made Taylee's immense talent shine even more.

With some kids, you have to hide them beneath flash

and sequins and glitter and makeup, and hope no one would notice they had not a shred of dance ability.

Not with Taylee.

Tate carved at his steak, but mostly pushed it around on his plate, and I could tell something was bothering him.

"Okay, spit it out. What's up? Who is trying to kill me now? Did I make some other psycho dance mom mad? Is someone going to kidnap me before the evening performance?"

He didn't respond to my joking, so I knew it was serious.

"Please tell me."

"Taylee has to leave tonight." My heart sank. I knew the news had been coming, because I knew her safety was always an issue. Andrew Fallon had violated all kinds of rules by allowing her to stay with me, although he had camped in my living room for the entire two days leading up to the performance.

But I did not want her to go. And my reasons were not selfish, for a change. She wanted to stay here. She didn't want to move and start all over. This time, all alone.

"Where is she going?" I asked, tears clouding my voice, and making the bisque tasteless. I put my spoon down.

"I don't know, Jenny. And even if I did, I couldn't tell you."

I thought of poor little Taylee, who was right now surrounded by her fellow dancers in a dressing room at the Eccles Center, where they were playing cards and eating junk food and waiting for the next performance. Both the matinee and the evening performance were sold out, and I stood to make an even tidier profit this year than last. I would be able to pay my dad back, put a little money in the bank for all the lean months ahead, and hopefully invest in some new socks.

"I'm not hungry anymore. I can't stand the thought of her all alone."

"I know. I wish there was another way, but there isn't. She isn't safe here, now, even though they kept her involvement out of the press. Especially since we don't know who was driving the Humvee that chased you and Marlys down. Could be another psycho dance mom, but . . . Someone could find her. She has to leave, Jenny, in order to stay alive."

I understood, but didn't like it anyway. "And does she know?"

"Yes, Andrew told her about an hour ago. As soon as her performance is over tonight, they'll be leaving."

"Can you take me back to the Eccles Center? I want to spend as much time with Taylee as I can, before she has to go."

THE evening performance went off with only a few hitches. One of the buffoons peed her pants and had to be pulled from the lineup at the last minute, as we couldn't salvage the costume. Her mother was willing to let her dance with a big wet stain. I was not.

Taylee did an awesome job, and only a few people noticed when one of the other fairy corps members danced right off the stage and into the orchestra pit. She survived with only a few scrapes and bruises.

When the performance was over, the girls gathered around excitedly, as they always did, and I got lots of hugs and thank-yous. I needed to get out front to the foyer and say good-bye to our audience, but I also needed a moment alone with Taylee.

Marshal Fallon stood guard in front of the door where she was changing, and as soon as the gaggle of girls were done hugging me, I headed to him.

"You better take care of her."

"I will. I always do."

"You didn't do such a great job this time," I reminded him.

"Well, that's because I didn't count on a certain kooky dance teacher getting herself—and Taylee—into a lot of hot water," he countered, amusement coloring his voice.

"I didn't cause this," I said.

"I know. I promise I'll take care of her, Jenny."

"I'm going to need to know she's okay."

"That's not possible. No one can know where she is."

"I'm going to *need* to know she's okay," I repeated.

He leaned down and gently kissed my cheek, and then straightened up. "I'll do my best."

Then he opened up the door and let me into the room.

Taylee was dressed, a small overnight bag sitting on the counter. She was looking into the mirror, as though she saw a stranger there, and her small, heart-shaped face was forlorn.

Her name would change, as would her life, and I was so worried about where she would end up, and who would care for her, that my stomach was tied in knots. I wanted to whisk her out of there and hide her away, but knew I was not capable of keeping her safe. Not from the demons who were after her. After all, they were much bigger demons than the psycho dance moms that had threatened and destroyed her life here in Utah.

"I'm so sad you have to leave, Taylee."

She turned away from the mirror and faced me.

"I know. I'm sad, too. I want to stay here. I want to stay with you."

"I know. I'm sorry about all of this, and about your mom. I guess you saw her when she was, uh, well . . ."

"Yeah, I did. I called 911."

"You did? Sheesh. No one told me. No wonder they knew you were in danger."

"The dispatcher said they would keep me safe, but I knew they wouldn't. I called on a pay phone, and it was late and dark, and then I heard something before I could tell them it was Krystal, so I hung up and ran. I figured the only way I could stay safe was to hide, or to get to you."

"I didn't help you much, did I?" I asked her, feeling a pang in my heart. She'd had so much faith in me. A lot more than I deserved.

Tears filled her eyes and mine responded in kind, and I moved forward and pulled her into a bear hug. "I'll always remember you. And wherever you are dancing, I want you to think of me. Never, ever, ever let them stop you from dancing. One day you will be the best, and I'll see you again. One day you'll be safe again." It would be a while, I knew. Probably until her father died. Maybe after that, if the hit went further than what I'd been told.

I pulled away from her and reached into my pocket, pulling out a small gold chain with a dangling pair of tiny gold pointe shoes on the end. I'd had to borrow the money from Marlys to purchase it, but she gave it willingly, insisting I not pay her back, as she sobbed thinking of little Taylee without parents, alone, and her life in so much danger.

I would pay her back, but I appreciated her thoughtfulness.

I put the necklace around Taylee's neck and fastened the clasp, and then turned her shoulders to face the mirror, so she could see the necklace.

"No matter where you are, you keep this on. Keep it on like you do this one," I said, patting the cross I knew she had hidden under her leotard. "I don't know where you got it, but I know it means a lot to you, and that probably means there's a memory attached to it. So I'm giving you another memory. I will always remember you, and hope you'll do the same for me. And if you ever find yourself in a bad situation, you come to me. I'll be here."

She nodded, the tears spilling over. She reached up to hug me, and whispered in my ear, "It was from my teacher. The one who died. He believed in me. Thanks for believing in me, too."

A knock on the door told us it was time for her to go. After Marshal Fallon escorted her away, I cried some more, not sure who I felt worse for—her or me. I prayed that she wouldn't spend the rest of her childhood collecting "memories" as she moved from place to place, but would find somewhere to call home. I also prayed that my praying wouldn't doom her to a worse fate, since asking God for help never worked out real well for me. That thought made me cry some more. Maybe it was just an emotional meltdown that had been coming for days, ever since all the chaos had erupted in my life.

"Jenny?"

I looked up and my eyes widened as I saw Monica standing in the doorway. She wore a bag lady's outfit, and her hair was died a horrendous shade of brown, but there was little doubt it was Monica.

"What are you doing here? And where the hell is my costume for the Sugar Plum Fairy?" Wow, where had that come from? After all, the production was over for the year, and given all that had happened, a costume seemed like peanuts. But still . . .

I considered the fact that Monica was a lot more unbalanced than I had realized, and that she had regularly tried to strangle me—in effigy. A little catch of fear blocked my breathing.

"I didn't get it done. That's why I had to leave. When I tried to go to the store, I saw the cops watching my house, and I realized I had to get out of there. But I just came back to tell you I'm sorry."

"Sorry for not making the costume?"

"Oh no, you put a lot of pressure on me. It's your fault I couldn't get the costume done. No, I came to apologize for the bomb."

"*You* are the one who set off the bomb?"

"Well, I figured you'd have to put off the performance, and that would give me a few more days to get the costume done, because it was not working out like I had planned. And I ran out of the material you wanted, and I had to order more. Then my cat found the feathers in the bag, and thought they were a big bird and attacked and ate them, and that was an entirely *different* mess that you do not want to know about."

I suspected I did not. I looked around, but the building was pretty much abandoned now. So much for greeting my adoring public. And here I was, with a psychotic incognito costume designer, who was carrying who knew what weapons in her big, bag lady purse.

"Anyway, I'm sorry about the bomb. Just wanted you to know that. Oh, and also, I'm sorry about the attack outside your house. I really was just trying to get you to postpone the performance, so I would have more time. Now, I've got to run."

"Whoa, let me get this straight. You figured that attacking me would delay the performance and give you time to finish the costume? And when that didn't work you set off the bomb?"

"Yeah, but I forgot how damned stubborn you are."

"You're pretty small, and whoever attacked me was not. There's no way . . ."

"Oh, I have this really cool fat suit. It's awesome. I got it . . . Well, never mind where I got it. Anyway, I used it to throw you off my trail. You turned out to be more of a fighter than I figured, though. Good thing I'm not a guy."

"Wow. Unbelievable. And now you risked getting caught to come and apologize?"

"Of course. I do have manners, you know." We heard footsteps and her eyes widened. She quickly slipped on a pair of oversized sunglasses, which, with her hair, attire, and the bag she carried made her look like an aging Olsen twin.

"Bye, Jenny," she whispered, as she scuttled off down the hallway toward an exit.

Tate rounded the corner and watched her disappear with puzzlement.

"Homeless person get inside somehow?"

"Monica."

"Monica?" His voice rose a notch and he pulled his phone off his belt and opened it, his body poised as if about to run after her. Then he turned to look at me, shaking my head, and a grin formed on his face. He dialed the police dispatcher, then put his hand over the phone to ask me to give him a good description. He relayed that information to the dispatcher, then hung up.

"You aren't going after her?"

"No. We still have cops all around this place, since Taylee just barely left. She won't get away."

"She might. She's sneaky. She's been getting away with things for years. I mean, think about it. If Sandra Epstein hadn't died, and all that other stuff hadn't happened, you wouldn't even have known she was a fugitive."

"True, but our force is good. They'll get her."

I didn't feel like arguing with him, but I suspected she was long gone.

TATE escorted me home, following behind me as I drove my pink Bug to the front of my apartment building, where, for a change, there was a spot. Maybe my luck was turning.

I got out of the car and locked it, then turned to watch as Tate Wilson stepped out of his police vehicle and walked toward me.

"Thanks for the meal, again, and for following me home, but I think I'll be okay now."

"Actually," he said, his voice a low sexy growl, "I think you and I have some unfinished business. This case is over, you know. I believe I mentioned what I wanted to do when this case was over?"

My heart raced and I could feel a thunk-thunk in my ears, and I got warm in places that hadn't been warm since the last time he gave me that look, his cobalt blue eyes searing into me.

I gulped, and said, "I'm really tired. I think maybe another time."

"You don't mean that."

"I don't mean that. Wait, I mean, yes, I do. I mean it."

"No, you don't."

"No, I don't," I admitted. I was terrified—both of what would happen if he did come in, and what would happen if he didn't. "But, I have to know."

"Know what?"

"Where the hell do you keep disappearing to? Do you

have a girlfriend? A wife? You keep taking off without explanation. I don't do wives and girlfriends."

He raised an eyebrow and a silky smile slid across his face, and I blushed. "I did *not* mean it that way. And I'm serious here."

He sighed, and then smiled. "Invite me in, Jenny T. Partridge, and I'll tell you anything you want to know. Anything at all."

"Would you like to come in, Tate?"

"Don't mind if I do," he answered, and he turned and escorted me up the walk, the gentle pressure on my back just enough to send shock waves through all my senses.

I unlocked my door, and we stepped inside, then I relocked the door, turning the dead bolt. He surprised me by pressing me tightly against the door, and he moved into me, putting his hands on my neck and lifting my hair, kissing my neck and back where they were left bare by the tiny black dress I had worn for the performance. His left hand moved down to caress my backside and I shivered with desire.

He turned me to face him, and kissed me, desire coursing from his tongue into my mouth, and I lost all rational thought as pleasure ran through my body. His left hand raised my dress and caressed my behind, covered only with a thin layer of panty hose and a very, very brief thong, and then it dipped down dangerously close to a place that hadn't seen any male interaction in quite a while.

"Wait, wait, please wait. You haven't told me yet. Where do you go?"

Tate pulled away slightly, and then sighed. "I didn't exactly tell you the truth."

Oh great. I should have known. "Married," I said, despair I couldn't hide tingeing my voice.

He chuckled. "God, no. It is another woman. No, not a woman. She thinks she's a woman, but she's still a child. Seventeen, and before you freak out she's my half sister. Product of an affair my father had years back. My mother pretends she doesn't exist. My father sends her mother money, and a few presents on holidays. In short, she is not acknowledged as a Wilson. And predictably, it has impacted how she acts. She gets in trouble. A lot. And when she does, I bail her out. So there you have it."

"Well, that's a bit of a downer. Here I was thinking you had this great mysterious past, and instead . . ."

"Downer? Mysterious past?"

I couldn't help myself, and a giggle escaped.

"You are messing with me," he said in a low growl, and then resumed his exploration of my womanly parts, and I melted back against the door. He ran his fingers across the inside of my thigh, rasping through the nylons, and I gasped, and my heart pounded so loudly it sounded like someone was hitting my door . . . Wait. Someone *was* pounding on the door.

Tate groaned. "Ignore it," he said into my hair.

"Jennifer. Jennifer, I know you are in there. Let me in. It's James."

James? Oh yeah, James. My friend who was always getting me into trouble, because he wasn't willing to admit that he was gay, at least to his mother. James. *James?*

I turned and unlocked the door, opening it to peer out at a frantic and disheveled James. Even worse than seeing James was realizing that he was holding a small carrying case that was barking at me, like the banshees from hell. Or wherever those banshees were from. Winkie the rat dog was back. I heard a sigh of disappointment behind me, but considering the trouble James kept getting me into, and the fact that he was my friend, I had to find out what was wrong.

"What do you want, James? This isn't a good time."

"You have to let me in, Jenny. Things are bad. Really bad. Turns out Cullin's wife thinks he was having an affair with you, since she didn't know Cullin was gay, and it also turns out she's pretty damn twisted. Not only that, but Mother is on the way over here, and we have to get our stories straight before she arrives. Please, Jennifer, let me in."

Turns out she thought I was having an affair with the dastardly Cullin? Affair? Our stories straight?

I was going to kill him.